THE DRIVE HOME

SEAN KELLY

THE DRIVE HOME

A Tale of Bromance and Horror

Emerald Inkwell
Eugene
2016

Published by Emerald Inkwell

© 2016 by Sean Kelly

Inspired by and written in the Pacific Northwest
First Edition,
Published 2016

ISBN: 978-0-9965382-0-6

Emeraldinkwell.com
info@emeraldinkwell.com

This book is a work of fiction. Any names, characters, places, and incidents are either the product of the author's imagination or are used fictitiously. Any resemblance to actual persons, living or dead, events, or locales is entirely coincidental.

Cover art by Chelsea Zehetmir

This book is dedicated to so many people,
but a few in particular were invaluable.

*To **Dustin Taylor** and **Chelsea Zehetmir,***
my two best friends,
who revitalized my passion for writing
and did everything in their power to support me.

*To **Grandpa Ben Kelly***
who, before he passed, told me I could do anything.
I wish you were here to see this.
We all miss you more than you'll ever know.

*And, finally, to **my dad**,*
who, as far as I can remember,
is the only reason I ever picked up a book.
This is all your fault, you Irish bastard.

Introduction

Better Late Than Never

I

If you really want to hear about it, you'll probably want to know where I was born, what my lousy childhood was like, et cetera, et cetera. But the truth is that, while I come from a "high-functioning" dysfunctional family, my childhood wasn't that lousy and where I came from is significant, but not what's important. What is important is where I'm headed and how I plan on getting there. And, as I can only assume that you're sitting there reading my novel, you should know that this is where it all begins.

There's a lot to be said about writing a novel, most of which you've probably heard time and time again, whether it's from the opinionated and outspoken Stephen King, or the typical inspirational words of (Insert Successful Author's Name Here) encouraging would-be authors to follow their dreams. Although these were the very same words that inspired me to continue writing, I'll attempt to not bore you with the usual nonsense, but hopefully provide you with a unique perspective instead.

But before I let you loose to travel throughout the Pacific Northwest on a dark and eerie journey, I'd like to let you know who I am, what it took to arrive in the here and now, and prepare you for what's still to come.

II

Thinking back, it has become easier to pinpoint where…*this* all began. After twenty-five years of fading Christmas memories, there's only one that stands out clearly. For the life of me, I can't remember what age I was, but I was young. We were living in a cozy house on 49th Street in Springfield, Oregon, and I remember lying in bed, wide awake, waiting for one of my parents to come "wake me up" to open presents. As the bedroom door slowly creaked open, I leapt out of bed and sprinted down the hall towards the red and green blinking tree in the living room. I immediately reached for the nearest present with my name on it and tore it open.

After opening the box, I found my very first Game Boy, in all its heavy, gray, boxy glory. Little did I know that gray brick and the additional game cartridge I held in my hands were the keys to my future. And from the very first moment I plugged in *The Legend of Zelda: Link's Awakening*, I was hooked.

During my formative years, I merely assumed that I had an addiction to video games, which was a well-justified assumption. But it wasn't until I grew a bit older and my obsession with gaming was forced to share the limelight with girls and theater, that I had an epiphany that would shape my future forever. The video games themselves weren't what had me hooked. Don't get me wrong, I always have and will love gaming. But it was the stories with which I was obsessed. Tales, legends and anecdotes were my drug of choice, and, while I would soon stray from them, I would always come back to their sweet embrace. Looking back, it's hard to believe that I was too young and naïve to realize that my video games, and my dad reading me *The Chronicles of Narnia* on the bus home from school, were having a lasting effect on me and the man that I would soon become.

III

Up until high school, I had read a few books on my own, but most were forced upon me by my teachers, which, in turn, ruined any enjoyment I might have received from reading them. Which would also explain why some of my favorite books are the ones that I read before I hit high school. Early on, The *Chronicles of Narnia* filled my head with so many fanciful and extraordinary thoughts, yet nothing to do with Christian parallels and allegorical lions. Although my dad read them to me each and every day that we rode home on the city bus, I had to read and experience them myself. So I did. I read those seven books, with their original hand drawn covers—not the shitty ones with still images from the movies—over and over again to satiate my intrigue with the fictional world of Narnia.

Witnessing my newfound interest in reading the books, my dad stepped in, forcing one of his favorite novels upon me, for which I will always be grateful. The book in question is the one and only *The Catcher in the Rye*.

My dad sat next to me, the book in one hand and a Miller High Life—*"the champagne of beers"*—in the other. In an attempt to instill his love for reading in his young, video-game-addicted son, he said, "Tell you what, buddy. You read this book, my favorite book and prove to me that you can, I'll give you ten bucks." His offer was accompanied by an inquisitively raised eyebrow and a skeptical grin.

Pssh! Easy ten bucks, I thought, not fully aware of the value of a dollar or a good book. So, I read it as fast as possible. What I didn't know is that over the next few years he would drunkenly quiz me about every aspect of the novel. Which meant that while I enjoyed reading it, I was too young to appreciate the little things that made Holden Caulfield so great and I really didn't pay much attention to the nuances in the writing.

To this very day, my dad is still unsure if I ever actually read it back then...which I did, but because I couldn't remember and quote lines from the book verbatim, there would always be that seed of doubt in his mind. I read it again a few times, to prove to myself that I could, and it quickly became clear why Caulfield was so easy to relate to and I made a deep connection with the character. I never did quite understand why the book was so controversial, to the point that it required censorship and banishment, but maybe my foul-mouthed family, full of Irish mutts and Marines, are to blame.

After many years of failing my dad's many impromptu quizzes, I had finally proven myself worthy, or that I had at least read "the important parts" of *The Catcher in the Rye*. This led to my dad introducing me to his extensive Stephen King collection, which is likely the largest I'll ever come across.

IV

As excited as I was to read the works of my dad's favorite author, this was actually an unfortunate time for me to be introduced to King's writing. I'd heard so much about his books, but by the time *The Gunslinger* was finally placed in front of me, my attention span had been ravaged by the opposite sex. Girls kept me distracted from nearly every form of storytelling, even my beloved video games. But they did do at least one good thing for me back then. Girls were one of the main reasons I was drawn into theater, which I'll always regard as some of the greatest years of my life.

When I was young, I was cast in a play based on popular fairy tales and the rush of standing on stage in front of hundreds of people quickly became hard to beat. And as I progressed through middle school and the better part of high school, I focused a majority of my time on both acting and dating. Everything else in my life took a back seat, school included.

My sophomore year in high school—also my first year living in Spokane, Washington—began with being cast as the lead villain in the all-time classic *Arsenic and Old Lace*. That was followed by some creative writing courses, which led to me writing a few stories of my own. My main influences were the *Final Fantasy* video games and mafia movies like *Goodfellas* and my writing clearly reflected that. It didn't take long—although, maybe a little too long—before I made the connection between all of these so-called hobbies I'd come to love: the storytelling. By pursuing a career in writing, I had found a clear foot in the door of everything I've ever wanted to do.

As I graduated high school and began to take college courses, my path in life slowly took shape, and, although it was easier said than done, I finally knew how I wanted to follow my dreams.

V

My first inclination was to study video game development and learn to tell the interactive stories I loved so much as a child. What I failed to realize was that juggling a full-time job to pay rent, taking classes and trying to pen and program something worthwhile was a difficult task. So, I did what I could while surviving paycheck to paycheck. I worked *a lot*, and what time I had for classes grew smaller, which in turn, lessened the amount of spare time I had to write. I broadened my studies slightly and took classes focusing on acting, literature, art and drawing for media, computer animation, programming, and concepts of visual literacy. But as much as it pains me to admit, my schooling suffered the same fate as my passion for writing and was nearly forgotten about entirely.

After the better part of a decade, with a little help from my closest friends, something clicked on in my brain—broke the dam, if you will—and I grew an insatiable appetite for writing. I couldn't stop. It blew my mind how much time I found to peck away at the keys on my laptop. Like that, my addiction was back. The storytelling potential coursed through my veins, exuding a feeling of euphoria every time I finished a new chapter. With school, work, writing, et cetera, my brain soon felt like it was going to explode from being overworked and what I finally found, was that the answer to it all was...*write*...in front of me! Sorry, stupid puns are sometimes a guilty pleasure of mine.

I took some time off work, came up with a simple, terrifying thought and in an attempt to succeed in "writing what I know," I dropped it smack dab in the middle of my home: the Pacific Northwest. To continue with this theme, I took people, places, events and conversations from real life and placed them into something horrific. And as fucked up as everything I did to these doppelgangers was, I couldn't help but get a sick sense of enjoyment every time I killed off one of my friends or family members. After months and months of slaving away over a keyboard, I finally finished writing something I could be proud of. *The Drive Home* was finally born and the *tale of bromance and horror* had concluded. It was, by far, the greatest high I'd felt in years.

VI

That high brought me to a place that every aspiring author hopes to arrive at: I have a finished, polished book...now what? I sent the manuscript off to a number of publishers, receiving dozens of expected rejection letters. But that didn't faze me. I knew what I was getting into; rejection was just part of the process. And as much as I respect the stressful, painful process of traditional novel publication, I couldn't help but think there were better ways for me to achieve my dreams.

It was finally realized after one of my closest friends and I spent hundreds of long nights discussing our novels and our passion for writing (aided by the alcoholic conversational lubricant that is abundant where we come from). We covered everything from ways to market our published works to unique distribution methods we could undertake on our own. It didn't take long for us to decide it was time to take matters into our own hands.

The two of us had worked together for years and we both thrived when the success of a project was dependent solely on the effort we invested into it. When no one is telling us what we can and can't do, we find ourselves striving for greatness. This all led to the most important decision in our lives: the founding of a *Pacific Northwest Publishing Community*, which will forever be known as Emerald Inkwell. With a number of launch projects in the works, the first of which is *The Drive Home*, Emerald Inkwell is staged to do great and wonderful things.

With that, I leave you with something near and dear to my heart: a journey throughout the Pacific Northwest, fraught with love and lust, violence and heartbreak, foul language and family, and a little bit of inspiration on the side. *The Drive Home* is a dark and occasionally humorous tale of two best friends and an unfortunate series of events that will shake them to their very foundation. Enjoy and look forward to the amazing things to come. And the rest, as they say…*isn't* history, it's the future.

Sean Kelly
August 13th, 2015

"There is nothing to writing. All you do is sit down at a typewriter and bleed."

~ Ernest Hemingway

THE DRIVE HOME

1

IN AN UNUSUAL turn of events for the young, happy couple, Ben and Lynn argued for the first time in months. It wasn't only about money or happiness, or even sex, but in some ways, it was about all of that. If they could have foretold the future, just maybe, they wouldn't have fought that night. Maybe they would have watched a scary movie at home, enjoyed a simple dinner together, made love, and continued on with their routine, daily lives. But maybe that was the problem; maybe that's why things needed to change so suddenly. Their usual, everyday lives, had progressed into a stagnant haze of stressful work and a lackluster home life, which Ben finally rectified with two choice words: "I quit."

"Are you sure you should have done that?" said Lynn, as she stared into the bathroom mirror, brushing foundation onto her face.

"I had to, honey. I needed to focus. For once in my life, I needed to do something for me and I've always wanted to be a writer." Ben had only just broken the news to Lynn that he had become jobless for the first time since he was fourteen.

"But why would you just quit your job? Are you sure that's...necessary?"

"Well, yeah, I think it is. I've been working some shitty job my entire life and all I've ever wanted to do was be a real, published author. It wasn't until recently that I even felt like it was a possibility."

"Jesus, Ben. I think this is a bit drastic. Don't you?" Lynn continued to dress herself for their planned night out.

"Sometimes things need to be a little drastic. I've been completely un-drastic my entire life. Obviously, school was a terrible idea. Funny enough, the only class I didn't fail was creative writing." Ben tucked his stiff, inexpensive dress shirt into his pants and wrapped an old, light blue, checkered tie around his neck. As he tightened it, it felt like a noose cinching around his throat. He hated dressing nice. "I worked at that restaurant for seven years now. I've had the same piece-of-shit car since I turned sixteen. The only thing I've ever done that was anywhere near drastic was convincing you to leave Spokane and come back to Grants Pass with me." Sitting down on the edge of the bed, he continued talking to Lynn through the wooden bathroom door. He packed his neatly folded clothes into his suitcase, preparing for a last-minute trip to visit his father in Washington.

"And you know the only reason I left Spokane was because there wasn't anything left for me there," said Lynn. "My parents moved away, my sister moved into her boyfriend's house. It was just you and me." She smiled at herself in the mirror, curling her light brown hair, thinking that she'd won the argument.

"Well...look at it this way: it was the same thing at Joey's Pizza; there's nothing left for me, either. I can't work some miserable day job for the rest of my life. I just can't." Ben escaped into his head for a brief moment. "Someone once said, 'If you can still fail while doing something that's safe, that makes you miserable, why not take a chance doing something you love?' Can't you at

2

least understand *that*?" Ben sat atop his suitcase, forcing it closed before latching it shut.

"Look, Ben," she exited the bathroom and wrapped her arms around his neck. "If this is really what you want, you know I'll support you. But when...*if* you get this out of your system, I'll be right here beside you. I know that your boss cares about you too, at least he'd better after all these years, so he'd have to give you your job back. You know...if you wanted it, I mean." The condescension in her voice dug itself into Ben's heart. "I'll stop in and talk to him when you're on your way back, just to make sure he keeps a spot open for you."

"Alright," he hesitantly agreed, if only attempting to sound reasonable.

"But why rush into anything crazy? We've got the rest of our lives to figure out what we want to do." Lynn straightened his tie and pressed her hand against his chest. "Look, I know Taylor and Amy wanted to have dinner with us tonight, but why don't you two have a boys' night out? Then Amy and I will have a night in. The two of us haven't had any time to hang out in a while."

"Alright." He gave her a small, submissive peck on the cheek before she pulled away. "Why don't you give Amy a call? I need to go put some deodorant on. I love you."

"Okay, sweetie, I love you too." She gave him a quick peck. "And then, after you've vented all this out over a couple pitchers of beer, and slept on it for a night, we can talk about you quitting your job again in the morning." Lynn walked out of the room.

"But, I've already quit my...!" Ben shouted as Lynn disappeared down the stairs at the end of the hallway. "...job." He had made this career decision a long time ago; it simply took him a while to gain the courage to act on it, but if it would make Lynn happy, he would sleep on it for the night. Try to "get it all out of his system." But as much as he tried to convince himself that time would clarify his thoughts, something in the back of his mind told him that nothing would change.

Since he was a child, Ben had always aspired to be like his favorite author, Stephen King. The dark and twisted stories were his favorite, thrusting ordinary people into horrific and extraordinary situations. He couldn't stop reading them, even though his mother explicitly disapproved. She loathed the outlandish and horrid novels her baby boy was reading beneath his makeshift fort, strung together from Ninja Turtle sheets and dining room chairs. But her hatred for the books had never been enough to stop Ben from enjoying them. Thinking back, he couldn't help but remember the first book he'd ever read, in which he imagined himself as Holden Caulfield, vicariously living a rather unorthodox coming-of-age tale. Ben knew that the moment he turned the final page, the rest of his life would be spent telling stories like that one.

His mind continued to drift back as he stared into his own eyes in the bathroom mirror, while awkwardly attempting to put on his deodorant without untucking his shirt. A loud knock at the front door meant his ride had arrived. As he made his way down the stairs, he noticed Lynn in the kitchen, decanting a bottle of '93 merlot.

Wines have always been paired with various dishes: fish, steak, pasta. This particular style of wine, however, a merlot, was best paired with only one thing: women and their gossip.

Ben's brain had been hardwired to believe that their gossip consisted of talking about men and their "qualities," excessive shopping, and the weddings that had been promised to them years prior. Just thinking of such conversations sent a chill up his spine and reinforced his inclination to leave; that and the horn blaring from the car sitting in the driveway. Ben cracked open the front door, allowing Amy to push her way past him. He could smell the trail of Love Spell perfume as she walked by.

"Hi, Ben! Thanks for taking Taylor off my hands for the night." Amy immediately took off her coat, revealing an ankle-length, purple dress she had worn for their double date. "I can't take him anywhere, but you, on the other hand, well…he's your problem tonight." She had already made her way to the kitchen to receive the first course of the wine pairing.

"Come on, Ben, God damnit, the fight starts in ten!" Taylor yelled from the driveway. "We gotta get a good seat at the bar." He still hadn't learned the art of keeping his voice down while in small neighborhoods at eight-twenty at night. Most of the local residents were in their golden years and were in bed hours earlier. They would likely complain to Lynn in the morning. "Ben, come on!"

"Alright!" Ben shouted out the front door as Lynn walked up behind him, nudging him forward. "Jesus, he's obnoxious sometimes. Love you." He'd been subtly moved out the door at this point.

"Love you too, babe. Text me later." Lynn hastily kissed him on the lips and shut the door before he could turn away.

"Come on, lover boy, I'll give you big fuckin' kisses if you'll just get in the damn car!" Taylor honked the horn a few more times.

Ben walked around the front of the vehicle, its engine still rumbling, and climbed into the passenger seat. He slammed shut the heavy door of the primer gray '69 Firebird and glared over at Taylor. "Well, what are we waiting for, Jeeves? I pay you to drive, not sit around being an asshole."

"Rude, Ben, just rude. Maybe you *should* pay me, with how much I drive your broke ass around." Taylor had that stupid toothy grin he wore every time he tried to be funny. He put the car in reverse and backed out of the driveway. Being his usual reckless self, he drove fifteen miles-per-hour over the speed limit, hoping to get to the bar in time to watch the big fight. Luckily, no police cruisers patrolled the elderly neighborhoods and the bar was only a short drive away.

After a few minutes of awful country music and gripping the "oh, shit" handle fastened to the roof of the car, they swung into the parking lot of the Game Time Sports Bar.

"Damn, look at all these cars," said Taylor.

"No worries, man. I'm sure we'll be able to find a couple of seats."

They pulled into the only available parking spot on the side of the bar. They both walked towards the entrance, each admiring a gang of Harley Davidson motorcycles near the front door before opening it and going inside.

The sound of the first bell, signaling the start of round one, rang out from the TV, louder than the sounds of the light music and obnoxious patrons. Each boxer closed in quickly and the exchange of punches started immediately. Being the first high profile fight of the year, they would normally waste twenty dollars watching it on pay-per-view, but they figured their money would be better spent on cold beer. They only hoped it would be a decent fight, whether or not they paid to watch it.

Taylor pushed a path through the crowd of bikers that likely belonged to the Harleys out front. They made their way to a small, clearly makeshift table near the back wall.

"At least it's got a good view of the TV," he said.

Roland "Tall Can" Williams with a hard right to the body. An uppercut lands from "The Big Fish" and Williams responds with a barrage of blows to the Fish's head! What a shot that was, Henry. If Williams keeps this up, the fight isn't going to last very long.

A pretty waitress in the standard, low-cut referee outfit made good time over to their table. "What'll it be, boys?"

Ben ordered their usual. "Pitcher of hef, two glasses, please."

Taylor stared at the nametag dangling from her chest, his eyes quickly drifting to the view next to it. "Hi…Wendy." He couldn't bring himself to look her in the eyes.

"Coming right up." She winked at them, her eyes lingering on Taylor for an extra moment and set down a paper boat full of popcorn before walking away, swinging her hips. She was working hard for her tips.

"Thanks!" Taylor hollered back at her, hoping for another wink. "God-damn, she's cute. So," he said, changing the subject, "tell me, why the change in plans? One minute, we're set to waste a bunch of money at Benicci's on some overpriced dinner. The next thing I know, Amy's having a girls' night in with Lynn and we get to watch the fight. Gotta say, I don't know what you did, but I could sure as hell get used to it."

"Well, I quit my job," said Ben, tossing a piece of popcorn into his mouth.

"You're shittin' me. What did Joey say?"

"He was actually pretty understanding, but he wasn't very happy about it. He tried to get me to go down to part-time instead of quitting."

"Figures. That place will probably fall apart without

you. Who else is going to clean up everyone else's mistakes? Most of them don't know their asses from their elbows." That was one of Taylor's favorite sayings passed down by his father; he found that it satisfied his sense of nostalgia to throw it into conversation every so often.

Ben laughed a bit. "Yeah, I can only hope everything falls apart. Then maybe I won't feel like I wasted my time there. Lynn says that she gets it, but she thinks this is just a phase or something. Like I'm having a mid-life crisis—in my late twenties."

"Well, are you?"

A pitcher of foamy, golden beer and two glasses were placed on the table in front of them. "Here you go, guys. Anything else?"

"No, thank you," said Ben.

The waitress smiled again and moved on to her next table.

"Well?" asked Taylor.

The Big Fish lands a punishing blow! Williams is gonna feel that one in the morning.

"No, it's not just a phase...dick. I've actually wanted to write a book for a long time now. You know that. I think this way I can take some time to write a real, full-length novel. I've had a few ideas, but I just don't know what to write, exactly. And plus, tons of writers have quit their jobs to write full-time, why can't I do it?"

"I guess I never really thought about it like that, but it makes sense." Taylor grabbed the pitcher and filled his glass to the brim. A perfect pour, if you ignore the single stream of foam trailing down the side of the pint glass. "You could write about me, you know? I'd make a great story." That wide smile returned to his face.

"Oh, yeah, the life of a loan officer is epic. I know I'd

pay to read about some random guy filling out paperwork all day."

The Big Fish is down for the count! No one saw this coming, Henry...

"Yeah, yeah," said Taylor, playfully offended. "I was just joking. Don't worry, you'll figure something out, man. I know you will." He raised his glass towards Ben, who reciprocated.

"Thanks. This is just something I think I need to do. I know it'll be worth it in the end. It has to be."

Seven...eight...nine...ten! The Tall Can takes the bout! Unbelievable! What a knockout, Jeff. And with eight full rounds left, Henry. An absolute upset...

They both stared at the big screen. "What?" Taylor was shocked. "Out in the second round? What a gyp!"

"Thank God we didn't order this on pay-per-view," Ben added.

The bar's patrons booed and hollered at the screen. A beer bottle, tossed by one of the bikers, smashed into the wall behind the television. "Bullshit!" they shouted. "Get up you pussy!" A man, dressed in referee stripes similar to Wendy the waitress's attire, but with a flashy name tag on his chest that read "Manager," quickly ran over to the bikers, pleading with them to mellow out.

Ben and Taylor returned to their conversation, now that the fight had become irrelevant.

"You really quit your job, huh?" Taylor tossed some of the popcorn from the boat into his mouth.

"Yeah, I guess."

"You guess?"

"Yeah I...I should have put in my two weeks or tried to talk it over with Joey or something. I don't know."

"Don't worry about it. Sounds like you needed this."

Ben raised his glass. "I'll drink to that."

"So, how are you gonna get started?"

"Well, you know how I told you that my dad's in the hospital, up in Spokane? It doesn't sound like it's anything too serious." Ben refilled their glasses, then loosened the tie around his neck. "But I think I'm going to drive up there and take the scenic route. Maybe do a little writing, stop here and there. Try to get a little inspiration along the way."

"I think that's a great idea." Taylor took another sip from the warming beer. "Take a little time away from normal life, visit your dad and see if you can get some writing done. Maybe hit up a strip club or two. I think that's what you really need to unwind and get a little perspective on life." They both laughed a bit and silently imagined the beautiful sights at the nearest strip club.

"God, other than the whole strip club thing, you're dangerously close to sounding like Lynn."

"What do you mean, 'sound like Lynn?'"

"'Just get it out of your system.' I've already made my decision. This is what I want. I can't think of anything else I've wanted more."

"Alright, calm down, that's not what I meant. I just think you need to be smart about all your options is all." Taylor set down his glass, avoiding the uncomfortable eye contact. "Okay, look, Lynn wanted me to talk to you. Well, Lynn wanted Amy to get me to talk to you. I think if that's what you want, it's what you want. Just promise me you'll think about it, for Lynn."

Ben took a large swig from his beer, polishing off the glass and not saying another word.

"Look, Ben, forget I said anything. I gotta go take a leak real quick." Taylor gulped down the rest of his beer and got up from his seat. "When I get back, we'll just bullshit until they kick us outta here. It's not like you have to work tomorrow, right?" They both smiled at the thought. It had been months since they'd closed down a bar.

"Alright, sounds good."

Taylor took off towards the bathroom, pushing his way through the thinning crowds in the bar.

Ben stared off at the big screen as the sports network rebroadcasted the big knockout to make up for the leftover time meant to air a full-length fight.

The camera spun around "The Big Fish" sprawled out on the canvas.

Ben felt as though, at that exact moment, he could relate to the fighter. The feeling of being stuck, not able to change his current situation no matter how hard he tried, felt all too familiar. Something important taking place and everyone's eyes are upon you, waiting to see what you'll do. Will he get up and finish the fight, or stay down and be forced to deal with the humiliation of defeat?

That's how Ben felt about his life working for Joey, which is why, after seven long years, he decided to finally shit or get off the pot. After spending the better part of a decade sweating over five-hundred-degree brick ovens and doing all the shit-work, he knew it was time for a change.

Although he'd made his decision and knew he would have to live with it, he couldn't help but feel like he might have made a mistake. And while some mistakes end in tragedy, like "The Big Fish" dropping his left, hoping to counter with his right, Ben knew that he shouldn't let that stop him from going for a big, knockout punch. He had to take that chance and hope that his mistake would change things for the better. Like a bruised and battered young woman who stays in a violent relationship only long enough to fall in love with the male nurse treating her most recent string of injuries. He felt that taking that chance was worth it, worth hoping that his mistakes would end up like the young lady at the hospital, and not like a washed up prize fighter, embarrassed in front of the entire nation.

2

AN UNFORTUNATE TRUTH in this world, is that everyone, man or woman, must make a few decisions in life that don't make any sense. A few mistakes that defy common logic and can make or break the next few years of one's life. It's how we grow, how we—as human beings—learn and evolve. Ben had only ever made two such mistakes.

While most initial reckless decisions are made before reaching one's formative years, Ben's first reckless decision was during his freshman year of high school. He'd gone nearly all year with straight As and a four-year plan for graduating with a slightly higher than 3.5 grade point average. After heading off to college, Ben would begin his career and then start a family; that was the plan his own family expected of him. Throughout high school, every homework assignment he would turn in was returned with a large red "A" and scribbled comments like "Excellent work!" or "This is college-level writing; keep it up!" Ben never had any reason to doubt his future.

At least until he met Morgan. She had a popular reputation amongst the boys in high school and she was cast as a bit of a slut. Quite characteristically, she loved every minute of it.

Ben was never the type of guy to "make any moves," but he still managed to keep Morgan entangled in her longest relationship to date, only two short months. As proud as Ben was of this, Morgan made it abundantly clear that if they didn't take their relationship to the next level, they didn't have a future together.

That's when Ben ran into his first big mistake: sex. It dawned on him once that it might have been an error in judgment, but he, along with every other man in existence, would never truly admit to that. His parents knew that something had changed in him once his report cards began showing up with steadily decreasing grades. But there was nothing Ben could have done to prevent it; he was powerless during that time in his youth, when the opposite sex becomes the most important thing in life. Drinking warm beer at parties and the freedom of learning to drive weren't far behind.

Finally, after Morgan got the "attention" she craved from him, she ended their relationship the very next day.

Ben's second life-altering mistake came one week after high school graduation. He had been with Lynn for three years and they hadn't yet talked much about their future. The week following graduation, they decided that with no money, no job, no plan—and no idea what to do next—they would pick up and move away from their lives in Washington to start one life together. They packed their bags and moved back to Ben's small hometown of Grants Pass, Oregon. And although Ben hated his eventual job at the pizza place, he considered moving to Oregon with Lynn one of the greatest mistakes he'd ever made.

His most recent choice to quit his job without two weeks' notice was looking to be Ben's third, and most regrettable mistake. With everyone telling him to get it out of his system, he was worried he might start to believe that his dream job was truly just a phase. It may take time to learn whether or not his choice was a brilliant or a poor decision, but chances were that it wouldn't take long to find out. Ben knew he would never regret leaving his job and he knew that going all-in with something he loved was the best decision he could make. But while he couldn't wait to visit his dad on his trip, he couldn't help but feel a little concerned. Concerned because once he arrived in Spokane and came face to face with his old man, he would feel like that awkward student in high school again, being scolded for yet another childish decision. Just like in high school, his dad would tell him to "do what you gotta do to provide for a family, even if it makes you unhappy," but eventually his dad's mind would drift and he would move on, reveling in the visit from his only son.

Bryan, Ben's father, always claimed to understand the things Ben did to get himself in trouble, usually because Bryan had been in trouble for worse when he was a boy. But like his father before him, Bryan wouldn't let a little thing like cancer stop him from teaching his only son one more lesson.

That scared the hell out of Ben. Yet in a weird, nostalgic sort of way, he was almost looking forward to the tongue lashing, if only for old time's sake. He couldn't help being nervous, primarily because his dad would be having surgery in the morning. With a few free days between quitting his job and his dad getting out of surgery, Ben decided to take advantage of the extra time and enjoy a more relaxed trip up to Washington. This way, he could begin his new life as a writer and start his first novel. The first step, deciding what to write about, would be the most difficult.

With any luck, and a little liquid courage, Ben and Taylor would think of something brilliant. Maybe he could use Taylor's help just this once to get started.

3

"HEY, COME ON," said Taylor as he returned from the restroom. "Let's get the hell out of here." His face was more distraught than usual.

"Hmm?" Ben looked up at him. "What, already?"

"Yeah, let's…uh…let's go see your dad…right now." Taylor looked around frantically, watching for something. "You can get started on your story and, well, you know me. I'm not one to turn down a road trip." He smiled awkwardly as he anxiously danced around next to the table. "Besides, I still haven't met your old man. So, you know, let's go see him."

"Wait, what are you talking about?" Ben wasn't sure how their conversation had escalated so quickly. "Well…" he thought to himself for a moment. "I guess it couldn't hurt if you tagged along, but we don't have to leave yet. Come on, let's finish the pitcher at least."

"Look, I got in a little argument in the bathroom and I'm pretty sure he's friends with those biker dicks. So, we should probably go. Now." Taylor grabbed his coat and made his way towards the door.

Ben continued to process the plan he'd inadvertently agreed to.

As long as the two of them had been friends, Taylor never instigated arguments with anyone, let alone strangers. Especially while taking a piss in the men's room.

A loud yell from the bathroom drew Ben's attention as a large man wearing a leather cut flung the bathroom door open. The biker's face filled with confusion and rage as he tried to decide whether to hold his aching head or his clearly broken—and gushing—nose. "Where the fuck did he go?" The biker shouted over the whistle from his nose.

"Ben! Time to go. Now!" Taylor disappeared out the front door.

Without hesitation, Ben got up and jogged after him, both of them forgetting to pay their bill. He hurried out the front door and Taylor stopped in front of him to fish for the keys in his pockets, which he found deep in the right one.

"Start the car, there's something I've always wanted to do." Taylor threw the keys towards Ben and gave him a reassuring smile. "Trust me."

"Wait, do what!?"

"Just start the God-damn car."

Without any more hesitation, Ben ran over to the Firebird and climbed in to start it.

Taylor took off towards the line of motorcycles parked outside the front door. "I'm sorry, ladies," he said sincerely to the bikes. He ran up to the nearest one, a navy blue Panhead, and kicked it as hard as he could, sending it tumbling into the Sportster next to it, then into the one after that, and so on like a line of twenty-thousand-dollar dominoes. "Ha! That felt great!" Taylor spun around and, in true *Dukes of Hazard* fashion, jumped through the passenger-side window of the car. "Drive!" The squeal of the car's tires whistled through the air as it fishtailed out of the parking lot.

"What the hell's wrong with you?" Ben's eyes

jumped back and forth between the road and his paranoid best friend.

"Oh, man, that was freaking amazing!" After adjusting in his seat, Taylor eyed the road behind them, making sure they didn't have a tail as they made their getaway. "Oh, I wish we could have seen the look on their faces. Pricks." He spun back around to sit properly in his seat.

"Jesus, Taylor. What was that? What happened back there?"

"Well, he pushed me against the wall and cut in front of me at the urinal. Told me to 'move, faggot,'" Taylor said, mimicking a tough biker voice. "I got a...little pissed and I...pushed him back."

"His face was gushing blood, dude."

"Okay, so I pushed his face into the big metal thing on top of the urinal, whatever. I've never done anything like that before. I'm still so...pumped!"

Ben ran his hand through his hair. "Look, I'm all up for getting in fights every once in a while. Hell, I'll even get your back, but a little warning would have been nice." He paused and exhaled loudly. "You at least could have let me finish my fuckin' beer."

"Sorry, it was kind of a spur-of-the-moment thing. You know?" Taylor leaned back against the head rest and closed his eyes. "I guess your 'taking chances' talk kind of got to me."

"It *was* kind of badass, though. I always knew you were fucking nuts." They both smiled and laughed a bit, coming down from the adrenaline pumping through their veins.

Taylor had never been in a real fight before, but they talked about the appeal of it often.

"What did it feel like?" asked Ben.

"That's kind of a gay question." Taylor laughed at Ben's expense. "Seriously?"

"Yeah, I'm gonna be a writer, you know? I've hit someone before, but I have to hear about other people's experiences too."

"You know when you're a kid and you're on a bike or a skateboard and you're at the top of a big hill? Or you're getting ready to try out your makeshift ramp to jump over something way too dangerous?"

"Oh, the good old days. Like that time we built that shitty ramp to jump over the creek?"

"Yeah, exactly. You hit the ramp and the only thing to go through your brain is: 'was this idea good or completely fucking stupid?' But it's too late to back out anyway and your heart's still racing and the adrenaline pumping. I don't know how else to really explain it."

"I think I get what you're saying. You're still lucky you didn't get your ass kicked back there."

"Luck had nothing to do with it." Taylor felt extremely full of himself after his so-called fight. "Hey, where are you taking us?"

"Back to my place. I figure we can watch a movie or something with the girls before we leave in the morning. And let 'em know we're okay after that show back there."

"No, we can't go back now, I'm too pumped. We need to do something else, some more bro time before we have to head back home." Taylor looked around, hoping to see something that could keep them out for a bit longer. "Screw it. Let's hit the road, let's go to Spokane, right now."

"Come on, Taylor."

"Yeah, why not?"

"We need to pack and tell the girls where we're going; you need to request time off. They'll shit a brick if we just left."

"I've got a pen and a slightly soda-stained legal pad in the back that you can use. We'll stop and buy whatever else we need on the road."

Ben stopped the car in the middle of the street and thought for a moment. Even the periodic honking from passing cars couldn't interrupt the debate taking place in his mind. Ben never could master the art of listening to his gut. That feeling eating away at him, telling him that leaving would be a bad idea; he chose to interpret that as his gut telling him to take a risk and do something a little crazy. "Alright, fine, but what about the girls?"

"You have a cell phone, don't you? We'll call them from the road. That way they can't try to stop us. Imagine how Lynn would feel if when we get back, you had your book fully written and all you had to do next was get it published. And Amy, well she'll have Lynn to complain about me to," Taylor said smiling.

"I don't know, Taylor, maybe it's not such a good idea."

Taylor jovially slapped him on the arm. "Really, Ben? Have I ever steered you wrong?"

"Yeah, all the time. I think the easier question would be when haven't you?"

"Hey, screw you, pal." Taylor didn't find the joke as funny as Ben did. "Would you just trust me this once?"

Ben glared at Taylor for a moment, one questioning eyebrow raised above the other. He averted his eyes back to the road, flicked on his turn signal and made a wide U-turn on the dark, empty street. The blacktop quickly raced beneath them like the sea flowing beneath a speedboat leaving the harbor.

Taylor chuckled then leaned back in his seat, closing his eyes again. "I knew you'd see it my way."

They drove through the empty city streets until they reached the edge of town. The open road stretched out before them, seemingly never-ending. Driving slowly through the dark—both of them running on fumes from the lack of sleep—they carried on through the night, eager to make the trip. Due to the conservative speed limits surrounding Grants Pass, they only made it a short ways out of town before the sun started to rise.

Bright scarlet rays of sunlight crept over the horizon to their right, instantly blinding Ben's weary, sleepy eyes. The thought of dozing off tickled his upper eyelids. He had hoped for a second wind, but the persistent hum of the engine sung like a siren's lullaby. It had been hours since he had seen Lynn and she was likely worried sick. With one hand on the wheel, Ben fumbled through his pockets to find the new iPhone he'd purchased the week before. Hidden amongst the loose change and gum wrappers, he found it. Glancing to and from the screen, his thumb pecked at the keypad, searching for Lynn's cell phone number. He knew that she wouldn't likely be awake, but he felt he could at least leave her a message, so he pushed "call."

The line rang once.

A thick beam of light slapped Taylor across the face, causing him to squint and stir in his seat.

The phone rang again.

Taylor's eyes opened and he glanced over to see Ben using his cell phone. In an unprecedented moment of reaction, he snatched the phone from Ben's hand, rolled down the passenger-side window and flung the phone with all his might into the passing fields.

"What the hell did you do that for?"

"Who were you calling? Lynn?" Taylor readjusted in his seat. "Do you really think that she would just let us drive off like this?"

"I just bought that fucking phone…" Ben hit the steering wheel. "Yeah, I think she would. Before we went out last night, she was actually pretty supportive about the idea." He wasn't sure if he even believed his own words.

"That's because she knew that you would still have to come home and get permission from her. If she answered, she would just badger you until you agreed to go back home and talk about it before you make any…" Taylor mocked quotes with his fingers. "…drastic decisions."

Ben hated to admit when he found a kernel of truth in Taylor's words. "Well, she did tell me not to do anything rash."

"Exactly. That's because she knew you wouldn't. To tell you the truth, Ben, you are a bit predictable."

God, I hate it when you make a good point, Ben thought. It wasn't sound enough reasoning to justify throwing his new phone out the window, but Taylor made a good point nonetheless.

"And now that she and Amy have had all night to bitch and moan after we didn't come home, it's probably in our best interests not to talk to them. At least not until they've had a chance to cool down." Taylor stretched his arms out in front of him.

"But, we *will* call them, right?"

"Of course, what kind of boyfriends would we be if we didn't? We just need to put a little distance between us and them first."

"Alright." Ben raised his arm to see the fuel gauge hidden behind it. "But we need to stop at the next gas station. You're paying to make up for throwing my shit out the window. Then you get to drive, I need to get some sleep. I've been running on fumes for a couple hours now."

"Sounds good." Taylor stretched his arms wide, until

his elbow hit the partially rolled-down window, causing it to tingle violently. "Ow, that frickin' hurt. I think I got enough sleep, but I'm a bit hungry, though. I haven't eaten since lunch yesterday."

"Yeah, we didn't get anything before we left the bar last night."

A sign flew by them for the only gas stop for another hundred miles. "Joe's Gas-and-Go!"

Ben pulled into the dusty driveway and stopped at the only gas pump without an "out of order" sign dangling from it. They sat for a moment after the bell rang to signal that a car had pulled up. Since they were still in southern Oregon, it was illegal for them to pump their own gas. So, they continued to wait for the attendant. After a couple minutes of waiting, without anyone coming to provide any assistance, they stepped out of the car to stretch their legs and crack their backs. It was quiet for miles around the gas station, no other cars or buildings—they definitely were not in the city anymore. Another minute passed before they decided to enter the general store connected to the gas station. Inside felt deserted, much like the acres of grassland around it. No clerk or attendant in sight. They walked down the aisles picking out snacks they hadn't seen in stores for years. They would be lucky to find any food that hadn't passed its expiration date. Even the small candy bins were labeled "Penny Candy."

Ben hadn't seen penny candy since he was ten. The media would have had a field day if they knew there were still businesses selling candies labeled "Sugar Cigarettes."

"Hey, Ben, look at how old these beer bottles are," Taylor said, staring through the glass display case. "I don't even think they make this brand anymore."

"Hey!" A gruff, impoverished voice erupted from behind them, causing Taylor to drop a bottle. "What you want?" said the short, bearded man behind the counter.

Ben eyed the dirty, blue overalls, spotted with tattered holes. "I'm sorry." He didn't understand why he was apologizing. "Didn't see you back there. We just, uh, need to pay for some gas and get some snacks for the road."

"Well, hurry up. Git' your shit and leave." The short, hairy man sat back down behind the counter.

Taylor made a surprised face at Ben. For being the only customers around for miles, they thought they would get a bit warmer of a welcome. Taylor grabbed some likely expired bags of chips and a six-pack of beer. He raised the bottles and blew a thin layer of dust off of them.

Ben picked up a few power bars and some sodas. Each of them took handfuls of the most important thing for any road trip: jerky. Beef jerky was undoubtedly the food of choice for any journey. A few pepperoni sticks apiece would be enough to hold them over, but after seeing the little jar on the counter full of silver-dollar jerky, they each had to grab a handful.

"This is it," Taylor said as he and Ben set their items down on the counter. "And go ahead and just fill us up with regular."

"I'll bag up your stuff, but you boys can pump your own damn gas." The angry little man carelessly stuffed all of the groceries into paper bags and then jammed his finger into a few buttons on the antique cash register.

"What do you mean? It's your job. We're not technically allowed to do that." Ben said. The hairy man just glared up at him from beneath his trucker cap and spit some of his dip out onto the floor. "Okay, whatever, I used to live in Washington. I know how to do it."

"Forty-six sixty-five."

Taylor pulled out his wallet and handed the man a

fifty-dollar bill. The man snatched it from his hand and shoved it into the cash register, then sat back down without another word. Taylor looked over at Ben, who shrugged and raised his eyebrows, then took the bags off the counter and made his way towards the door. "Um...keep the change...I guess." Taylor tapped the counter and followed Ben outside. When the door closed behind him and he was sure that the crazy little man hadn't followed them out of the store, he shouted over to Ben. "Jesus, that was weird! At least he was nice enough to bag everything for us."

"Yeah, no kidding," said Ben, his mouth already full of the jerky they'd just purchased. "A little stale, but still good." He set down the groceries on the passenger seat and pulled out a one-liter of Coke.

Taylor walked around to the driver's side of the car and stood for a moment. The usual sarcastic and lively tone had left his face as he stared back into the shop. The intensity in his eyes looked as though they would burn right through the mini-mart's glass door.

"What's up?" Ben asked.

Taylor kept looking for another moment.

Ben had seen that same look just before Taylor had wrecked the motorcycles back in Grants Pass.

"Hang on, I'll be right back," said Taylor. "I just want my change for that fifty."

"Dude, don't worry about it. It was only like, four bucks. Guy probably needs all the tips he can get with that shitty attitude of his."

"It's alright, it'll just take a minute. I promise. I'll be right back." Taylor removed his fingers from the door handle and rushed back into the store.

Ben twisted off the cap from the soda and took a big swig, then opened up a bag of chips. His hunger masked the stale taste of the salt and vinegar crisps. He walked over to the pump, unscrewed the gas cap and set the bag of chips on the roof of the car so he could begin filling the tank. It had been a while since he'd done it, but the familiar sound and penetrating smell of gasoline escaping from the nozzle reassured him that he was doing it correctly. He glanced over at the building every so often, waiting for Taylor to emerge. Five minutes had passed before he started to worry that something bad had happened to Taylor. The thought of a crazed, spiteful hillbilly brandishing a shotgun seemed like a strong possibility. Just as he was ready to gather his courage and check on his friend, Taylor appeared through the door, holding a crumpled bill in his hand. He jogged over to the driver's side, snatched the chips from on top of the roof, then climbed in. Ben shook off the dripping nozzle into the tank and returned it to its holster, then screwed the gas cap back on until it clicked three times. He sat down in the passenger seat, where Taylor teasingly waived the fifty-dollar bill in his face.

"There, that was easy."

"How did you get the whole fifty back? And what took you so long?" Ben pulled the seatbelt down around him.

"I told him that he was…very rude to the only customers around for miles and that, just in case he didn't know, it was illegal for customers to pump their own gas in Oregon. And, finally, that it was illegal for him to not give me the rest of my change back." Taylor clicked his seat belt into place and shoved the bill into his pocket. "After I explained all that, he hollered for a minute and I was pretty sure he was going to pull a gun or something from under the counter. But after he was done fuming, he realized what a dick he was being and gave me a full refund." Taylor smiled with relief that things had gone his way.

Ben couldn't help but be happy that the crazed hillbilly didn't unload any buckshot into Taylor's chest. "Huh. That actually is pretty lucky." Ben still didn't know if Taylor had done anything crazy, like before they left Grants Pass. "Cool, I guess. That means you can buy some beer from *this* decade in the next town then."

"I guess that's fair. But you'll have to buy some beer eventually, though." Taylor started the Firebird and drove off down the road. The next town was less than two hours away from the station. There they could relax, maybe try to get some writing done and if they were still feeling lucky, take a risk by calling the girls. Hopefully, they could avoid any sort of a tongue lashing that might accompany such a call, but that might prove to be a difficult task.

But Ben knew he would have to take that risk eventually.

4

AFTER DRIVING ALL morning, with little to no sleep, Ben and Taylor mutually decided to make their first stop in Eugene. An old friend lived there, who they hadn't seen in over a year and were excited to finally visit.

Brandon had left Grants Pass a few years ago in order to start his own Irish pub near the University of Oregon. The last time Ben had spoken with him, Brandon said he had been doing well and that his bar had been growing in popularity. Both Ben and Taylor found it hard to believe that Brandon, with all the stupid things they had done together as children, would be responsible enough to own and manage a business. But, to everyone's surprise, he had done it.

As they pulled off of the I-5 exit onto Franklin Boulevard, they found themselves right between the towering buildings of the University of Oregon and the beautiful city skyline looking towards Autzen Stadium.

Taylor looked over at their reflection in the enormous, glass basketball arena as they drove past. A group of transients dressed in tie-dye clothes and playing guitar sat on the sidewalk with large cardboard signs, shamelessly asking for money.

"I love it here; it's so beautiful. At least during the summer," said Ben. "Last time I talked to Brandon, he said it rains most of the year, though." He rolled down the passenger-side window to allow the pine-scented air to fill the car.

"Yeah, it'd be better if there weren't so many hippies and hobos," said Taylor, resisting the urge to yell obscenities at the passing transients.

"Careful being so judgmental. Lynn swears she used to be a hippie."

"Yeah, but the difference is that you convinced her to shave her armpits and wear a scent other than bong water."

Ben couldn't help but laugh at Taylor's loathing for hippies.

"Lynn still likes patchouli oil for some God-awful reason. I can't stand it and I think she knows that. She puts it on whenever she's pissed."

"Sucks for you. I told Amy I was 'allergic' to patchouli." Taylor kept driving until Franklin Boulevard split in two. "Where is Brandon's bar, anyway?"

Ben snatched Taylor's phone from the center console's cup holder and dialed their old friend's number. "I have no idea, hang on." The phone rang a few times before Brandon finally answered. "Hey, Brandon, we're in town. Where the hell is your bar?" He listened as Brandon gave him directions. "O'Donnell's on Eleventh? Alright, we're on Eleventh now. Should be there pretty quick." He hung up the phone. "Just keep going this way. Brandon said it should be on the left after some ugly nightclub."

Taylor watched as they passed by auto dealerships and college bars. Just beside a rundown, brick nightclub was the big, green sign with the name "O'Donnell's" on it. He pulled around to the side of the bar and stopped near the back alleyway. They climbed out and he put four dollars' worth of quarters into the parking meter.

Ben held open the front door while Taylor walked into

the bar; it was dead inside. Only two older patrons were seated at the bar.

Their old friend had gotten a bit hefty over the past year. But as he stood behind the counter, he chatted up the customers, laughing as loud as ever until he finally noticed Ben and Taylor.

"Ben, Taylor, holy shit it's good to see you guys!" Brandon shouted over the soft Flogging Molly song playing from the jukebox. He ran over to them, wrapped one arm around each of their necks and squeezed tightly. "God, how long has it been?"

Taylor choked out an answer as he tried to break free of Brandon's grasp. "It's been about a year and a half, I think."

"You've been avoiding me for a year and a half? I oughta kick both your asses."

"Let go, God damnit." Ben broke free before Taylor was released. "It's good to see you, too, buddy."

"I can't believe it. So, what's new with you guys?" Brandon had already moved them over to the bar and taken up his position behind it. Without asking, he pulled a six-pack of bottled beer from the cooler and placed it in front of Ben and Taylor. He took two of the beers and set them in front of the other two patrons. "On me, guys." Then he returned to his old pals at the other end of the counter. "And what the hell are you doin' in Eugene?"

"Same shit, different day!" shouted Taylor, opening his beer.

"Well, I finally quit my job at the pizza place," said Ben.

"Really? I gotta say, I didn't think you were ever going to actually leave that place. What was it, five, six years there?"

"Seven."

"Seven!? Awful!" Brandon cried out. "Those were the good old days, though, weren't they? All three of us working there."

Taylor raised his beer. "We sure did have some good times, didn't we? Cheers, boys."

"Cheers," the others said as the bottles clinked together.

"Taylor, do you remember when we used to leave our phone numbers on cute girls' receipts?" Brandon felt like gloating about past conquests.

"Yeah, but it never worked. I tried it at least a half a dozen times with no luck."

"I got it to work once," Ben casually interjected.

"Bullshit! You've had a girlfriend; no way you would have done that!" Taylor shouted in disbelief.

"Ask Brandon," said Ben. "He told me I couldn't do it, so I did. It's not like I actually did anything about it. I just wrote my number on a girl's check and she just said 'thanks' and 'goodbye,' but she did give me the 'fuck me eyes,' though."

"This is unbelievable." Taylor was pissed he'd been outshone by his two best friends. "Mind if I get something on tap? This light beer sucks."

"No, help yourself. Sorry about the light beer, trying to watch my girlish figure." Brandon ran his hands over his "feminine" curves. "Oh, careful of the handle on the reach-in cooler, it's busted."

Taylor tugged on the reach-in cooler's handle and it snapped off, scraping up his hand. "God damnit, Brandon. Fix your shit hole."

"I'm not going to take offense to that, because I know you're just jealous of our 'accomplishments' from back in the day. What do you say, Ben? Do you think my bar's a shit hole?"

"No." Ben smiled back at Brandon, enjoying the tortured look on Taylor's face. "I think it's a beautiful bar. I wouldn't change a thing."

Taylor finally managed to retrieve a couple pitchers from the cooler and began pouring beer into them.

The three of them always knew they could make themselves at home when they visited one another. No secrets, no barriers, just the best of friends. That's why Brandon didn't care about letting either of them empty the taps or raid the coolers. His beer was their beer and he knew that they would always do the same for him.

"Oh, shit, guys. I almost forgot the Ducks are playing. Game started about twenty minutes ago." Brandon fumbled around behind the counter and eventually found a television remote. He flicked through the channels on the flat screen hanging behind the bar until he found the green and yellow uniforms sprinting down the field at Autzen Stadium.

"That's terrible; I didn't even know the season had started," Taylor said as he poured a few pints from one of the pitchers. "Who are they playing against?"

"Washington State."

"This early in the season? Wow."

Other than growing up together, Duck football is what bonded them. When they were younger, they would get pumped for the upcoming seasons and watch the games at Ben's house. While they worked at Joey's, Saturdays quickly became their favorite days to take off from work. They would grill, try their hand at making hot wings and drink large amounts of bottled beer while screaming "OOOOOOOOO!" at the television. That small ritual brought them all closer together and while Lynn didn't care too much for football, she would watch and laugh as they made asses of themselves, attempting to match the noise level at the stadium.

Ben didn't always watch football. He'd gone to games as a boy, but never got into watching them on television. Eventually, after he'd moved to Washington, the passion simply faded away. One day, after returning to Grants Pass and after he and Taylor got off work, they caught the last half of a Duck game. Just like that, Ben fell right back into old habits and the thrill of being a Duck fan. "Okay, so, looks like we're up by two touchdowns, second quarter's just starting." Ben felt around on the counter for his beer, keeping his eyes focused on the screen. "God, I hope they have a good season this year. We've taken the Rose Bowl, now we just need to take the Championship."

"No kidding," said Taylor.

Their favorite running back in years flew down the field after receiving a handoff.

"Go. GO. GO!" they all yelled.

Touchdown! shouted the stadium announcer, quickly followed by the ceremonially loud blow horn.

"Yes, that was fucking amazing!" shouted Taylor.

"That had to have been, what, like seventy yards?" Ben asked rhetorically.

"I'll drink to that." Brandon raised his bottle and they all clinked their drinks together, followed by chugging down the better half of them. "God, I love football."

"I know. I feel like it's been ages since last season." Ben turned to Brandon. "Lynn is actually starting to get into the Ducks, too. She watched a couple games with me last year; I even got her to yell 'O' before each play."

"Yeah, you did." Taylor smiled, hoping someone caught on to his poor innuendo.

"Shut up, Taylor." Ben paused for a moment. "But yeah, yeah I did." He smiled back, insinuating just as poor innuendo.

Once halftime rolled around, they'd finished their second round of drinks and Brandon needed a smoke. All three of them went out into the back alley, leaving the two patrons alone in the bar.

"They're regulars," said Brandon. "No need to worry 'bout them."

Whenever they drank with Brandon, they couldn't help but indulge their other vices. Ben and Taylor didn't smoke often, but never shied away when Brandon offered them a cigarette. They quickly finished their smokes and took turns pissing behind the dumpster, hoping the others wouldn't try to knock each other over by kicking at the back of the knee. But just in time for the second half kickoff, they returned to their seats at the bar.

The other two patrons had left while they were outside. With the bar now empty, excluding the three of them, Brandon turned off the "Open" sign and locked the front door, then turned up the volume on the TV. They talked and drank for hours, until the field at Autzen flooded with fans, celebrating the Ducks' victory over Washington State. With most of the day gone, they continued to drink and talk into the early hours of the morning. An abundance of beer bottles littered the counter tops, accompanied by empty pitchers and half-smoked cigarettes. Back in the company of his old friends, Brandon had reverted to his usual flamboyant self, the intoxicants slowly changing him into a sassy black woman. His arms flailed as he recalled old memories with his two favorite people, until a swing of his massive arm knocked over the bottles, like a strike at the bowling alley.

They quickly moved over to the pool tables, playing an odd version of three man pool. Ben won a few games in a row, forcing Brandon and Taylor to tackle him to the ground, drunkenly wrestling for a few minutes before Ben managed to break free.

The more intoxicated they became, the more rambunctious they got, which, in turn, meant more bottles would pile up and more pool balls would find their way onto the floor. All three of them needed a night like this. A night to unwind and enjoy life a little.

Ben needed to unwind. He felt as though he were stuck between a rock and a hard place, between Lynn and his dream of becoming a writer. As much as she claimed to support him, he could tell she didn't truly believe he had what it takes to become a published author.

Taylor had earned himself a job at one of the local credit unions, which meant more money and better hours, but he hated it. His job as a loan officer meant he got to determine whether or not someone qualified for a loan. It was easy to imagine how many friends this life made him. He and Amy were hoping to start a family soon and he did his best to do what any good potential father would do: provide for his soon-to-be wife and unborn child.

Other than this rather slow night, Brandon's business was, in fact, doing quite well. Few Irish pubs truly captured the essence of Ireland, short of the color green and a few paper clovers tacked on the walls, but his did. The menu consisted of traditional Irish meals like corned beef and cabbage, and breakfasts filled with blood pudding and rashers of bacon. The two most promoted items were twelve kinds of genuine Irish whiskey and good, old-fashioned Guinness. Brandon often chose to play authentic music straight from the Emerald Isle to help provide an actual pub experience. He'd modeled it after a pub he'd visited during a high school trip to the Isle, so he knew what it would take to emulate the real deal. But the success didn't cause his need for celebration. Brandon left Grants Pass for good to start his business.

He left his family, his not-so-serious girlfriend and, most importantly, his best friends, but now they'd come to visit him. There was rarely a greater cause to celebrate.

They always supported one another. A few years back, when Ben knew he wanted to be a writer, Brandon and Taylor both told him to follow his dream and to leave the pizza parlor in the rear view. Brandon even offered him a job at the bar when it first opened, so that Ben could write as much as possible, but Lynn didn't want to move. She loved Grants Pass too much to make any drastic changes. But finally, Ben had the chance to follow that dream.

As the clock in the bar struck three a.m., and none of them were in any shape to drive, Brandon offered Ben and Taylor a place to stay for the night in the bar. "It's not a problem, guys. As long as you don't mind sleeping on a couple of shitty cots. I got me a nice comfy place upstairs. Bed and all."

"No, that's fine," said Ben.

"Can't I come sleep with you?" asked Taylor. "I'll let you be the big spoon."

"As appealing as that sounds, I've got a meeting early tomorrow morning, down at the court house. So, as much as I'd like to hold you close all night, I've got to get at least a little sleep."

"Fine," said Taylor, jokingly.

Brandon ran upstairs and brought down a couple of green cots and some blankets. "Night, assholes. It's been fun. If I don't see you guys in the morning, feel free to make something to eat and leave out the back door. And don't be strangers, guys."

All three of them quickly passed out the moment their heads hit the pillows. Ben could easily sleep for twenty hours, but they planned on waking up at eight. Five hours of sleep would be better than none.

5

THE MORNING CAME and the light shined through the green, stained-glass windows of the bar.

Ben woke up first, stretched and took his morning piss behind the dumpster in the alley, forgetting about the indoor restroom.

Taylor stirred awake shortly after and went to the inside toilet to pee. "Brandon up yet?" he asked as he walked out of the bathroom, zipping up his jeans. He made his way behind the bar and over to the stairs leading to Brandon's room. "Hey, Brandon, you up?" No one answered. "Huh, guess he's already gone. Didn't he say he needed to be up early for something?"

"Yeah, I think so," said Ben, clutching his head tightly. "God, my head fucking hurts."

"Yeah, it feels like someone dropped a safe on your head, huh?"

"Worse."

"Mine too. Maybe you should learn to hold your booze better."

"Ha, ha." Ben walked over to the kitchen door and noticed a piece of paper taped to it. "Hey, looks like he left us a note." He read it out loud:

Hey guys, I had a great time seeing you two again. We have to get together soon to celebrate your book, Ben. I had to take off already, but feel free to make something to eat and have a beer for the road if you want, just leave out the back. Keep in touch. ~Brandon

"I didn't know he had such nice, girly handwriting," said Ben.

"Huh, neither did I. It's almost as pretty as yours. Well, that sucks that he had to leave so early." Taylor snatched the note from Ben's hands and crumpled it before tossing it to the floor behind him. "Oh well, I guess we should probably get outta here, anyway."

"Yeah, probably. We'll stop back by on the way home." Ben went into the kitchen and opened the industrial refrigerator, taking out a few eggs and some bread for toast. He cooked up their quick breakfast and after a few minutes of arguing, he convinced Taylor to clean up after him.

With their bellies full and the protein helping to fight one hell of a hangover, they left the bar, locking the back door from the inside before shutting it. Seeing Brandon did them a lot of good and provided a needed sense of nostalgia for them both. A bit of respite they wouldn't soon forget.

"So, where to next?" asked Taylor, pushing Ben out of the back alley and quickly into the car's passenger seat.

"Well, when I was a kid there was a neat place just outside of Salem. I've been wanting to go back for years and last night has me feeling pretty nostalgic. I think it'll be nice to see it again." Ben tried to remember the name as he climbed into the passenger seat and Taylor sat behind the wheel. "Um…Mt. Angel. Yeah, that was it."

"Mt. Angel, huh? Sounds sexy. I'm in."

"Come on, Taylor, you don't have anything else to do and you're over a hundred miles away from home. Of course you're in." Ben awkwardly turned around and fished through the junk in the back seat, eventually finding a notepad on the floor. He turned to a fresh page and took his favorite pen out of his pocket, in hopes he could begin brainstorming. "But let's just drive. Doesn't really matter where we go. If we see somewhere nice, we can stop."

"Sounds good to me. Just drive and see where it takes us."

"Exactly."

Ready to continue their long journey north, Taylor pulled back onto I-5 and merged into the fast lane. Before they realized it, they were an hour outside of Eugene and only a short distance past Albany, and with the alcohol still being purged from their systems, they both drastically needed a pit stop. Usually, they would pull over to the side of the road and use nature's bathroom. But the roads were narrow and the shoulders even narrower. Luckily, they passed a sign for a rest stop and were happy to park somewhere for a bit. It didn't take long before they saw the exit ramp leading to a small parking lot, hidden behind the tree line.

Before the car could come to a full stop, Ben jumped out and sprinted for the restroom.

The air outside smelled of pine trees and fresh rain. Inside the restroom, however, the stalls and steel urinals smelled like a shack in an overpopulated Hooverville settled beneath a bridge. The worst of the lingering stench emanated from two steel toilets and their desperate need to be flushed.

Ben's overwhelming need to take a piss overpowered the stench and he decided to forgo flushing the toilets.

Taylor followed shortly after, throwing open the heavy, rusted door. "Ugh, it smells like shit in here."

"Well, it is a bathroom on the side of the highway." Ben finished his third shake and zipped himself up. He proceeded to wash his hands, not realizing the dispensers were out of paper towels. "You want to chill out here for a bit?"

"In a bathroom?" Taylor laughed as he scooted up close to the urinal and Ben glared at him. "I'm just fuckin' with you. Calm down." He spoke louder to drown out the sound of liquid drumming against the metal backsplash. "But yeah, that sounds good, I think we got a few more beers left in the trunk." Taylor shook off and followed Ben out of the restroom, forgetting to wash his hands.

Ben retrieved his notepad and pen from the car then walked over to a poorly maintained picnic table near the edge of the clearing.

Taylor grabbed a few refreshing beverages from the trunk and their snacks from the back seat then met Ben at the table.

Moments after sitting down, Ben found himself immediately accosted by a beer bottle soaring towards his chest.

"Oh, shit. I just realized I forgot a bottle opener," Taylor said, fretfully. "How're we gonna drink beer if we don't have a bottle opener?"

"No worries, watch this." Ben placed the bottle's cap on the edge of the wood table and slammed the heel of his palm down on top of it, removing the cap. The beer started to foam from the top and Ben met the lukewarm, rising suds with his lips. "A little warm, but not too bad."

"Damnit, Ben, I was trying to mess with you." He pulled a flat bartender's tool from his back pocket. "I took it from Brandon's bar."

"No worries, I 'borrowed' a couple beer mugs. They're stashed in the trunk." They both laughed as Ben realized how much he hated it when they thought alike.

"So, you figure out what you're gonna write yet?"

Taylor sat down on the table top next to him.

"Nah, I'm still thinking. I really wanted to write a sci-fi story. When I was a kid, I always loved the idea of travelling through space, seeing alien worlds, sexing up green women—you know, the usual stuff."

"Naturally."

"But science fiction fans are hard to please. Believe me, I am one. I would know."

"That'd be really cool, but I get it. You have to be really specific and technical when it comes to writing sci-fi stuff. Otherwise it just doesn't sound realistic. As realistic as science fiction can be, anyway." Taylor chugged down half his beer. "If not that, what else were you thinking?"

"I don't know. I thought about writing something realistic. Like an *Indiana Jones* story or something, or maybe a mystery book. I don't know."

"That's where it's at. People love mystery or treasure hunting stories. Oh, I got it! What about an archeologist who finds the remnants of an ancient society buried beneath the pyramids?"

"That sounds great, but it sounds like it's been done before. Doesn't it?"

"Yeah, more or less. Let me know when you figure it out, though. I'd love to help. You know I always have great ideas. Ah, like this." He turned to Ben like he'd had a life changing epiphany. "You're searching for Hitler's hidden treasure stash." He was shaking his head up and down, as if to say *that's the one.*

"Well, that's good and all, but I don't know enough about Hitler and Nazi treasure to write about it. But don't worry, I'm trapped with you in a car for another four hundred miles, so I'm sure once I figure it out, you'll be the first to know."

"True. True. Oh, hey, check it out." Taylor pointed to a small Prius parking near their car. Two girls climbed out of the car and started walking towards the restroom. Taylor's eyes were locked onto them like an ass-seeking missile. Taylor often sought praise for his finely tuned rack radar. He could spot a pair of Ds from a block away. His attention was clearly focused on the girls as they walked across the parking lot. "Holy...shit, would you look...at...that," he said, mesmerized.

Both girls wore tight yoga pants—Taylor's favorite— one with the word "Juicy" written across her backside and the other read "Love," two letters on each cheek.

"Oh, don't worry. I'm already there." Ben's eyes were less obvious when it came to observing the opposite sex, a trick he'd learned from years of being in a relationship.

"Hey, ladies!" Taylor shouted over to them, but they quietly giggled and disappeared into the restroom. "They love me. Oh, shit, that's what you should do. Write a 'romance' novel." He smirked and shook his eyebrows, obviously meaning verbal pornography. "Oh! A lesbian romance novel, with pictures and not so many words. The title: 'Fifty Shades of Scissoring!'"

"Yeah, I'm still kind of a closet romantic. A closet lesbian, if you will, but I've never been very good at romantic stuff." Ben turned and grabbed his notepad off the picnic table and retrieved his pen from behind his ear. "Ask Lynn. She'll tell you I'm pretty much the least romantic person she knows."

"That's just because she's waiting for you to put a ring on her finger. That'll make women say all sorts of weird shit. You give her a ring and you'll become the most romantic guy in the world." Taylor quickly sucked down the rest of his beer and popped off the tops of two more bottles. "Hurry and finish your first one."

Ben followed Taylor's instruction and moved on to his next bottle.

"So, a mystery-type novel," said Taylor. "Like a 'who-done-it' sort of thing? What can we do?"

"Yeah, more or less, but I want to steer clear of sounding like a game of *Clue*."

"What about a cop following an international jewel thief? That would be like a mystery, turns out it's, like, the police captain or something."

"A little *Pink Panther*-ish, but it could work." Ben jotted down some notes on his pad. *Cop trailing jewel thief, big twist in bad guy reveal and who done it, NOT like Clue, but a murder mystery.* He wanted to ensure that he wouldn't forget the ideas in case he chose to use one of them, especially since they'd been drinking. Both of them tended to forget the million-dollar ideas they came up with every time they drank. Between bullet points, Ben would stop and look up at the canopy, enjoying the dark green leaves penetrated by thin slips of sunlight.

Taylor continued to eyeball the restroom doors, waiting for the girls to exit. Every so often, he had to claim that he wasn't being creepy, but it's hard to defend noticeably gawking at the women's restroom. But finally, after a good fifteen minutes, the girls exited and Taylor slapped Ben on the chest repeatedly with the back of his hand until he averted his eyes from their upward gaze. "Why won't you look, Ben? I mean, come on, their asses are begging to be read, over and over again."

True, true, thought Ben. "I already looked earlier. Their asses aren't going to have changed in the last fifteen minutes. Besides, I have a girlfriend and so do you, for that matter." He downed the rest of his drink, hopefully ending the conversation.

"Yeah, but it's not like we're *doing* anything, just

looking. You think Lynn doesn't check out random 'hot' guys on the street or when she goes out with Amy?"

"I know she does, but still…"

"And don't take this the wrong way, Ben, but there are a lot hotter guys than you out there. So, she knows she can do better, but she loves you for you. Looking at a little eye candy's not going to hurt anyone. That's why God invented eye candy…to be ogled...and hopefully tasted."

"I don't know if everything you just said convinced me, or just pissed me off. Dick." Ben punched Taylor in the arm as hard as he could while sitting on a bench.

Taylor jumped to his feet and stood directly in front of him. "Okay, Ben. What if they were naked?"

Ben paused cautiously, waiting for some sort of justification for this highly unlikely scenario.

"Say a pipe burst in the bathroom, spraying them so hard that their clothes were ripped from their wet bodies and you missed it. What then?"

Weak reasoning, but a fair question. "I guess that…I…would have missed out. But I looked anyway; you're acting like I was fighting you the entire time or something."

"I know you did. Just giving you a hard time. Someone's gotta do it." Taylor finally realized that the girls had already driven away. "Come on." Taylor chugged down his beer and threw the bottle as hard as he could at a tree. "Let's get outta here before it gets too late in the day."

Ben stood up with his beer, pen and paper in hand.

"Hey, come on, already." Taylor motioned at Ben to finish the beer faster.

Fuck it. Ben guzzled down the rest of his beer and followed in suit with Taylor, smashing his bottle against the same tree. It nearly slipped his mind that he still needed to call Lynn. If he didn't do it soon, she might get worried and call the police. "Hey, asshole, since you threw mine out the window, let me use your cell. I'm gonna call Lynn real quick, so we don't forget later."

"Yeah, they've probably had enough time to cool off. She's probably going to be pissed when you tell her where you are, though." He tossed his phone over to Ben, who sat on the hood of the car. Taylor didn't keep many numbers in his phone, not even Lynn's. Luckily, Ben was able to remember it, seeing how he hadn't physically typed in her number in years.

The phone rang a few times before Lynn answered. "Hello?"

"Hey, honey, it's me."

"Ben, where the hell are you? It's been two days! You never came home. I've been worried sick!"

"Yeah, sorry about that." Ben tried to quickly think of an excuse. "Let me just start by saying that this is pretty much all Taylor's fault, as usual. He started a fight at the bar and then, somehow, convinced me to take him on my trip to see my dad. Then, he talked me into leaving that night. I think we both had a bit too much to drink to make any good decisions."

"No shit, Ben. You could have at least called me."

"I know. Taylor thought you guys might need a little time to cool down. And he threw my phone out the window while we were driving. Can you believe that? I honestly have no idea what he was thinking."

"I don't know what *you* were thinking, Ben. Are you coming home, then?" Lynn's voice changed from worried to livid.

"Well, honey," Ben said, hoping that using her pet name would calm her. "We're already quite a ways away from Grants Pass. We've come this far; we might as well just keep going."

"That's the stupidest thing I've ever heard." Any concern she had left vanished. "You need to come home. I'm pissed and we need to talk about this."

"Look, it's not just my decision." Ben tried to keep his focus on the conversation as Taylor turned on the radio inside the car and jumped from station to station. "It's his car; he wants to drive up there either way. I'm…going to keep going. You know I need to go see my dad, Lynn. This is important to me." Ben started to have trouble concentrating as Taylor began shouting the lyrics to a gangster rap song on the radio. Growing more irritated, Ben tried to make hand signals at him to turn it down, but with no luck.

Taylor wouldn't run the risk of ruining his rhyming streak by stopping to turn a dial.

"Fine, but just get home as fast as you can." Lynn's voice continued to increase in intensity. "And call me the moment you reach Spokane. Okay?"

"Okay, I promise."

"And we're going to talk about all this shit when you get home."

Ben knew calling her might have been a bad idea. "Yeah, I know." He got up off the hood of the car. "I love you?" His question was met with the sound of silence; she had hung up.

"…Cali is where they put they mack down, gimme love!" Taylor shouted, then finally decided to turn the volume down. He poked his head up over the door of the car. "So, how'd that go?" he yelled. "Terrible, right?"

"Yeah, she was pretty pissed."

"Told you she would be." Taylor's smug attitude irritated Ben.

"You know Amy's going to be pissed, too. You

should probably give her a call."

"No, I called her yesterday from Brandon's bar."

Ben couldn't believe what he'd just heard. "Are you kidding me? And you couldn't remind me to call Lynn?"

"I figured Amy would tell Lynn where you were. Besides, she has more of a temper than Amy. I didn't want to ruin our night with Brandon."

"Look, just try to be a bit more...considerate, next time. Alright?" Ben walked around to the passenger door. "That was pretty fucking uncool."

"Alright, I'm sorry. I didn't mean to cause any problems."

Ben knew that wasn't the truth. He could tell that behind all of Taylor's kind words, and the way he acted around Lynn, that he hated her bitchy attitude. "Yeah, sure," said Ben.

They had remained at the rest stop long enough, so they buckled up and prepared to hit the open road again.

"So, how do we get to this Mt. Angel place?" Taylor attempted to steer the conversation in a "not his fault" direction.

Ben pulled the map out of the car door to study the exact directions. "Let's see. So, keep driving 'til we get past Salem and Keizer, then turn off right near the end of the Keizer city limits. Then just follow the road for a ways. We're not too far out."

Taylor backed out of the parking space and sped out of the rest stop. "Alright, let's hit the road, Jack." He continued to mumble the lyrics to the Ray Charles hit until the rest stop faded from the rear view mirror and became nothing but a distant memory.

6

AFTER SOME TIME on the highway and a number of winding back roads—filled with the obnoxious sounds of two men singing along to their favorite rap and country songs—the Firebird quickly found itself driving down Main Street in Mt. Angel. Had they not been watching for the small town, they might have passed right through it. Mt. Angel had a small population and looked as though it had been pulled from an old western film, on old western with German-inspired architecture. Like most dusty Old West movies, Main Street stretched from one end of the town to the other, only a couple miles long. Were it not for the annual Oktoberfest celebration, the town's largest attraction, few would likely have ever heard the name.

Taylor quickly fell in love with the picturesque, small town and drove up and down its side streets for over an hour while Ben slept in the passenger seat. In all his years living in Oregon, Taylor couldn't believe that he'd never been to Mt. Angel before. He drove past the police station and a local sausage manufacturer, making his way towards the towering, brick steeple in the center of the town. As he neared the enormous church, he slowed the car to a light stroll and peered out the window, taking in everything the church had to offer. "I'm definitely coming back here some time." He drove back to Main Street, passed by the police station again and parked in front of a small convenience store. In an attempt to scare his best friend awake, Taylor shook Ben a few times, shouting. "Get up, asshole! We're there, we're there!"

"Fuck off," said Ben, shoving Taylor away from him and attempting to fall back asleep.

"We're in Mt. Angel, dude." Taylor put the car keys in his pocket and stepped out of the car.

After forcing himself to open his eyes, Ben climbed out and followed Taylor to the hood of the car.

"So, what is there to actually do in this town?" asked Taylor.

"Other than Oktoberfest, which isn't for another few months, I have no idea." Ben rubbed his eyes one last time and walked out to the back of the car, examining the town. He looked left for a few seconds, then to the right, hoping that something interesting would catch his eye. Across the street he saw a small barbershop, with an old white man sitting out front, reading the newspaper. Near the far end of town, he could see a run-down bowling alley that hadn't been maintained since the late Sixties and an auto shop, bustling with the sounds of socket wrenches and air compressors.

"Well, it's not quite noon yet. What do you want to do?" asked Taylor, standing next to him.

"I don't know. I just woke up." Ben blinked and clenched his eyes vigorously.

Taylor looked around, trying to think of something to do. "I got nothing."

"I gotta pee." Ben started walking down the street.

"Where're you going?"

"To find somewhere to take a piss."

"Alright, meet you back here in a bit then?"

"Yeah. If you want, grab some beer or something inside," said Ben, pointing back at the store. "Maybe I'll see if I can find somewhere to relax and write for a bit."

"Alright, see ya in a bit, then." Taylor walked off in the opposite direction, examining all the buildings around him. Before disappearing from sight, he stopped and took out his phone, snapping a few photos of a wooden boy carved into the side of a white building adorned with diagonal brown beams across the outside.

Ben continued down the sidewalk, looking into the windows of the stores. The strangest storefront he passed showcased hundreds of tiny, carved German shepherds. "Creepy," he said out loud before continuing on down the street. Not far from the carving shop, a white sign, dangling above a storefront, caught his attention. "'The Sour Kraut?'" It took him a moment to connect the dots. "Well, that's a little racist, but I'm in." He shrugged his shoulders and went inside.

A portly man stood behind a bar, wearing all black with a folded white apron around his waist, talking into an old flip phone. He waived at Ben as he sat at one of the barstools. "No. Alright, I gotta go. Okay, buh-bye." The bartender hung up the phone and approached Ben. "Sorry about that. My nephew's a little shit; stole his mom's credit card. Sometimes you just want to take 'em out back and…beat 'em with a hose."

Ben couldn't help but laugh in agreement. "Yeah, I've got a few family members like that. I'm actually surprised that you're open. Seems like nothing's open this early around here."

"Of course I'm open. This place is my pride and joy. I'd be open twenty-four-seven, if they'd let me."

"This is your place? So, if you don't mind me asking, how'd you come up with the name? I feel like you'd catch a little flak for that."

"Oh, the town fucking hated it." The bartender's foul

language caught Ben by surprise. "At first, they said no," continued the bartender, "but then I started coming up with…let's just say 'more interesting' names."

"Like what?" Ben asked.

"Let's see…oh, first, you know the big church up the road?"

Ben nodded.

"I pitched the 'Easy Alter Boy.'"

"Bullshit."

"Swear to God, man. To be expected, they shot that name down immediately. So, then I said 'Okay, how about the 'Judgmental Nazi' or the 'Crispy Hebrew' instead?'"

It was hard for Ben to believe how openly crude and intolerant the bartender was acting, but he couldn't help letting a little laughter slip.

"But eventually, they came to their senses and let me keep The Sour Kraut." The bartender crossed his arms, satisfied with his story.

"That is probably the worst and funniest thing I've ever heard."

"Oh, speaking of funny and terrible things, you like dirty jokes?"

"Sure." Ben smiled. "Whaddya got?"

"Okay, I'll start you off with an easy one. Do you know why altar boys' hair is always parted?"

Ben shook his head.

"Because the priest is always saying 'yes, my son,'" he said while mocking a priest stroking and parting a boy's hair near his groin.

Ben laughed out loud. "That's pretty terrible, but I've heard worse."

The bartender's belly shook as he chuckled out loud.

"I'm Ben, by the way."

"Nice to meet you, Ben. I'm Chuck."

"Nice to meet you, too."

"So, you like the really inappropriate jokes, huh?"

"I'll admit that sometimes the gross and awful jokes are the best ones."

"Okay, I've got another one for you. You thirsty?"

"Um…that's not a very good joke, but yeah. Do you have any actual German beers? I was hoping to find one somewhere in this town."

"Definitely, can I recommend one?" asked Chuck.

"Yeah, for sure."

"Try this." Chuck grabbed a chilled glass and pressed it down on a glass rinser before stepping up to the taps. He began pouring from the second tap in from the right, with an ornate, wood-carved handle. A golden pale beer filled glass, settling in a perfect pour. "My favorite," he said as he set the beer down in front of Ben.

Ben raised the glass to his lips and sipped the chilled liquid from beneath the inch foam. "Holy…shit—that's delicious."

"Right?" Chuck had a huge, satisfied grin on his face.

"I should have brought Taylor here. He's gonna be pissed that I didn't bring him."

"Who?"

"Oh, my friend and I are both in town. We're doing a little research and exploring a bit. We split up 'cause I had to…oh, right. I forgot I had to take a piss. Where's your bathroom?"

Chuck pointed at a door with a faceless silhouette of a man wearing lederhosen, on the door. "Right there."

"Thanks. I'll be right back and then I want to hear that joke."

"I'll be here."

Ben disappeared into the bathroom and quickly

emptied his bladder before returning to his beer. "Oh, that's better. Sorry, where were we?"

"Right, here's another easy one. What do you get when you cross a fifty foot rooster and an M&M?"

Ben took a drink while he waited for a punch line.

"A giant cock that melts in your mouth, not in your hand."

"Okay, that's pretty good," Ben said smiling. "What else you got?"

"You know why there are no straight pride parades, right?"

"Why?"

"Because they're all fucking gay."

Ben spit out a little bit of his beer.

"Okay, last one for now…maybe. We'll see." Chuck widened his stance and prepared to tell the next joke, which apparently required his entire body. "Anyway, two male ranchers walk out to the edge of their property and see one of their sheep with its head stuck in the fence."

"Okay," said Ben, suspicious of the punch line.

"The first rancher unbuttons his pants and drops trou. He grabs the sheep and starts fuckin' it," Chuck said, thrusting excessively, "until he finally finishes. Then, he steps back, pulls his pants up and looks at the other rancher and says, 'You want to get in on some of this?' So, the second rancher unbuttons his pants, takes 'em off, then pulls the sheep out of the fence and sticks his head in the hole."

*What? I don't get…*Ben only had to think for a moment before it clicked and he started laughing uncontrollably. "What? That's terrible!" he said with a huge smile on his face.

Chuck began chuckling again, his enormous belly shaking up and down. "You like that?"

"Yeah, that was a pretty good one." Ben drank down a few gulps of beer, then rolled up the sleeves of his shirt. "Oh, shit. I should probably get going. How much?" he asked pointing at the half-empty pint glass.

"Don't worry about it, on the house."

"You sure?"

"Yeah, you let me pick your drink and tell you jokes I wouldn't say in front of my mother…again. Just come back sometime, and hey, bring your friend."

"I'll do that. Thanks, man." Ben extended his arm over the counter and Chuck reciprocated, shaking Ben's hand. "Maybe we'll stop by before we leave town."

"Sounds good, Ben. Nice meeting you."

"The same." Ben finished his beer and walked towards the door, but stopped before opening it. "Hey, are there any libraries, or anywhere around here to do some reading, maybe get a little writing done?"

"You're a writer, huh? Why doesn't that surprise me?" Chuck scratched his temple. "I think the only library is at the school, but there's a bookstore down on Main Street. Cute girl works there. Little nerdy, though."

"Okay, cool. Thanks again and have a good one." Ben waved goodbye and Chuck waved back. He exited the bar making his way towards where they'd parked the car. As he passed by the convenience store, he noticed Taylor inside, examining the beer selection in the enormous coolers. Ben continued down the sidewalk and noticed a sign on the small building next to the barbershop, which simply read: "Bookstore." *Maybe the "little nerdy" girl will know a good place to get a little inspiration around here*. He jogged across the street and nodded as he walked past the old barber, still sitting in the lawn chair out front of his shop. The barber only snarled at him and turned away. *Okay, dick*. As Ben approached the storefront, he peered through the bookstore's windows, but saw no one inside. Expecting it to be locked, he pulled on the door, which opened and chimed as he walked through it.

A few seconds later, a young girl—around the same age as Ben—walked out of the back room carrying a stack of books. She unintentionally hid her face behind the tower of books, attempting to balance them as they swayed back and forth, teasing at a possible collapse. After managing to carefully set the books down on the front counter, she accidentally knocked an old copy of *King Lear* to the floor in front of Ben's feet.

He knelt down and picked up the book, placing it on top of the stack.

She smiled and her pasty white cheeks changed to a rosy red. "Thanks," she said, brushing a strand of hair behind her ear.

"Don't worry about it." He smiled back at her.

"How may I help you?" She pushed her glasses up close to her eyes.

"Well, to be perfectly honest, I'm trying to write a book and I'm looking for somewhere to get a little work done. I thought I might find an avid reader in here who might know a peaceful place to feel inspired. You wouldn't happen to know anywhere nice to write in this beautiful weather, would you?"

"Well..." She looked down while she thought for a moment. "There's a small coffee shop not too far away from here; they have some outside tables. Or...there's a nice park a few blocks away. It's really pretty. It's my favorite..." She hesitated for a moment. "I...I could show you where it is. If you want?"

"That would be great. I'm Ben." He held his hand out.

"Ashton," she said as she placed her hand in his, accepting his light shake.

"It's nice to meet you. Are you sure it's alright for you to leave the store?"

"It's almost time for me to take my lunch. It'll be fine. Besides, it's not like I have any customers." She walked over to the front door and spun around the small "Open" sign to read "Closed" and placed a small "Out to lunch" sign in the window. "Come on, it's not too far."

Ben followed her out of the store and waited for her to lock up. As they walked down Main Street, he noticed the barber had disappeared from his chair on the sidewalk and a "Closed" sign had been placed in the window upside down.

Neither of them spoke as they walked down the street, only sharing a bit of eye contact and a periodic smile.

"That barber guy is a bit creepy...don't you think?" said Ben, attempting to strike up a conversation.

"Yeah, he's kind of a weird one. He is nice though; he brings me an apple every day around lunch time."

"Oh." *I am an idiot*, Ben thought. "Sorry, I didn't know you knew him that well." It became obvious that neither of them were very good at small talk. Unsure if the silence or the German beer—with a higher-than-average ABV—spurred his attempts at conversation, he decided to try and break the ice with a few jokes and make her smile, to make up for his earlier stupidity. "Two peanuts walking down the street, one gets a-salted."

Ashton smiled slightly.

"Two muffins, baking in the oven. One says to the other 'Man, it's hot in here.' The other one looks over and screams, 'Holy crap! A talking muffin!'"

A quickly silenced laugh broke out of Ashton's mouth.

As they reached the end of the block and prepared to turn the corner, Ben noticed Taylor leaning against the driver-side door of their car. He tried not to attract

Taylor's attention, for fear of what he might think was happening with this unfamiliar, pretty girl. But he wasn't that lucky.

Taylor turned his head and watched them reach the corner. He raised his arms and shrugged his shoulders as if to say, "Who the hell is this?" and "What about our plan?"

Ben waved him off with a hand behind Ashton's back and they continued around the corner.

"It's just up there. Do you see the trees around that big gazebo?" asked Ashton.

"Yeah, looks beautiful." Ben tried to think of something more to say before she decided to return to the store. "So, what do you do with your free time? Besides reading. Do you do any writing?"

"No, I wouldn't be any good." She looked down and brushed the same rogue strands of brown hair back behind her ear. "I do love to read, though. You said you were a writer. Have you written anything I might have read?"

"No, not yet. I'm working on it, though. I'm trying to write my first novel."

"Well, who knows, maybe I'll end up reading your book someday." She looked up at Ben and smiled a petite smile.

"Actually, I haven't really started yet. I'm still trying to figure out what to write. All I've ever written is a few short stories. Nothing like a full novel. I've always liked mysteries, or fantasy novels. But, I think I'm steering towards something a bit more realistic and gritty for my first novel. I'm open to suggestions, though."

"You should write a love story." She began acting playfully dramatic. "Something that pulls on the heart strings and maybe makes you cry by the time you get to the end. Every good story should be about love."

"Oh, so you're one of those?" Ben joked.

"Yup," she said, smiling with a sense of pride.

"I'll keep that in mind, but I don't think that's really my style. I've never really been much of a romantic." They were both smiling comfortably by the time they reached the park.

"Well, here we are. I should probably get back to the shop."

"Are you sure you can't stay for just a bit? You haven't been on lunch that long."

"Um...I guess it couldn't hurt, for just a few more minutes, at least."

Ben pointed to a picnic table near the edge of the park and they sat down. "Are you from around here?"

"Yep, born and raised. What about you?"

"Born and raised in Grants Pass. Mostly raised there, anyway. It's actually a pretty small town, sort of like this one, only less...old-timey-looking."

"Old-timey-looking?" She thought his description of her town was cute.

Ben shrugged, not knowing how else to describe it.

"Grants Pass is a ways from here, isn't it?"

"Yeah, a few hours south."

"I've never been there before."

"It's alright. Not quite as memorable as this place, though. I love all the German-ness."

"What brings you all the way up here? Just looking for a change of scenery to write your book?"

Ben couldn't help but notice that every time she mentioned his writing, she didn't sound condescending or patronizing. He even noticed a flicker of excitement in her voice and how her face lit up whenever she said "your book." "No, not exactly. My dad is pretty sick. He's hold up in the cancer ward in a hospital up in Spokane. But, he's having surgery…today, actually. The doctors said he should be awake in a day or two. So, we're actually heading up there to see him, but I also quit…" Ben felt a strange urge to be honest with her. Maybe it was because he knew he'd never see her again after today, or maybe because he actually had feelings for her. So, he told her the truth. "I actually got fired from my job, so I'm taking a bit of time to do what I love while we drive up there. An 'involuntary career shift,' if you will."

"We?"

"Oh, right, my friend, Taylor and I. He's at the store right now stocking up on supplies. We drove his car up here; it was sort of a spur-of-the-moment decision to take off."

"Impulsive, huh? I like that." She nervously looked down at the ground, kicking at the dirt beneath her feet. "You must not have anything keeping you…tied down…if you can just up and take off like that."

Ben could decipher the real question beneath all the small talk and he knew what answer he *should* tell her. But he was worried the truth might ruin the good time they were having. Plus, he hadn't been viewed as clever or interesting in years and he enjoyed the extra attention. "Nope. Nothing 'keeping me tied down' there." Ben played at being naïve, but the moment the words slipped past his lips, he knew he shouldn't have said it. If Lynn were to find out about it, their relationship would be over. Nine long years, down the drain.

Taylor wouldn't say anything to Lynn about the "girl from the bookstore." He would most likely say "Good for you, man, you need to get out there and talk to people more often, especially pretty girls." Taylor knew Ben would never actually cheat on Lynn, and other than her periodic fits of "bitchy-ness," he actually liked her. As

Ben thought about Taylor and Lynn, Taylor's words echoed in his mind: "Lynn probably does the same thing when you're not around."

"That's good." A big smile lit up Ashton's face, snapping Ben back to the moment. Her smile was gorgeous; the perfect compromise between "awkwardly tiny" and looking like the Joker. She adjusted her glasses and looked back up at him. "What was your job, before all this?"

"I worked in a pizza place for seven-plus years. It got real old, real quick."

"Do you mind if I ask…what did you get fired for?"

Ben didn't feel the need to hesitate before answering. "Well, my boss was a bit of a hard ass, which, on its own, is fine, but he never appreciated all the work I did around there. He really didn't acknowledge anybody's hard work; he wouldn't even let staff keep their tips."

Ashton shook her head in disapproval, intently listening to Ben's boring work story.

"I usually did most of his work, too. You know, all of the running-the-business type stuff. I even dealt with staff management and scheduling. I asked him for a raise or a promotion, so I could actually get some sort of compensation for all the extra work I did."

"What did he say? Let me guess, he said 'no,' didn't he?"

"Well, not exactly. He offered me a ten-cent raise, which is virtually worthless, even to minimum wage employees. So, I told him *that* and then it kind of escalated from there, and he fired me."

"Oh, wow. At least you stood up for yourself. Most people can't even do that. They deal with a condescending boss in a job they hate, for years, for…shit pay." She clearly didn't swear very often.

"That's how I saw it." Ben felt that, if he swore too, it would make her feel more comfortable around him. "I've always felt that if you're gonna work for shit pay, you should either be miserable in a job you love doing, or be happy in a job you hate doing."

"Exactly. That makes a lot of sense." She laughed and put on her cute, tiny smile again.

"So, what about you? What do you want to do?" Ben asked.

"Well, I like working in the book store, but I think I want to be a literary agent one day. Read all day long and help new writers"—she pointed at Ben—"like you. You know, help find budding new authors."

"Tell you what. Sometime, I'll let you represent me, when you're ready to get started. Hopefully by then, this novel will have taken off and your job'll be a piece of cake."

"I'd like that." Ashton placed her hand on top of Ben's and looked away, her cheeks blushing. After looking down at her watch, she noticed the time. They'd been talking for the better part of her lunch and she only had a few minutes to get back to the bookstore. "Oh, shoot! I have to go." She climbed down from the table top and before walking away, looked back to Ben. "Good luck with your book. I think whatever you write will be amazing. You better look me up after you make it big."

"Yeah, I'll do that." Ben tried to think of something quick to say before she left. "Hey, um…thanks again for bringing me here. I can feel the creativity flowing already."

Ashton walked up to Ben and planted a small, wet kiss on his cheek. She quickly looked away and continued on her course back to the store. Halfway up the block, she looked back and gave him one last smile. If Ben remembered one thing from the town, it would be her warm, petite smile. It had been years since Lynn had looked at him like that, let alone a complete stranger. As Ashton walked up the block, Taylor walked past her, but she avoided any eye contact as they passed.

Taylor, refusing to deviate from the norm, turned to watch her as she walked away. His "up and down of the goods" returned with a verdict of a two—awkwardly carrying grocery bags—thumbs up.

Ben got up and took one of the bags from Taylor.

"Her ass...was...amazing. Who the hell was she?"

"She runs the bookstore down the street. Nice girl."

"Nice is definitely the word I would choose, that's for sure. Did I see her flirting with you, you sly devil, you?" Taylor looked teasingly surprised.

"Shut up."

"Oh, I see. *You* were flirting with *her!*" Taylor's fake shock only came across as irritating.

Ben turned and walked back to his spot at the picnic table.

Taylor chased after him and pulled a couple of beers from one of the bags. "Calm down, I'm just kidding. Here, cheers." He popped the bottle caps off with the bottle opener he'd stolen from Brandon's bar.

"Did you grab my notepad from the car?" Ben took a big swig of his beer. "Oh, God, that tastes freaking good. What is that?" he asked as he examined the bottle.

"Yeah, here. It's a new summer beer from Malt Mountain Brewing." Taylor pulled the legal pad from the grocery bag. "So, you still haven't told me what you're writing about. It's me, isn't it?"

"Yeah, because the most interesting thing I can think of is you." Ben hoped Taylor would catch his sarcasm.

"Oh, come on. You know you love me."

Ben let out a half-hearted laugh, still distracted by his

conversation with Ashton. "That's what Ashton and I were just talking about."

"What, you loving me? And who the hell is Ashton?"

"Ashton. The bookstore girl." Ben pointed in her general direction and took another drink. "She said I should write a love story."

"Eck," Taylors face said it all. "Love stories are usually fuckin' terrible. They're always the same stupid thing, over and over again."

"That's pretty much what I told her, more or less. In your actual, honest opinion, what do you think would make a good book?"

"Oh, I don't know. I don't read."

"You wanted to help me write this book, but you don't read?"

"Hey, I watch a lot of movies! I think that qualifies me to know a good story when I hear one. No faith. When are you going to learn to trust me?"

"Well, if it hasn't happened by now..." Ben shrugged his eyebrows and chugged some of the beer. "What about a fantasy story, you know with elves and goblins and shit."

"Eh, it's been done. There's no way it'll be better than *Lord of the Rings*. What else you got?"

Ben took his pen out of his pocket and scratched his head with the tip. "Um...zombie outbreak?"

"God no, it's been waaay overdone nowadays. Don't get me wrong, everyone loves a good zombie story, but I don't know if we need any more, at least right now. Got anything else?"

"Jesus, alright, um...you are damn picky, you know that?" Ben could already feel the well running dry. "Let's just stick with what we talked about before. We both kind of like the whole murder mystery thing."

"I think it's a great idea. You just have to come up

with an interesting mystery that hasn't really been done before."

Ben kept quiet as he pondered what sort of story he could tell. He began to scribble notes on his pad, while Taylor chugged down his beer and stared up at the partly cloudy sky.

Taylor watched the clouds with a sense of purpose, hoping they would reveal the perfect story idea, like a colossal Rorschach test. He took one final swig from the bottle until it was empty, then tossed it behind him into the grass.

"Really?"

"What?" Taylor shrugged and reached for another beer. "They pay people to clean up these parks."

Ben took a large drink from his beer, noticing how much was still left in the bottle. "I don't know what to write about. I feel like there's an idea right on the tip of my pen, but I've got no clue what it is."

"Well, finish your beer. It's a known fact that booze makes you more creative." Taylor smiled. "True story."

"Oh, sure, I've heard that before..." Ben made his condescending attitude clear. Still, he went ahead and finished his beer, just in case Taylor was right.

"I've got it!" Taylor spun around to face Ben. "What about a black widow?"

"Like the spider? What does that have to do with anything?"

"No, 'black widow,' like a lady who kills men. Like a hooker or something."

"That's an interesting idea; there's not many female serial killers. Or what about a hitchhiker that kills people that pick her up?"

"Hasn't something like that been done before, like in the movies? Wasn't it was called, like, 'Hitchhiker' or something."

"Yeah, I think you're right. Ugh, God-damn!" Ben set down his pen and pad. "I can't even focus. I don't even know where to start."

"It's that girl, isn't it? From the bookstore. You like her, don't you?" Taylor grew excited, picking on Ben like a pre-pubescent boy with his first crush.

"That's the thing, I don't even know her, but...yeah, I guess she was pretty cute. But I have Lynn and she loves me. That's all that matters."

"I know, but you can still look. That doesn't make you a bad guy. This trip isn't just about visiting your dad or writing your book. It's also about broadening your horizons a little bit, man. Loosen up. Live a little!"

"I know that, but I'm not going to chase after another girl, Taylor."

"That's not what I'm saying. And that doesn't mean you can't talk to her. When was the last time you talked to a girl? Just randomly, no intention of hitting on her."

Ben was stumped. He couldn't remember the last time he'd talked to a girl that he wasn't living with or working around.

"Exactly!" Taylor exclaimed at the silence. "Because you've got a girlfriend, you've never felt like it's okay to talk to someone of the opposite sex that you don't know. Why is that?"

"I don't know. I guess you're right." Ben had never put that much thought into it. "Never thought I'd hear myself admit you were right about something."

"Tell ya what. We'll finish off the beer I got, but I'm gonna go get us one more six-pack for the road. And while I do that, I'll see if—what was her name? Ashton?"

Ben nodded.

"I'll see if Ashton is still at her store so you can say

'goodbye' before we leave town."

"Taylor, don't."

Taylor had already hopped off of the table and began running towards the convenience store.

Ben decided to take advantage of the alone time by doing a little uninterrupted brainstorming. He started writing down names, locations, professions and plot points that interested him. Anything that entered his mind, even if it had nothing to do with a murder mystery. He wanted to ensure that if he thought up a good idea, there was no chance of him forgetting it.

The time flew by in the small park as the sun started to fall towards the horizon and a light breeze blew through the trees.

Ben only stopped writing for one brief moment, to simply listen to the rustling of the leaves around him. Before too long, he was able to narrow down his list of ideas to a few key ones, the "black widow" among them. He contemplated sinister cult leaders and mass murderers, serial killers and televised crime dramas. All the ideas intrigued him, but none of them stood out as original and unique. Distracted, he set down his pen and looked back up the road. Although Ashton was out of sight, he couldn't help but picture her sitting beside him. Their conversation replayed over and over again in his head. His "single brain" repeatedly pointed out the numerous missed opportunities that he could have used to flirt or impress her. Unfortunately—or perhaps fortunately— monogamy had made him rusty and each opportunity he recognized slipped away. While he knew that not acting on those impulses was for the best, he couldn't keep it from gnawing away at him. Attempting to regain his focus, Ben shook his head and reinserted his nose firmly in his notepad. He began scribbling away again. At first, he didn't realize how little attention he was paying, but then he reviewed his most recent notes. He had no idea that most of what he'd written were words like "Angel" and "Ashton." Shaking these thoughts from his mind was beginning to prove difficult. All he could do was press on with his writing.

Somewhere around a half hour later, Ben realized that Taylor still hadn't returned from his trip to the store. "What the hell's taking so long?" He closed his notepad and slid the pen back into his pocket. Standing up, he grabbed the last two beers before walking back towards Main Street. As he walked along the sidewalk, he could hear the increasingly loud sound of sirens and spotted the flashing of red and blue lights on the pavement around the corner. Worried that something had happened to Taylor, he ran up to the street corner, frantically looking for his friend.

Taylor stood, leaning back against the car door as he'd done before, this time covering his mouth with a shocked look on his face.

Ben ran up to him to find out why he never returned to the park. "Hey, what happened to you?"

"Jesus, Ben...I'm sorry."

"Its fine, man. I just got a little worried is all."

"No, not that. I came back up here and bought another six-pack. And while I was in the store, I saw an ambulance and cop cars drive up to the bookstore. A few minutes ago, they wheeled out a body. It was covered by a sheet, but I saw some long brown hair hanging off the side. I think it was her, Ben."

"Holy shit..." Ben leaned back onto the car and covered his mouth with his hand. "Do you know what happened?"

"One of the cops came around asking some questions;

sounds like she was murdered."

"What? But we *just* saw her earlier today."

"I know; it's kind of unsettling. If you would have gone in there twenty minutes later…you could be fucking dead, dude."

They both stood next to the car, in utter shock. Without another word, they both stood silent for a few minutes, quietly watching the emergency response personnel swarm the crime scene.

"Come on, man, let's…uh…let's get the hell out of here." Taylor placed his hand on Ben's shoulder and opened the driver-side door.

"But who would do something like this? To someone so young. That's…just…horrible."

"I know, buddy. Come on."

They slumped into their car, Taylor behind the wheel and Ben in the passenger seat, feeling the heavy weight of the tragedy. Ben felt the weight of the loss; he felt as though he'd met a kindred spirit and even made a close friend. Taylor empathized with his best friend, because that's what true friends do for one another, and neither of them had ever been so near such a tragic event. It was clear to Taylor that Ben was infatuated with her, even if he wouldn't fully admit it. So, he suffered with his best friend, and for him.

Although Ben had only known Ashton for a short time, he wished he could have been able to help her. Maybe if he had shown up twenty minutes later, just maybe, he could have done something to save her. Or he could have taken her away from the bookstore sooner, *before* it all took place, or he could have kept her at the park longer. *I should have done something*, he thought.

As they drove out of town, they both stayed quiet. Even as the town disappeared from the rear view mirror, they weren't sure what to say to one another. So, Taylor continued driving in silence, not even turning on the radio.

It took a couple of hours before Ben—lost in his thoughts—drifted off to sleep, his head firmly pressed against the glass window. As the night quickly fell and the cold air cooled the glass, Ben's unconscious mind quickly returned to Main Street. Back to where he'd first met Ashton.

7

WHILE BEN AND Taylor continued their long drive towards Spokane, hoping to forget their time in Mt. Angel, a middle-aged detective would soon be woken up from a well-deserved night of rest back in Eugene.

Detective Dan Sawyer had only returned home and fallen asleep for a few hours before his cell phone began violently vibrating across the night stand, instantly waking him from his sleep. Reaching for the phone, Dan's clumsy hands felt around on the stand, knocking his cell to the floor. "God damnit." He leaned over the edge of the bed and fished for his phone beneath the white bed skirt.

His wife rolled over and placed her pale hand on his arm. "Who is it, sweetie?" she asked, still half asleep.

"It's…work. Shit." The cold phone felt like an ice cube as he opened it and pressed it against his cheek. "This is Sawyer."

"You *just* got home. Can't they call someone else?" asked his wife.

Dan raised his pointer finger to his mouth and shushed her so that he could hear the dispatcher. "I'll be right there," he said as he shut the phone. Climbing out of bed, he planted his bare feet firmly on the frigid floorboards. Still groggy from the lack of sleep, he stumbled over to his dresser and put on a pair of underwear, then a tee shirt to wear beneath a button up. "Double homicide, I have to go."

"Can't they call someone else? You're not the only detective on the force, you know."

Dan continued to dress himself, ignoring his wife's pleas for her husband to stay in bed with her. She held the top sheet against her bare chest and insisted he come back to bed. He listened to the familiar words he'd heard her say dozens of times before, but continued to ignore them. Fully dressed, he removed the Springfield nine-millimeter he kept locked in the top drawer of his nightstand. Once it found its place, firmly secured in the holster beneath his left arm and his badge properly dangled around his neck, he knelt down on the bed and leaned over to his wife, interrupting her pleas by giving her a kiss on the lips. "I'm sorry, I have to go." He gave her a quick peck on the cheek. "I'll be back soon…I hope."

"I love you." The underlying tension in those few words alone relayed how upset she truly was.

"Love you, too." Dan grabbed his keys from the bowl by the front door and climbed into the run-down, but trusty, Plymouth sitting in the driveway. He started the car and waited for the windows to defrost, breathing hot air into his clasped hands for warmth. Eventually, once the windows became clear and the car brought itself to a comfortable temperature, he backed out of the driveway and left for the crime scene. The streets were empty and it only took Dan a few minutes to make it across town. He passed the university campus and continued down Broadway until he spotted the familiar yellow tape surrounding the entrance to a dimly lit alleyway. The alley sat between a small Irish pub and an empty office building. He parked across the street from the crime scene, just beneath an old lamppost. Before he could climb out of the car, his partner made her way over and opened the door for him.

"It's about time you got here, Dan. Sheila must not have been very happy," she said, shutting the door behind him.

"No, Lyle, no she wasn't," Dan joked. "So, why did you have me pulled out of bed at…" he checked his watch, "…two in the morning?"

"I really like Sheila, you know. But this job is gonna drive her away, eventually."

Not really the time, Lyle. "I appreciate the concern, but I'd appreciate it if you'd mind your God-damn business." He shot her a friendly, sarcastic smile.

Detective Lyle smirked at the frustration written across his face. "Okay, after my first run over the scene, I would say it looks like your standard double homicide. I'm thinking a drunken disagreement, or maybe an angry spouse." Lyle paused a moment before taking another shot at Dan. "Sound familiar?" She casually played off the remark and looked back at him.

His eyes shot daggers back at her. "What makes you think an angry spouse did this?" He raised the tape for her to pass under.

"They were both out here in the alley. One was standing back here." She pointed to a body next to the dumpster. "The other was leaning against the wall of the bar. My first theory was a couple of…*lovers*, were out here and someone, a spouse maybe, caught them and put an end to it. Hell, maybe a hate crime against the gays."

"I think you've been watching too many TV shows, Lyle." Dan squatted down next to the first victim to examine the body. "Looks like blunt force trauma. Skull is smashed in something fierce."

"The lab geeks haven't found the murder weapon yet,

but they're pretty sure that a pool cue was used to surprise the victims. Then, to finish the job, was some sort of heavy brick. Like a cinder block."

"Makes sense, from what I can tell." Dan walked over to the second body. "But tell me, if this is just some simple lovers' quarrel, what am I doing here? Couldn't anybody else handle this?"

"Well, that was just my first theory, seeing how that guy's...*thing*...is out. But this is where it gets interesting. We may have a lead and this might just be more than another murder. The only helpful evidence we could find from the estimated TOD was the security camera at the deli, across the street." She pointed over near Dan's car; the deli sat a short distance up the block. "The tape showed a gray Firebird parked in front of the alley that left early yesterday morning. A woman walking her dog found the victims a few hours ago."

"The point?"

"Anyways, a police report was just filed, yesterday evening, up in Mt. Angel." She opened a file in her hand. "It states that during a murder investigation, a similar gray Firebird was spotted in the town, then leaving the scene."

"Okay, now you've got my full attention. Who was their victim?"

"A young girl who worked in a bookstore. She died from asphyxiation, though. She was beaten, but not to this extent. I know it's a bit of a stretch, but this vehicle may be our only connection to this murder. And how many gray Firebirds do you think are running around Oregon?"

One of the uniformed officers walked over to Dan and Lyle, the security tape in his hand. "There was nothing else on the recording. The camera was at a terrible, high angle. We could only see the bottom of the driver's side door. No faces. Sorry, detectives."

"Thank you. Go ahead and log that tape into evidence," Lyle said to the officer, then turned back to Dan and handed him her notepad. "Well, that's why I had them call you in. If someone in that car is responsible, then more people may be in danger. Two connected crime scenes is just bad luck. If we get a third, we may be looking at a serial killer. And since you worked with those FBI profilers a while back, I thought this had your name written all over it."

"Huh…" Dan thought to himself for a moment as he slowly examined the crime scene, hoping to connect some invisible dots. "What do we know about our two victims?"

"The fat one actually owns the bar." Lyle pointed at a name on the notepad. "Brandon Hemsworth, twenty-six, Grants Pass local. The other vic had no ID. Teeth were smashed up; hands too, so no clean prints. So, I think we send the bodies down to the lab and have them run the DNA through the wringer. Probably our best bet to ID him."

"Alright, run the DNA let me know if we get a match. Tomorrow morning I'll take a drive up to Mt. Angel, talk with the locals there. Maybe they'll know a bit more about our mystery car." Dan closed the notepad Detective Lyle had given him.

"You want me to go with you?"

"I don't know if Sheila would be too happy if I took you on vacation and not her." Dan didn't want to be rude, but he preferred the solitude.

"Some vacation. You'll be busy tracking down a murderer while I sit in a motel room eating take-out. I know I wouldn't be much help, but it just doesn't feel right, you know? We've been partners for years now. You going off and doing this alone, it's just bad juju."

"Don't worry, I'll be fine. I'll just be doing a little recon is all." Detective Sawyer examined the bodies once more for any additional information. The unidentified victim had no wallet, no cell phone and nothing that might tell Dan who he was. But he made note of it on the small notepad he kept in his inside coat pocket. The only distinguishing mark was a tattoo along the bottom of the victim's forearm in old Latin text. "*Nam et ipsa scientia potestas est,*" Dan read out loud.

"What the hell does that mean?" asked Lyle.

"Huh." Dan smiled as he translated the words in his head. The irony made him laugh. "For, also, knowledge itself is power."

"What's so funny about that?"

"The fact that we don't know a God-damn thing about him. A little more knowledge about the vic or the killer would go a hell of a long way." Dan stood up. "Find anything useful inside?"

"Haven't been in just yet, care to do the honors?" She led him to the back door of the bar and opened it, following Dan inside. As she walked around the extremely dirty tables, she carefully examined the scene.

"It looks like the owner didn't have any time to straighten up the place." Dan walked around the pool tables, examining the beer bottles and empty pitchers scattered across them. "We're not going to get anything from in here. There's no way to tell if the killer was even a patron. This place is too much of a God-damn mess." As he made his way to the main counter, he noticed a collection of a dozen empty beer bottles. Next to them was an ashtray, full of snuffed out cigarette butts and a few full ones that had been forgotten about shortly after they were lit. Once he realized they hadn't been moved and had burned down to the filter, he started to get a strange feeling in the back of his mind. "Hmm…"

"What is it?" asked Lyle.

"I'm not sure yet. Could be nothing." Dan put the ashtray out of his mind, but couldn't shake that strange feeling, like it was something important. "Have 'em take a photo of this, will you?" He asked Lyle. "And run the cigarettes for prints and DNA, too."

"All of 'em?"

"Why not?"

"Sure thing." She flagged over a uniformed officer to begin taking pictures and another to collect the evidence.

Looking around the room, an incomplete game of pool caught Dan's attention. He walked over and counted the balls on the table, to see who was winning and the same strange feeling hit him again. "Alright, I don't think we're going to get a whole lot more. Bag and tag everything and get me a full report by tomorrow."

"On it," replied the nearest officer.

"I'll stop by the precinct in the morning before I head to Mt. Angel. Be sure to include any autopsy findings in the report." Dan walked over to the back door, removed his badge from around his neck and shoved it into his coat pocket. "Now, if you don't mind, I'm going to go back to bed and if I'm lucky, my wife won't passive-aggressively punish me by yanking the blankets off me all night."

"Good luck," Lyle smiled and waved him off. "See you in a little while."

Dan left the scene of the crime, climbed back into his Plymouth and drove off towards home. As he hit the driveway, he hoped the headlights shining into the bedroom wouldn't wake up Sheila. He knew she was already angry with him for leaving in the middle of the night and the last thing he wanted to do was exacerbate the situation. He cautiously slid his key into the door handle, trying to think of a way to avoid the potential argument awaiting him.

No lights were on inside the house.

Good sign, he thought. Due to how often he would come home late, or leave in the early hours of the morning, he had become extremely familiar with sneaking from the entry way to the bedroom down the hall.

Unfortunately, so had his wife. And any other time, she would have been awoken by the squeaking floor boards. But, by pure luck, she was still fast asleep in their bed, unaware of her stealthy husband's entrance.

First, Dan quietly removed his clothing and tossed everything to the floor, including his holster, then he slid into the bed. As he lifted up the covers, he noticed Sheila lying there, still completely naked, with only a thin white sheet tucked beneath her. He took that as a good sign.

Whenever Sheila went to bed angry, she wore as many layers as she could stand, each one typically consisting of the most unflattering clothing possible. Gaudy, thick flannel pajamas were the sexiest attire in her passive-aggressive wardrobe. But due to her lack of clothing that night, Dan could rest easily, knowing that she wouldn't be too upset in the morning. After thirteen years of marriage, Dan had become accustomed to Sheila's habits and moods. Over time, it became easier for him to take advantage of these quirks, or to avoid them entirely. But he couldn't ignore the sight of her lying naked next to him. Knowing he should try to sleep, he peeked under the covers again pulling the thin, white sheet until it broke free from beneath Sheila's arm. The moonlight crawled through the blinds and reflected off of her pale skin beneath the sheet.

Dan couldn't take his eyes off of her. He found everything about her intoxicating, even after all these years. The light freckles scattered across her arms and shoulders were his favorite. Back when Dan used to "play the field" he never thought he could enjoy freckles, but Sheila's drove him crazy. Good crazy. He scooted close to her and kissed one of the freckles on her shoulder, then again on her neck.

A pleasurable moan crept out of her.

Once he started, he couldn't stop himself. Soft kissing quickly turned into passionate love-making. Dan would be lying if he claimed he wasn't at least attempting to make up for leaving in the middle of the night.

And she was happy to let him "make amends."

As Dan lay back, satisfied and exhausted, with Sheila cozily nestled in his armpit, he finally drifted off to sleep.

The alarm clock's buzzer sounded only a few hours later, at eight a.m. Dan felt as though he'd just closed his eyes, now he had to get up and start his day all over again. He followed his usual morning routine of kissing his wife, taking a quick shower and getting dressed. Finally, he secured his gun in his holster and dangled his badge around his neck again.

Sheila, her anger subdued by his tenderness earlier in the morning, made him a simple meal to begin the day: eggs, bacon and hash browns. A simple meal, but easily Dan's favorite.

"Thank you, sweetheart," he said choking down his meal. "It's delicious."

"I know," she said with a proud smile.

"So, there's this thing I have to do for work today."

"Uh-huh," she mumbled suspiciously.

"I'm following up on a lead and I have to drive up to Mt. Angel. Sounds like I'll be back tomorrow, unless something happens with this lead."

"Alright."

"Wait, alright? That's it?"

"Yup. You're a good detective. You have to do what you have to do to catch the bad guys."

Dan found himself speechless at her unexpected composure. "Yeah, I guess."

Sheila walked over and gave him a kiss before walking towards the bathroom. "Oh, my sister is coming to town this weekend. Richard left her for his secretary, so she'll be staying with us for a little while."

There it is. With that miserable shrew Jackie coming into town, maybe I'll stay on the road a little longer, he thought, but would never dare to say aloud. "I love you!" he shouted down the hall.

"Love you too, honey!" she yelled back before entering the bathroom and turning on the shower.

Dan finished his breakfast and drained his mug of coffee before heading off towards the station. He flipped between the pre-programmed radio stations in his car, settling on a foul-mouthed, conservative talk show. After getting his daily fill of biased news, he parked in his designated spot in front of the station and headed inside. Once he sat down at his desk, Lyle placed the manila file containing the report he'd asked for on his desk. "Morning, Jo, anything new on the double?" Dan realized he needed another boost of energy before tackling the mountain of paperwork on his desk and walked over to the coffee machine to pour himself a cup.

"Nothing new yet," said Lyle. "They're working on the autopsy now. DNA is off to the lab, but results won't be back for a couple days."

"Figures. You'd think trying to catch a murderer would be considered a rush job." Dan quickly downed the rest of his coffee and set the dirty mug on his desk. He started thumbing through the report to ensure he had all the facts he would need. "Alright, I'm just gonna take the Plymouth to Mt. Angel. At least then I can smoke in the car."

"Does Sheila know you're smoking again?"

"No and she's not going to find out, *is* she?" Dan's eyes glared at Lyle until she nodded in agreement. He sat back down at his desk and stared at the stacks of paperwork he needed to catch up on, hoping they would spontaneously burst into flames. "Look at all this God-damn paperwork. There's crack-heads and rapists running rampant out there and they want me to sit behind a desk and fill out paperwork. You know what the worst thing about it is? You forget to dot an 'I' or cross a 'T' on one of these forms and the prick walks on a technicality."

"Yeah, seems a little bit back-asswards, doesn't it?"

"You're telling me." Dan looked over at the captain's office and noticed him reading the newspaper. "Shit, I still have to tell the captain I'm going to Mt. Angel."

"You haven't told him yet?"

"When would I have had the chance? He would have ripped me a new asshole if I'd have called him from the crime scene this morning." Dan rubbed his eyes, still trying to fully wake up. "And before I deal with his bullshit, I need another cup of coffee." He returned to the coffee pot and filled his mug, blowing the steam from its surface before taking a sip. Then, he smiled as the warm liquid reached his stomach.

"You think he'll just give you the go-ahead to leave?"

"I think if his choices are: have me sit at my desk and fill out paperwork or track down a violent murderer, he'll make the right decision."

Lyle smiled in agreement.

"Alright, might as well get this over with." Dan set down his mug and picked up the case file to show his captain. He knocked on the office door and walked right in. "Captain?"

"Come in." His boss sat behind a large oak desk with a copy of the *Emerald News* hiding his face. He bent the newspaper to see who had interrupted his morning reading. "What do you need, Dan?"

"Did you have a chance to look over the case file for the double from this morning?"

"No, why? Something special about it?"

"At first glance, no, but the only viable lead is the interesting part." Dan opened the file and placed it in on the desk in front of the captain. "The security camera across the street from the crime scene picked up the driver's side of a gray Firebird arriving and leaving the scene of the crime. There were no other leads."

"Sounds like it's about to go cold."

"That's where the lead comes in. We received a report about a homicide up in Mt. Angel yesterday. A gray Firebird fitting the same description was spotted in the area. The timeline matches with the TOD of our vics." Dan placed his finger pointedly on the blurred partial image of the Firebird. "This car is the only connection we have and if we don't follow this lead, more people may be in danger. I'm going to leave soon for Mt. Angel to follow up."

"And you're just comin' to me with this now?" The captain slammed shut the file on his desk and stared up at the detective.

"We just finished examining the crime scene this morning." *When the fuck should I have told you?*

The captain glared for a moment, trying to determine if he should allow Dan to leave. "What time were you thinking of leaving? You taking a cruiser?"

"I'm hoping to leave as soon as possible. I don't think

I'll need to be gone for too long either. And I'll just take my car."

"Does Sheila know you're smoking again? I mean, why else would you take that boat instead of a cruiser?"

"Jesus, what's with everyone today? What're you, the cigarette police?"

"Alright, alright, forget it…just, keep track of your expenses and keep me updated if you learn anything. I always told you your past work with the Bureau would come in handy one day. If this case gets any bigger, it could be a career-maker."

"Glad to hear it, Captain." *I don't really care about my career, only catching whoever did this.* Dan turned around to prepare for his road trip.

"Oh, Dan, one more thing. Make sure you finish your paperwork before you go, don't want to fall behind on that."

It was difficult for Dan to hide the lack of enthusiasm in his voice. "Yes, sir." He turned and headed out to his desk, settled into his chair and prepared for the mountain of papers he needed to fill out.

"How'd he take it?" Lyle picked up his half-filled cup of coffee and finished it.

"Surprisingly well, but you know him. 'Finish your paper work!'" He puffed out his chest and did his best impersonation of the captain.

"Well, hurry up and get out of here. I'm tired of sitting across from you. I think we need a break."

"I appreciate the sentiment, but you're not the only one." Both of them buried their heads in their paperwork, signing and scribbling away. Even at Dan's hurried pace, his paperwork still kept him until the early afternoon. Finally, when Dan was about to give up and stay in Eugene to finish everything, Lyle noticed his irritation and decided to give him a bit of relief.

"Alright," she said. "What do you have left? I'll take care of it."

"Thank you, Lyle." Without hesitation, he picked up the small stack of remaining work and passed it over his desk to her. "Would you mind checking on Sheila while I'm away?"

"Of course I will."

"Thank you so much; you're a life saver." Dan gathered up his things, filled his Thermos with lukewarm coffee and walked with Lyle downstairs to the parking lot. "Let me know if we find out anything more, will you? Like, when the DNA results come back."

"Will do. Be safe, Dan." She waved him goodbye and returned to her desk upstairs.

Dan got in his car, tossed the file into the passenger seat and drove out of the parking lot. It wasn't a long drive to Mt. Angel, but he hoped to arrive as soon as possible and put this whole case behind him. From the moment he became involved, it had been nothing but trouble and he was certain it would affect his home life. In his younger days, the most important thing in his life was making detective, but since he met Sheila, he was ready to settle down and start a family. For a brief moment, he considered retiring from the police force, taking up a job at his cousin's car dealership in downtown Eugene. One step at a time, though. First, he would finish this case, move on to the next one and, when the time was right, tell Sheila about retiring. Eventually.

8

AS BEN DRIFTED off to sleep—forehead pressed against the car window—his mind continuously replayed the events of the day before, repeatedly watching himself from the moment they arrived on Main Street. Each time he replayed the events, his unconscious mind attempted to work out various scenarios in which Ashton might have lived, but each sequence ended the same way. The more he replayed it, the more he attempted to figure out who might have done something so heinous. *Could I have seen him at some point throughout the day?* In a sudden shift of perspective, his mind began watching the events through an unfamiliar pair of eyes.

The unusual point of view made Ben feel as though someone had been watching them since their arrival in Mt. Angel. Whoever it was, they watched as Ben and Taylor parted ways near the convenience store. Things grew eerier as the watcher ignored Taylor completely and followed Ben to The Sour Kraut, then trailed him back to the bookstore and stealthily watched through the window as he met Ashton for the first time. It hid from sight as Ben and Ashton left the store, following them as they made their way down the block to enter the park. Hugging close to the ground, it neared Ashton, close enough to stroke the long brown hair that draped down her back. Low grunting and heavy breathing erupted as it reached out, contemplating the act of petting her lightly, but stopping within inches of her scalp. As they sat down on the picnic table, the haunting eyes pulled away, hiding behind a nearby tree, peeking out at them. Periodically, when Ben would make contact with her or they would stop and stare into each other's eyes, the angered wheezing grew erratic and violent, verging on howling.

As Ben finally said "goodbye" to her, and Taylor soon joined him at the picnic table, their stalker worked its way around the park, focusing on Ben. While he sat on the tabletop, writing and enjoying a cold beer, the heavy breathing intensified, quickly followed by enraged growls. The anger boiled over, forcing the stalker to run from the park and what seemed to be its prey, sprinting back towards the bookstore before bursting through the front door. It surprised Ashton and quickly leapt on top of her, violently swinging its arms, striking her in the face repeatedly.

Ashton's swollen eyes overflowed with blood and tears streaming down her face. She tried pleading for her life, but only garbled, incoherent cries emerged.

The pleas fell on deaf ears and the beast on top of her continued to strike her in the face with its pitch black fists. Its hands were dark as a starless night sky as they wrapped themselves around Ashton's throat. A shadow, tightening its grip, squeezing and pressing her throat against the wooden floor.

Her suffering seemed endless. Until it wasn't. She no longer struggled. Her breathing ceased and instead of fighting off her attacker, her arms fell limp to the floor.

The shadowy beast, heaving over top of her lifeless corpse, stood up and calmly walked over to the large storefront window. It watched as Taylor crossed the street and entered the convenience store. As it stepped closer to the window, the reflection of the sinister figure appeared as jet black as the shadowy hands that had removed the life from the young bookstore girl. Its gaze reflected back, seemingly staring at Ben. It's small, menacing eyes burned bright red, like unstable dwarf stars, igniting the empty space around them. They etched themselves into Ben's mind. He was never there, standing in that room, but the dark figure's eyes were staring directly into his own. Locked, piercing and frightening. Blood dripped off the shadowy figure's hand as it pressed against the glass.

They stared at one another for what felt like a lifetime and in an instant, the colorless beast spun around and grabbed Ben by the throat.

Ben snapped awake, panting heavily and soaked in sweat

9

TAYLOR JERKED THE wheel as Ben jolted awake. "Shit, Ben, you okay? He guided the car back into the center of the lane before looking at Ben with concern.

"Huh? Yeah…um…I'm fine." Ben pressed his hands against his eyes and rubbed them vigorously.

"You looked like you were having one hell of a dream. You were tossing and turning like crazy."

"I saw her…Ashton. I saw her die." Ben ran his hands through his hair as he stretched his arms.

"What do you mean? You were back at the park; how could you have seen her die?"

"No, it was…just a dream. Only it was so clear, but now it feels so fuzzy at the same time." Ben couldn't remember everything from his dream, but the image of that shadowy figure, wringing the neck of that innocent girl, would prove difficult to shake. "That's it…" He ripped off his seatbelt and reached into the back seat, frantically searching for his notebook.

"What's 'it?' What are you looking for?"

"I figured it out. I think I know what to write." Ben found his notebook in the back side of the space beneath his seat.

"Well, tell me. What is it?"

Ben ignored him and started scribbling on the pad. He wrote for a moment, then scratched out what he'd just penned and continued writing. Again and again he did this until finally, a smile emerged on his face. He had finally written the first line of his novel.

Jake started his journey across the country, completely unaware of the beast that stalked him, starving for revenge.

"Can I see it?"

Ben passed him the pad. "It's about us, well...sort of. Write about what you know, right? A man travels across the country, going to visit someone. Hell, maybe his dad." He waved his hands in the air as if to say, *We've got something here!* "But as he goes from place to place, someone is stalking him looking to make the main character feel the pain that the stalker feels. So, this stalker kills everyone the guy comes in contact with."

"Creepy, dude. That's a little dark, don't you think?" Taylor placed the notepad on the steering wheel in front of him, carefully holding it in place with his thumbs as he read what Ben had written.

"Yeah, I know it's a little sadistic after what happened, but it feels *right*. If that makes any kind of sense."

"I like it; it's good." Taylor handed the notebook back to Ben. "Definitely gives off a certain feeling of suspense. Just leave me out of it, will ya? I think if I have to read about myself getting brutally murdered, I might just shit my pants."

"Don't worry, I won't use you. You'd definitely make an...*interesting* character, though."

"Hell, I'd be the star of the show. Oh, can I be the crazy guy? I can do crazy."

"You don't have to tell me, Mr. Piss-Off-A-Bunch-Of-Bikers-Like-A-Crazy-Person." Ben got back to work filling out his notepad, trying to create an outline for his new idea while it was still fresh in his mind. He started by writing about their time in Mt. Angel, expanding and exaggerating a bit. His writer's spirit took over as he started making up names and places. Even though he had these ideas, he wasn't sure where to begin or what the meat of his story should be. *What do I say after that first line?* Soon, another idea took shape: *Tell the story from the killer's perspective.* With only his terrifying dream holding the idea together, he wrote down a few details about Ashton's death. And in an homage to someone he'd met, who loved reading, he decided on the first victim: *a young girl, tending to a bookstore.*

Taylor continued to drive on towards their next destination and Ben wrote for another hour before eventually taking a break. They soon reached a long stretch of highway, walled in by tall, magnificent pine trees. The forest around them grew thick and became the only thing around for miles on either side. Although the evergreens were a familiar sight throughout Oregon, they were a beautiful change from the expansive, open farmlands. "Hey, Ben," said Taylor. "Why don't we stay here for the night, camp out? I haven't done that in ages."

"In the car?"

"No, not in the car." Taylor made a "look around you, dumbass" face.

"Right, the woods." Ben laughed. "It's funny. I was just thinking the exact same thing. This is going to sound a bit weird, but this place would be great for a murder." He looked over at Taylor, smiling.

"You're right. That did sound weird. Probably shouldn't say things like that out loud when other people are around." Taylor thought for a moment. "Matter of fact, don't say that around *me* anymore…creeper."

"Whatever. Let me check and see if I can find a good campground somewhere." Ben pulled out a big, bulky map from the car door and scanned over the Oregon wilderness with his finger. "Here, we go. We're not too far away from a 'Belle Vista' campground. The map has four stars next to the name."

"Sounds good enough to me, but we need some camping gear. Any towns nearby?"

"Well, the campground is still a little while away. Looks like about…ten minutes from us is a small town. And I mean, *really* small. But we should be able to pick up some stuff there."

"Alright." Taylor followed Ben's directions and took the next exit off the highway. It didn't take long before they arrived at a small stretch of road, with a couple buildings on either side. The words "small town" were an overstatement. Taylor parked the car in front of a store, across from a small gas station. Above the entrance was a hand painted, wooden sign that simply read "General Store." The sign was weathered and worn, with the paint chipping away.

Ben stepped out of the car and leaned through the open passenger window. "Anything you want?"

"Nah, you know me. Besides, when camping, you really only need a few things." Taylor counted on his fingers. "Beer, wieners and a sleeping bag. Get me that and I'm good."

"Can't say I'm surprised *wieners* made your list, but if you think of anything else, give me a shout." Ben patted the roof of the car before heading into the store. As he walked inside he immediately found a small section of camping supplies. It mostly consisted of basic equipment: sleeping bags, camping chairs, lanterns and other supplies. Ben picked out a couple of sleeping bags and foldable chairs, forgoing the lanterns, but picking up a small starter fishing rod, still in the packaging. *Campfire'll be enough light for us.* He gathered the standard camping food: hot dogs and marshmallows, some cans of beans and chili, and last but not least, enough beer to last them the rest of the night. With the short stretch of road—so small it would barely even be classified as a town—their lack of any delicious, wheat-style beer wasn't surprising, so Ben simply picked out a good old-fashioned lager and forewent their usual favorite. It was a slight struggle, carrying everything all at once, but he managed to get it all to the checkout counter and only had to backtrack for a sleeping bag he'd lost in the beer aisle.

A tiny, elderly woman, wearing a heavy flannel shirt sat behind the counter watching a small black-and-white television. As Ben set the second sleeping bag on the counter, she stood up with a big, heartwarming smile on her face. "Hello, sweetie, how are you doin' today?"

"I'm doing okay, thanks. How about yourself?"

"Oh, I can't complain. The sun is out and the store's been busy all day. So, I'm as happy as can be. I haven't seen you around here before. What brings you my way?" She started typing on her register and bagging the supplies.

"I'm actually going to visit my dad in Washington. He's in the hospital. My friend and I are taking a road trip up there." Ben pointed out to Taylor sitting in the car, playing some ridiculously addictive candy game on his phone.

She paused from inputting prices to lean over the counter to look in the direction of their car, but could barely see Taylor through the grimy glass door. "Oh, I'm so sorry. I hope your father's doing alright. Is it serious?"

"The doctors don't think so, but he hasn't been himself since he got sick."

"Well, let's hurry and get you back on the road again!"

She finished adding up the items on the register. "Anything else, sweetie?"

"Unless you have some jerky that you're hiding around here, I think that's it."

"Well, as a matter of fact, I make my own. Something I picked up from my Gerry, God rest his soul." She pointed at the dusty menu on the wall behind her. "He used to pride himself on his meats, so I do my best to honor him that way. What kind do you like? Spicy, smoky, or oriental?"

"Hell, I'll take a little bit of everything. Do you mind if I try a piece of the oriental first?"

"Not at all." She reached down beneath the counter and pulled out a few jars filled with strips of jerky. She held out an open container over the counter.

Ben reached in and took a fat piece; he could instantly smell the sweet scent of teriyaki. He tore off a bite and enjoyed the magnificently juicy flavor. It was, by far, the most tender piece of jerky he'd ever eaten. The first bite tasted like a perfectly cooked and seasoned steak, and the meat nearly melted in his mouth. "Oh my God. I never tried your husband's jerky, but I doubt it could have been better than this. Fill me up, please. How much?"

"Tell you what, if you promise to take a piece to your dad, it's on the house." The old lady pulled a handful of strips out of each jar and shoved them all in a paper bag. "Here and tell him I hope he feels better." She smiled a smile that could only be described as genuine and sincere, and she finished bagging the rest of the supplies.

Ben handed her a few bills and she handed him back his change.

She sat back down on the wooden stool behind the counter and returned to her television show.

It had been years since anyone had been that kind to

Ben. Grants Pass—and, he guessed, every other city across the globe—was filled with rude people living their everyday lives, with no thought towards one another's feelings. No one had the time of day to spend on anyone but themselves. The only people he'd ever found in his own town that were genuinely kind were the proprietors of a small mom-and-pop restaurant.

It was run by a tall and skinny old man named Steve. Steve could tell you the name of every customer that ever set foot in that small diner. And, other than the occasional gray mustache hair in the food, he made some of the best breakfast in Oregon. He used to operate it with his wife, Candy, until she passed away. She was even kinder than Steve. More memorable was her funeral. She chose to have the reception at her favorite spot in town, her own diner. Those two made up for everyone else that was ever unkind to Ben. No matter how rude people may have been, Steve and Candy made each day a little better.

Ben couldn't help but be reminded of those two after meeting the old shopkeeper. "Thank you so much. Really, I'll make sure he gets some and that he knows where it came from. He'll love to hear about you." Ben pressed his back against the door, said, "Goodbye," and walked out of the store backwards, balancing everything he'd purchased.

"Bye, sweetie."

He carried everything over to the car and tossed the sleeping bags through the window at Taylor, who tossed them into the back seat. After placing the grocery bags onto the floor in front of the passenger seat, he tossed the folding chairs into the back and sat down with the bags between his legs.

"What took you so long?" shouted Taylor.

"I just met the nicest old lady inside. She gave us a

shit-ton of free jerky."

"Oh, I think I'm in love. Maybe I should go in and say hi." Taylor laughed as he started the car and they returned to their route on the highway. He held his hand out in front of Ben without saying a word. When nothing happened, Taylor shook his hand up and down near Ben's face.

After a moment, Ben realized that Taylor was after a piece of the jerky. He looked in the paper bag that the lady had given him and fished around for a piece that was covered in tiny jalapeno seeds and red pepper flakes. She hadn't mentioned how hot the spicy jerky was, so Ben could only hope for the worst as he set the piece in Taylor's hand.

Without looking, Taylor tore off a large piece with his teeth and swallowed it. It only took seconds for his face to turn to a bright Tabasco red. He began panting hysterically, frantically searching for something to drink. "Jesus fuckin' Christ! What the hell is wrong with you? Give me something to drink. Give me a beer, quick!"

"You're driving, you can't drink a beer." Ben couldn't hold back his delight at Taylor's suffering, gripping his stomach in laughter.

"God damnit, give me something to drink!"

Ben decided to give him one of the beers he'd bought. It was difficult for him to get the cap off with Taylor reaching for the bottle.

After ripping it from Ben's hands, Taylor downed half of the beer immediately. After swishing the liquid around in his mouth, his face returned to its typical pale tone and not the bright red it had been a few seconds ago. "That wasn't so bad." His face was still sweating profusely. "It was actually pretty freaking good."

"Really?" Ben couldn't stop laughing.

They drove for another ten minutes before the sign for the Belle Vista Campground peeked out through the brush on the side of the road.

Taylor quickly turned off the highway onto an improvised gravel path. Thousands of tiny rocks crushed beneath the tires as the Firebird neared the campground.

Ben's dad used to habitually tell him, "You can always tell a good campground by the length of the drive after you leave the main road." And this campground was one of the good ones.

They pushed on down the road into the deep, lush Oregon woods.

"Ben, are you sure there's a campground out here? I feel like we're about to drive into the beginning of a slasher movie."

"Yeah, the map shows one out here. Just keep driving. We've got to be almost there." Ben continued to examine the unfolded map.

After they pulled around a large corner—between two walls of thick, dark pine trees—a small, steel trailer marking the entrance to the campground revealed itself.

Outside the oversized tin can, a heavyset woman with a short, Ellen DeGeneres hairstyle rocked back and forth in a worn, blue rocking chair. She watched as the gray Firebird stopped in the middle of the gravel road and she snuffed out her half-smoked cigarette on the arm of her chair. The wooden steps from the porch bowed beneath her as she walked down to meet the campers. "Welcome to Belle Vista Campground."

Taylor and Ben stepped out of the car, but left it running.

"What brings you all the way out here?" she asked.

"Looking for a little inspiration." Ben reached for his wallet. "How much for the night?"

"Twenty-five."

"Jesus, twenty-five a night? That's crazy." Taylor started to climb back into the car.

"Well, believe me, this campground is worth it. *Obviously* it's beautiful." She spit on the ground next to her. "Also, we'll give ya'all the free firewood you need. We have great fishing spots within walking distance of each lot and although it's not in the spirit of camping, fully functional restrooms, showers and all."

"Alright, you've sold it. Twenty-five it is." Ben held out two bills totaling twenty-five dollars.

"You know we could just drive off into the woods and camp for free, right?" Taylor said before Ben could give her the money.

"You could," the lady replied. "But have you ever camped in such a beautiful place as this? Plus, I think I remember seeing some pretty college girls down in lot seventeen. Said they were here for the end of summer break or something."

"Alright." Without hesitation, Taylor ran over and snatched the money from Ben's hand and gave it to the heavyset woman. "I agree; you've sold it."

"The name's Loraine and I think lot nineteen is open. Closest spot you're gonna git." She turned to walk back up the warped steps to her rocker. "Grab some firewood before you go. It gets cold at night."

Both of them grabbed a stack of firewood and tossed the logs into the trunk, then climbed into the Firebird. They drove down the gravel road, at the posted five miles-per-hour, passing by lot seventeen.

"Would you look at that…" said Taylor as a few of the college-aged girls ran across the street in front of them, causing him to step on the brakes. The girls were running from the showers; two of them wore long towels, wrapped around their bodies and smaller towels around their heads. Their bare feet slapped the pavement beneath them. "Did you see that, Ben? She just smiled at me."

"Please, I think you only see what you want to see."

"I think this is the best idea you've had yet." Taylor stepped on the gas pedal and swung into lot nineteen.

They each took a section of the large tarp Ben bought from the store and began lashing the corners to the nearby trees with rope and bungee cords. Now that the shelter was up, they kicked and brushed the ground beneath it, looking for any uncomfortable rocks that might attempt to stab them in the back while they slept. Next, they rolled out their new sleeping bags and stacked the wood in a teepee formation in the fire pit.

Taylor removed a small gas can from the trunk of his car and shook it vigorously. He could hear what little gasoline was left sloshing around in the bottom. "Just enough to start a fire! Got a light?"

"Yeah, here." Ben tossed him a book of matches he kept in his pocket.

Taylor poured what was left of the gasoline over the wood pile and struck a match. The initial burst of heat from the ignition created a scorching aura around the fire pit. The heat was a welcome sensation as the night began to creep over the forest. Rays of light that had been peeking through the tree tops began to wither and fade. The gasoline finally burned off of the wood in the fire pit, which created bright, red-hot coals beneath the thickest planks.

Ben and Taylor stood within the heat radius, warming themselves before deciding on what to eat for dinner.

"Hey, throw me a beer," said Taylor.

Ben lifted the cooler from the trunk and set it a few feet from the fire. He pulled out a beer bottle and lobbed it over the flames into Taylor's hands. Then he took one out for himself, popping the top with the bottle opener Taylor had stolen. "I gotta say, I prefer a wheat beer during the summer, but I do love a cold Bud every now and then." Ben took a deep swig of his cold beer. "What do you want? We got canned chili, some hot dogs and a bag of giant marshmallows." He unfolded a camping chair and tossed one over to Taylor, who did the same.

"I'll take a can of chili; I know how much you like the wieners."

"Oh, you know it." Ben made his irritated sarcasm blatantly clear. "But I think I'm gonna have some chili too, that's why I bought more than one can, dumbass." He sent a can of chili soaring over the flames before he sat down.

Taylor was barely able to catch it due to the bottle of beer taking up the majority of his attention.

Ben took out his pocket knife and jabbed a large hole into the top of the can for ventilation, then Taylor did the same. "Another good trick I learned from my dad when I was in the Scouts." They placed their dinners into the fire near the brightest red coals they could find.

"Did I ever tell you that I was a Boy Scout, too, when I was little?" Taylor picked up a stick and poked at the coals, sending ash and embers soaring through the air.

"No shit, really?"

"Yeah, back before my dad left. That was the last thing I remember about him, and the Scouts for that matter. But the last time we had a troop meeting, we made one of those stupid little pinewood derby cars."

"Oh, I fucking loved the pinewood derby race. It's a shame they only did it once a year. By far, the best thing about the Scouts."

"Right? My dad and me always won, too. That was at

least one thing I was always good at." Taylor was lost deep in thought, staring into the crackling flames.

"What *did* happen to your dad? Did he just take off or something?"

"Yeah." Taylor's eyes were still lost in the flames. "Something like that anyway. The last thing I remember was building those God-damn derby cars. The next thing I know is, I wake up one day and he's just…gone. Mom said he ran off to 'be with his real family.'"

"That's tough, man. I'm sorry." Ben let the words sink in. "What a dick."

"No shit. And what're you sorry for?" Taylor finished his beer and hurled his bottle out into the tree line as hard as he could. The bottle smashed, echoing through the campground. "It's not like he ran off with *you*. Right?" His eyes brightened a bit and he smirked, looking at Ben to approve of his joke.

"Oh, you know, we had two kids and a little, yappy Pomeranian together." Their usual joking and sarcasm began to work its way back into the conversation. Ben hoped his words would lighten the mood a little. "I'm surprised you haven't made your way over to lot seventeen yet. Introduce yourself to all the pretty girls."

"You know me, I can't 'stalk' girls on an empty stomach. You wanna go over there after we eat?"

All the sunlight had disappeared, only the glow from the scattered campfires lit up the night.

"I don't know, man. I really should get some writing done. I haven't done a whole lot since we left Mt. Angel."

"Look, we barely knew that girl. You need to move on and keep writing your God-damn book. Tell you what, I'll head over there and if any of the girls are dorky bookworms I'll bring one or two back for you. Well, I'll bring one back for you. Maybe…"

"Yeah, sure you will." They could see the chili was ready now; the sauce bubbled through the holes in the top of the cans.

Taylor grabbed the pair of tongs Ben had picked up from the store and pulled the cans from the fire. They poured each can into cheap, tin mugs and drank down their meals before they had a chance to get cold. Taylor placed his mug on a rock next to the fire pit and got up to get one more bottle of beer. "I'm off to see the show! Be back in a bit," he said, walking out into the woods, towards lot seventeen.

Ben retrieved his notebook and pen from the backseat of the car, then sat back down in his chair next to the fire. He stared at the empty page, his mind churning but coming up with nothing. Hoping to stimulate his brain, he tapped the tip of the pen on the paper over and over again until something came to mind.

He felt as though her death was somehow his fault; there had to have been something he could have done to save her.

He couldn't keep his mind from gravitating back to their... time with Ashton. This time, though, he wasn't looking back in regret, but with a sense of intrigue. It was growing easier to take what Taylor said to heart: "Move on and write your God-damn story." So, that's what Ben decided to do. After that first idea came to mind, more continued to pour out, like the faucet had been turned on and the handle broken off. Most ideas weren't anything more than words or phrases, but a few strong sentences came to mind. Ben tried to not focus on Ashton and her killer, but his thoughts and ideas continually reverted back to his gruesome nightmare. After deciding to steer into the skid, he wrote down everything he could remember about the dream, no matter how chilling each thought was.

The dark shadow's breathing was deep, full of hatred and loathing for the prey it continued to stalk.

After a short while of deciding how the scene with the bookstore girl should play out, Ben decided to turn his attention to the current scene, the murder in the woods. "Who would be 'caught dead' in the woods?" he asked himself, smiling at the stupid pun. The first idea that came to mind was to use the unaware college girls as innocent victims. Use the age-old stereotype of misbehaving students who get brutally murdered in the woods. *That was too easy,* he thought. His second idea was an old man fishing down on the banks of the river, found strangled with a large amount of fishing line. *No, that's not right.*

He began to shift in his seat and fidget with the campground items around him, trying to think of unique and efficient ways to end someone's life. "Taking a tumble" into the fire pit, a tent stake to the chest; all good ideas, but nothing truly terrifying. He leaned back in the chair, his arm dangling below the armrest, until his fingers touched a small hatchet buried in the dirt. A quick chill shot up his spine as he picked up the axe. He raised it high and slammed the blade down into a block of wood resting next to the fire. After slamming the hatchet into the wood a few times, he finally had it.

Neither of them noticed the man sneaking through the shadows behind them. He cunningly worked his way around through their campsite and hid behind a stack of firewood. His hand reached out of the shadows and removed a small hatchet from atop the stack. In an instant, he grabbed the elderly man from behind and struck him in the chest with the hatchet. The old man's wife watched in horror as her husband was struck repeatedly. The crazed lunatic turned his attention to the wife and grabbed her by the neck, slamming her head into the rocks surrounding the fire. He drove the hatchet into her neck, again and again, until her head separated from her body and the rocks around the flames were stained crimson with her blood.

Thoroughly frightened by his own imagination, Ben placed the hatchet he'd been fiddling with in his lap. He set down his pen and felt an eerie feeling that someone was watching him from the woods. Paranoia set in and he looked all around him, examining the dark spaces between the trees. As far as he could tell, no one was actually watching him from afar. His heart slowly settled and he began to calm down. Now that his heart had stopped beating out of his chest, he raised his beer to his lips.

"Holy shit!" a voice shouted from the tree line.

Ben spit out his beer and jumped to his feet, gripping the handle of the axe, preparing himself for his inevitable, bloody demise.

Taylor emerged from the shadows and stopped in front of the fire, a big smile on his face. "You missed out, buddy."

"Jesus Christ, Taylor." Ben's heart was racing and his bottle of beer lay on the ground, spilling out. "You gave me a fucking heart attack."

Taylor was breathing heavily after sprinting through the woods. "I walked up to the camp and I saw one of them changing. I could see through the little mesh window on her tent. That totally made up for the twenty-five bucks to stay the night. I need another beer!" He rushed over, pulled a bottle from the cooler and popped the top. The liquid inside disappeared like he was dying of thirst. "So? You get anything done?"

Ben laughed a little and regained his composure. "Um,

a good amount, actually. I think you were right, though. I think I'm actually starting to get over what happened back in Mt. Angel. It was terrible, yeah, but I think it gave me that emotional edge I needed for the story. I wanted to keep it realistic…and something that actually happened is pretty realistic, right?"

"A little gloomy, yeah, but realistic."

"Alright, then, read me a story. Tell me what you've written so far."

"Well, it's not really a story yet, just some bits and pieces, but what the hell." Ben began to read what he'd written so far. A few descriptions of the scenes he'd written and his ideas for the rest of the story. The dark tale he told fit perfectly with the crackling flames of the campfire, sounding eerily like an old, scary story he might have heard in the Scouts.

Taylor couldn't help but be impressed by Ben's determination to write the story. The work was beginning to sound like a real novel. And while the dark thoughts his best friend had coursing through his head were somewhat frightening, he was proud of Ben. "Have you thought of what you're going to call him yet, the killer?"

"Nothing that really catches my attention, but since we're driving across state lines, I've sort of taken to calling him the Highway Slasher."

"A little cheesy, but not bad. Don't worry I'll help you come up with something good."

"I think that I decided on one of two motives for the killer, too."

"Ah, I'm all ears."

"Well, the first idea is that the killer had someone close to him taken away by the protagonist. Like, accidentally, in a drunk-driving accident or something."

"Hey, don't knock the beer, man. That's the last thing

you need, one more reason for people to start complaining about how beer is so detrimental to society."

They both raised their bottles in agreement and took a drink.

"Well, the other is on a more personal level. The killer is a man who was obsessed with the protagonist's girlfriend and when the protagonist proposes to her, the guy snaps and ruins his life. He murders everyone that the protagonist comes in contact with."

"I like that one. It's a little more relatable. Also touches a little closer to home, 'cause I know I've fallen for girls that were with someone they shouldn't be."

"My thoughts exactly." Ben threw his notepad onto his sleeping bag and put the pen in his pocket. "So, it was a good show, huh?"

"Yeah, dude. You really missed out. When was the last time you saw a naked girl that wasn't Lynn or on a computer screen?"

"I don't know, probably the last time we went to a strip club together. So, like two years ago on your birthday."

Taylor shook his head in shame. "I'm telling you, man, you gotta take advantage of things like this. It's not every day that you get to see naked girls that you don't have to pay."

Ben smiled at Taylor's perversion. "Okay, perv. I'll let you buy me a lap dance when we get back home."

"Hey now, that's not what I meant."

Ben shrugged and smiled.

"You know it's not too late; you want to go back over there? Maybe with you there we can actually *talk* to them or something."

"No, I think I'm just gonna crash for the night. I got a bit of writing done, but now I think I'd just like to relax and listen to the sounds of nature."

"Really?"

With no better excuse, Ben simply looked at him as if to say, "Yeah, really."

"Alright, your call. Tomorrow, maybe. You want to do some fishing before we leave in the morning? I've got my old pole in the trunk and you picked up that kid's rod at the store. Sounds like we've got all we need."

"Sure, that'll be cool." Ben got up from his foldable chair and sat down on top of his sleeping bag. "Where do you think we'll be by the end of tomorrow?"

"We should cross over into Washington tomorrow. That'll put us at a little over halfway there."

"Good." Ben laid his head back on top of the sleeping bag and closed his eyes. "Can't wait to get to Washington."

"Never thought I'd hear those words come out of your mouth." Taylor got up and sat down on his sleeping bag. "Be ready to catch some fish in the morning."

"We'd better catch something, God damnit." They continued with the small talk for another ten minutes, staring up at the blue tarp hanging above them. The surrounding woods were utterly silent, except for the crackling of nearby campfires and the faint giggling from a couple lots away. Those sounds echoed like a soft lullaby, convincing their eyelids to pull themselves shut, as if they were being weighed down by sandbags. "God, I'm just gonna pass out 'til morning. I feel like I'm going to sleep like a rock."

Taylor passed out before he could say the same.

Looking over at the fire one last time, Ben finally realized that there were very few things as relaxing, inspiring, or life-affirming as camping in the woods. His eyes closed and he watched the flames light up the back of his eyelids. He allowed the overwhelming exhaustion to wash over him, sending him into a deep, inescapable sleep.

10

TAYLOR ONLY SLEPT for another hour before a loud ruckus from camp seventeen startled him awake. It took him a moment to realize what had awoken him: a few loud, high-pitched screams echoing through the surrounding trees. He climbed out of his sleeping bag and, for fear of what might be roaming the woods, pried the small hatchet from the block of wood where Ben had left it. After rubbing the sand from his eyes, he cautiously made his way down the gravel road that connected all the lots.

As he approached the lot where he'd been spying on the girls earlier in the day, he noticed a number of shadows dancing across the backdrop of trees. He had previously seen only three girls when he stopped by earlier, but now two male shadows joined them. A frightening thought crossed his mind: *the girls were in some sort of danger*. He prepared himself to play the hero and rescue the damsels in distress. As he moved closer to the camp, he played out the upcoming confrontation in his head, over and over again. Each time it ended with him being the obvious victor, but the closer he got, the more his gut told him that something wasn't right and the more his heart tried jumping out of his chest. Suddenly, something didn't sound right. The screams grew louder and became more playful than fearful. Soft giggles quickly permeated through the yelling. *They're having fun*, Taylor realized. After recognizing that the screams came from enjoyment, he ducked into the shadows and approached the tree line surrounding the lot. Although the girls were no longer in danger, his curiosity was piqued and he wondered who had thwarted his attempt at bravely rescuing the pretty girls. He pushed aside the foliage in front of him, just enough to see inside the camp.

A raised, red pickup truck had parked behind the line of cars in the driveway. Two college-aged boys dressed in full camouflage and trucker caps sat around the campfire. Another boy, wearing similar attire, chased two of the girls around with a squirt gun, trying to drench their white tank tops. It appeared that these two barely dressed girls were the source of the incessant screaming and laughter.

Taylor may have found out the cause of the disturbance, but he couldn't bring himself to leave his hiding spot in the bushes. Something kept him there, kept him watching. Watching as they continued to drink and make memories, like he and Ben had done in high school.

The few who weren't running around the campsite sat around the fire, drinking liquor from bottles and tossing the empties into the chest-high flames.

Taylor smiled as he remembered when he and Ben would steal bottles of whiskey from their parents and sneak off into the woods, or throw parties while their parents were away. Now that he was older, he couldn't believe that they used to add water to the bottles, raising the level of the booze, to avoid suspicion. Then he couldn't believe their parents never said anything about the obvious difference in taste. *They must have noticed*, Taylor thought. *Those really were the good old days, though*. Time had flown by in the blink of an eye. In no time, they were already twenty-five. A quarter of a century old. It had all flown by so quickly that Taylor worried that the next time he blinked, they would have already reached thirty. What bothered them more than their fear of aging was that it took them so long to realize just how fast time truly passes.

The kids in lot seventeen stirred an unfamiliar feeling inside of him. Jealousy tied a knot in his stomach and it was difficult for him to resist the feeling. Before anymore thoughts of wasted youth climbed into his mind, he turned to head back towards his own campsite, to return to his sleeping bag. As he started to walk away, out of the corner of his eye, the girl he'd spied on earlier in the day sprinted off into the woods, followed by the boy with the squirt gun.

She ran from the redneck boy and led him out into the forest, away from the light of the fire and their friends' line of sight. In a childish game of peek-a-boo, she ran and hid behind a large, split tree, poking her head out periodically to tease him. As she attempted to flee even further, the redneck boy managed to shoot her in the chest, but quickly ran out of ammunition. The now drenched girl took advantage of the opportunity and ran away again, fleeing towards the nearby river that encircled the entire campground.

For some reason, whether it was curiosity or intrigue, Taylor decided to follow them, using the bushes and trees to stay out of sight.

The river was a long walk from the campground. During the day it would make for an enjoyable hike, with a chance to relax on the riverbank once you arrived. At night, however, it was a clumsy trod through infinite darkness. By the time the residual light from the campfires faded into the distance, it quickly became impossible to avoid the surrounding tree trunks and their roots.

Rather than refill his squirt gun in the roaring rapids, the boy clad in camo tossed his gun to the ground and grabbed the soaked girl around the waist. She squealed with excitement as they fell down together, kissing heavily and laughing, not showing any signs of stopping.

While Taylor watched them roll around in the dark, he felt his grip tighten around the hatchet. The strange feeling that started to overwhelm him was no longer simple jealousy, it was something more. Something he couldn't put his finger on. Envy or admiration? Passion or exhilaration? Whatever it was, it quickly turned into a rising pressure, coursing through his veins. The nearest word to describe it could only be…rage.

Something strange happened next, something lacking mind and control. In what could only be described as an out-of-body experience, Taylor's consciousness felt as though it stepped back from his body, forcing him to only observe and give up any control of his limbs. Taylor's body stepped through the brush that had hidden him from the intimate campers. He walked closer to them, peeking out from behind the trees as he neared.

The campers were too distracted to keep a watchful eye on their surroundings.

Taylor watched as his body stopped next to the campers and raise the hatchet high above his head. With all his might, he slammed the axe downwards, burying it deep in the young man's back.

The boy screamed in agony before blood quickly filled his lungs and began pouring from his mouth.

Taylor used his foot to pry the hatchet from the boy's back and slammed it downwards again, intersecting with the previous wound. The body fell limp, turning into a lifeless, dead weight on top of the girl.

She let out a bloodcurdling scream as the blood stained her clothes and skin. Her hair quickly resembled a sandy beach, stained with a child's dropped, cherry snow cone.

Taylor kicked the boy off of her as she attempted to scuttle away on the forest floor. He casually sauntered over to her, his face lifeless as though his soul had disappeared from his eyes. His foot stomped down on her back, forcing the wind out of her lungs, silencing her attempt to scream for help. She attempted to regain her breath to scream for help a second time, but Taylor swung the axe into the side of her neck. She coughed repeatedly, each accompanied by dark, ruby blood splattering across the ground. Taylor used his foot to roll the girl onto her back and blood began cascading from the wound. One more swing nearly separated her head from her body. The woods fell silent again, as they had been before he had woken up.

As the life faded from her eyes, they stared up into the shadowy face of the man standing over her. Her final memory would be nothing more than a labored, beastly shadow, panting in the darkness.

Although the act was finished, the dark figure wearing a "Taylor suit" stood over the bodies, staring for what felt like hours, panting heavily, ogling his handiwork.

Taylor's consciousness, still watching over his blood-spattered body, looked on in horror, attempting to force his legs to turn and run away. A frightening thought passed through his mind: *what if this…monster, returned to lot seventeen and slaughtered everyone else? Or, worse, returned to the campground where Ben slept, unaware of what I've done.* But the man that used to be Taylor stood still over the corpses for another hour before finally moving again. He dragged the two corpses to the riverbank and kicked them in one at a time. In a moment of strange clarity, he leaned over the water and stuck his bloody hands in. He washed the stains from his hands, then stood in the shallow river. The water splashed up against his legs and he attempted to wash out the blood from his clothes. Nearly all the evidence of what he'd done had vanished.

After he climbed out of the river, he retrieved the bloodied hatchet and walked back into the woods, towards the campsites. He veered away from lot seventeen, giving himself a brief moment of relief before realizing he was walking back towards Ben. His oldest friend was now in danger. There was nothing he could do. Taylor watched as his body returned to their camp, stopping just short of the tree line, barely within the dim light of the smoldering fire. He stood completely still again, the same dead, nightmarish look upon his face, with his eyes firmly locked on the embers of the fire. The grip on the stained hatchet loosened, until it slipped from Taylor's grasp and fell into the bushes.

Ben began to stir and awaken, as though he knew someone was watching him. He sat up, still somewhat asleep and rubbed his eyes. After a big, exhausted yawn, he glanced towards what was left of the fire and noticed Taylor standing at the tree line.

Taylor noticed Ben making eye contact and like a thief fleeing the scene of his most recent crime, his consciousness snapped back into his body, leaving him to cover his own tracks. He frantically stepped over the brush in front of him and back into the full light of the fire.

"Hey, man what are you doing over there?" Ben asked groggily.

"Oh…I just, uh…" Taylor tried to think of a decent excuse. "I had to take a piss and then it all just, kind of *escalated* from there."

"Ah, gotcha. Yeah, I gotta piss, too. I'll be right back." Ben climbed out of his sleeping bag and stumbled towards the fire to warm up.

"Hey, you might not want to go that way. I wasn't really feeling very good." Taylor rubbed his stomach. "It got kinda…messy."

Ben laughed. "Alright, thanks for the warning. I'll go this way, then."

Taylor walked closer to the fire where Ben was able to see him clearly.

"What the hell happened to you? You're bleeding, man." Ben pointed to a splotch of blood on Taylor's temple.

"Oh…like I said, it got a little messy. I was already awake, so I walked to the river to wash up. I slipped and racked my head on a rock. I must have missed a little blood."

"Wow. That sounds…pretty much…awful. I never thought I would have to say anything remotely like this, but thank God I wasn't there to watch you take a shit." Ben laughed.

Taylor faked a bit of a smile and shied away before sitting down on his sleeping bag. "I just want to try and sleep. By tomorrow, I'll forget all about tonight and we'll hit the road again."

"You still want to do some fishing tomorrow morning?"

"I dunno. I just don't want to stay here." Taylor tried to think of a good excuse again. "It was a pretty long walk to the river from here, it was like a mile. Let's just start driving tomorrow and when we see a nice place, we can just stop and fish there."

"Yeah, that sounds good." Ben liked the idea of spontaneity. "Maybe we can find one of those 'hidden gems' that no one knows about."

Taylor smiled and laid his head down to close his eyes.

Ben walked a little ways into the woods, opposite the direction that Taylor had come from. He urinated on a tree trunk and returned to the camp.

Taylor had passed out already, curled up in his sleeping bag.

Fully relieved, Ben climbed back into his own sleeping bag and quickly fell back to sleep, completely unaware of Taylor's nighttime activities.

11

AS DETECTIVE SAWYER arrived within the city limits of Mt. Angel, he reached for his pack of smokes on the far side of the dashboard. He attempted to shake a cigarette out of the open hole in the top—one-handed—and mistakenly crushed the pack in his fist.

"Shit." He peered into the opening on the package trying to assess the condition of his last cigarette; it was ruined. The convenience store near the center of town would have to be his first stop. As it was later in the evening, the store was the only business still open. Dan knew that most of the cops at the precinct would have gone home by now, especially whoever was in charge, so a brief pit stop wouldn't hinder his investigation any further. He parked in one of the available spots directly in front of the store and went inside. "Evening, pal," he said to the young, high school boy behind the counter. "Pack of Pall Malls." Cheap smokes, but better than nothing. Besides, he didn't smoke for the taste.

"One pack of Pall Malls, got it." The boy looked uncomfortable as he searched for the right kind of cigarettes on the shelf behind him.

Must be new to the job, Dan thought.

The boy grabbed the correct brand of cigarettes and turned to awkwardly search for the appropriate buttons on the register. "Um…may I see your ID, please?"

"Are you serious?" Dan glared at him, hoping the boy would notice his coarse skin and wrinkled face, then he continued to stare until the awkward silence made the boy visibly uncomfortable.

"Oh…um, no. Sorry…sir. Four-thirty-six, please."

Dan handed him a five dollar bill, surprised at how inexpensive his smokes were for such a small town. That alone made the trip worth it. "Thanks, kid." It quickly dawned on him just how small this town truly was and he thought that, just maybe, the boy may know something about the Firebird. "Listen, kid, maybe you can help me. A few days back, a gray Firebird drove through town. You know anything about that?"

"Um…yeah I think I remember seeing a car like that. A guy came in and bought some beer. Then he left his car parked out front and walked down to the park. My shift ended at three, so I don't know when he left."

"He go into the bookstore by any chance?"

"I dunno. I can't see the store from in here. He did say he had a friend with him who was a big author or something. I thought he seemed like a pretty cool dude."

"Hmm…" Dan removed the clear plastic from his new pack of smokes and pulled out one cigarette, placing it between his lips.

"You can't smoke in here, sir." The kid realized his mistake the moment he finished speaking.

"No shit." The detective considered yelling at the boy to teach him a little respect for his elders, but resisted since he was out of his own jurisdiction. *Better play it nice.* "You see anything else?"

The kid shook his head "no."

"Alright, thanks, kid. Have a good one." He walked out of the store and pulled out his Zippo with the green shamrock on the front. The lighter sparked a few times before a steady flame took shape and he raised it to the end of the cigarette. After a long drag off of his cigarette, he stared down the darkening street towards the quarantined bookstore. He took one more puff then flicked what was left of the cigarette out into the street before climbing back into his car. Hoping to hear the familiar sounds of Judas Priest or The Ramones, Dan turned the dial on the radio, sifting through the white noise, until he finally found a clear station. The surprising sound of a banjo's country twang caused him to quickly switch the radio back off. Moving on, he drove down Main Street, looking into the bookstore's dark windows as he passed by.

The local precinct was a short drive. As Dan approached the building, the station looked dark, other than one dim globe shining on the entrance and the poorly lit hallway behind it. He parked out front and walked up the steps, pushing open the heavy double doors. The hinges were in dire need of maintenance and a loud creak squealed down the hallway. No one sat behind the reception desk near the entrance, no one to greet new arrivals.

"Hello?" Dan walked past the desk looking for someone, anyone, to assist him. "Hello? Lane County PD Detective Sawyer. Hel—"

"Sorry, sorry." A young boy, seemingly fresh out of the police academy, came sprinting out of the bathroom, still tucking in his blue, standard-issue shirt. "I'm sorry, how may we assist you today?"

"We?" Dan followed the boy over to his post at the desk. "Is there anyone else even here?"

"Um, no."

"Why in the hell would they leave you here all alone?"

"Well, everyone else went home to get a good night's sleep. It's been a busy couple of days. I'm here to 'uphold the appearance that we're keeping the town safe around the clock,'" the boy recited.

"You could start by turning some lights on around here. For a moment I thought that I was going to run into Freddy or Jason."

"Yeah, the boss is pretty strict on electricity usage. It kind of defeats the whole 'we're all home' vibe, huh?"

"Yeah, to say the least. So, I take it your captain isn't here?" Dan leaned onto the desk, putting his weight onto his right elbow.

"No, sir. He'll be back at six a.m. You said you were from Lane County?"

"Eugene, yeah. I'm investigating a double homicide that may be linked with a recent murder in your town. Can you access any of the files for me?"

"No, sir, sorry. I don't have access to the records. Are you talking about the bookshop girl?"

"Yeah, how'd you guess?"

"Well…we're not exactly busy around here and murders don't exactly happen here very often. Neither does random detectives showing up in the middle of the night, asking questions."

"Yeah, sorry about that. Name's Dan." He held out his badge and extended his hand to shake the boy's. "So, do you know anything about the investigation?"

"I'm not sure I can release any of that information without the captain's permission."

Dan grew tired of the childish attitude he had experienced from the town so far. "Look, is there anything you can tell me? Anything at all would help, off the record."

"Okay, off the record, someone saw a man enter the

bookstore in the early afternoon. The witness saw the girl leave with him and head towards the park. Stayed there for about an hour. No one knows what happened to this mystery man, but he disappeared later that day. That's about all I know. They don't really let me do any investigating."

"Not surprising."

The boy's eyes shot a look saying, *"What's that supposed to mean?"*

"I just mean, it's 'cause you're still young, is all. They'll stick you with the worst shifts and make you do all the grunt work. Don't worry about it, though, it's...hazing. I was in the same position once." Dan stretched the truth a bit to calm the boy.

"Really?"

Dan nodded.

"Well, look. I know I don't have any more information to give you, but I can make sure that the captain speaks with you in the morning. Do you have a place to sleep? You can stay in the crib if you'd like."

"No, thanks." The thought of sleeping on a thin mattress in a cold, cement room was more than unappealing. "Can you just...have him meet me at the bookstore in the morning? I saw it on my way in."

"Yes, sir. I'll have him come meet you first thing. Is there anything else we—*I* can do for you, Detective...?"

Before answering Dan pulled his smokes from his coat and held them out towards the boy, offering him one.

The boy shook his head "no."

"Detective Sawyer and no, that'll be fine. Thanks, kid." He put the pack to his mouth, pulled out a smoke for himself and walked out onto the front stoop. With nothing to do but wait until the morning, Dan drove to the bookstore and parked out front. A bit antsy for the next day's investigation and what clues he might find—if anything—he walked up to the dark windows and peered in. He pressed his forehead against the glass for a better look, the cherry on his cigarette leaving a black singe on the pane. Through the darkness, he couldn't make out any definite shapes, but he could distinguish the white, chalk outline of the body that once lay on the floor. Beyond that, all he could see were various shades of black nothingness. "Too dark to see shit," he said, finishing his cigarette and tossing it to the ground. He sat back in the driver's seat and tilted back his chair. Compared to the thin mattresses on the racks at the police station, Dan preferred the discomfort of his car. *Maybe the captain will be late for his shift, at least then I can get a little sleep.*

Wholly exhausted, he placed his hands behind his head and let out an exasperated sigh. With his eyes closed, he couldn't help but imagine what the crime scene looked like, only having the images from the Eugene case for reference. *Could this gray Firebird really be the killer? No experienced serial killer would be so stupid to use the same vehicle at two separate crime scenes.* His mind began to wander. *Maybe he started out small, some poor, misguided soul, quickly escalating up the serial killer food chain.* All he could do was speculate. He hated speculating. With his mind racing, he closed his eyes tighter, hoping to force himself to fall asleep faster. Sooner or later, he got his wish and drifted off to sleep.

Just as quickly as he'd fallen asleep, he was awoken by the loud rapping of a bronze signet ring on the window and the sunlight beating through the windshield of the Plymouth.

A stocky, balding man stood outside the car, holding two steaming paper cups filled with coffee.

Dan knew his Plymouth was an old piece of shit, but

he couldn't help being irritated by the man dragging his gaudy ring across the window.

"Morning, sunshine." The man's voice was muffled through the window. "Doug told me I'd find you here."

Dan couldn't help but know he was going to hate the man already. "Morning," he groaned back as he opened the car door.

"So, tell me Detective...Sawyer, was it? What exactly brings you to my small town?" The captain handed Dan one of the hot beverages.

"I'm sorry, I didn't catch your name." The hot cup heated Dan's icy fingers.

"Jerry."

"Dan." He took a sip of his coffee, wincing as it burned his tongue. "I'm following up on a lead that brought me here. I'm up from the Eugene P.D. We had a double homicide and the only lead was a gray Firebird leaving the scene. Rumor has it, that same Firebird was seen here around the time a young girl was murdered. Ringing any bells?"

"Hmmm...a gray Firebird?" The captain scratched his head with his ring hand. "Yeah, actually. We interviewed a young man standing near that car. Said that him and a buddy were makin' their way up towards Spokane. Something about a family member in the hospital."

"Did he notice anything suspicious around the time of the girl's death? Or was there anything off about him?"

"There was one thing. He said that his friend had visited the bookstore earlier that day and was seen walking with the victim, but witnesses say they parted ways and the boy wasn't seen anywhere near the bookstore until after we showed up. I didn't get a chance to follow up with him, though. The boy we spoke to seemed to cover all the bases."

Dan was astonished at the lack of quality police work. "He was seen with the victim and you didn't think it was necessary to question him *directly*?"

The captain shook his head and attempted to belch out a response, but was quickly interrupted.

"And now I've got a double homicide that is connected to *your* murder and you didn't follow up on a real, physical lead?"

"Now, you wait one God-damn minute. We don't have many serious crimes like this happen in our town." The captain spilled some of his coffee in a fit of anger. "When something does, it's usually a local matter, not some tourist, passing through town, stirring up shit."

Dan knew he needed to rectify the situation, or his investigation may end prematurely. "Look, I'm sorry. I've been run ragged over this case and I keep coming up with nothing but dead ends. I'm just a bit stressed. I'm sorry."

"It's okay, son. I've been there before. Let's just head into the crime scene and see if we can't shed some light on your case." The captain led Dan into the bookstore, giving him a clear look at the scene.

The chalk outline lay roughly where Dan expected it would be. In his time as an officer, especially the time he spent studying with the FBI, he'd seen a lot of death. He'd buried himself in case files, diving into the minds of murderers and serial killers, learning how they operated. Something about this murder, however, seemed different from the scenes he'd worked in the past.

They walked around the counter and stood around the chalk outline on the floor.

"What did the medical report say?" Dan said as he circled around, examining the scene.

"The perp forced their way into the building where someone slightly taller than the victim forced her to the ground and strangled her to death. The ME noted there was extensive bruising on the back of the skull and shoulders. That means he slammed her into the floor nearly hard enough to incapacitate her. She also mentioned that the killer continued to crush the throat for some time post mortem. We found some footprints leading over towards the window and then exiting out the front door. That's basically all we found." The captain took a satisfied drink of his coffee.

Dan looked down and could make out footprints near the window, still clearly formed in the dust, although slightly smeared from the recent traffic in the store. "Any forensic evidence on the scene?"

"None. The throat was wiped clean, no skin or blood under the fingernails. And the door was kicked in, so no prints on the handle."

"And no one saw *anything* at the time of the attack?"

"Unfortunately, no." The captain finished his coffee and tossed the crushed, empty cup into the corner of the room, missing the nearby trash bin.

Dan forced himself to hide his contempt. "Do you mind if I collect a few samples? Just dirt and hair to add to my report?" From within his coat pocket, the detective retrieved a small black case. Inside were a few small baggies and collection tools, including dust for finding fingerprints and thin plastic sheets for recovering them.

"No, go right ahead. We're done here. You're not going to find anything new, though."

Don't be offended if I don't just take your word for it, Dan thought to himself. He scooped up some bits of large dust and a bit of hair that presumably belonged to the young girl. It looked far too short for a girl's hair, though.

He found no prints near the outline and no blood spatter. But then Dan remembered something the captain had said: *"He stood over by the window."* Dan quickly walked over to the window and placed his feet in the prints, leaning in close to examine the glass. On a whim, he took a deep breath and slowly exhaled a warm burst of air. The faint outline of a handprint reflected back at him. He turned and faced the captain. "Did your men check the glass for prints?" Dan knew the answer already, due to the lack of powder or dust left over from their investigation.

"I'm sure they did; their report stated they didn't find any prints at the scene."

Dan turned back to the window and held his dust case up to his mouth. With one swift breath, a cloud of dust stuck to the pane of glass, clearly revealing a set of fingerprints. He shot an unkind look back at the captain, then returned his attention to the glass. After adding some extra powder to the window with a brush, he pressed a one-inch square of plastic onto each of the prints and pulled a satisfactory copy of all of them.

All five prints were smudged and smeared near the bottom as if the hand was pressed hard against the glass then dragged downward.

"There. Not perfect prints, but it'll be the nail in the coffin if we can catch this guy." Dan couldn't think of anything more to gain from the crime scene and was ready to leave the town as soon as possible. "Would it be alright to get a copy of your file on this case?"

"Yeah, I'll have Doug, the young man you met last night, print you up a copy." The captain followed Dan out of the bookstore and locked the building behind them.

Dan trailed him back to the station, where he walked past the awkward boy at the desk and gave him a slight nod as they passed by. He made his way to a small break table and poured himself another cup of coffee, sucking down the java as fast as possible.

The boy from the front desk ran by him, dropping papers from the file he was carrying, most likely running the errand of copying it.

Tired of waiting and eager to leave the small town, Dan walked out onto the front stoop again to wait outside. At least out there in the fresh air, he could smoke. He finished two whole cigarettes before the boy came stumbling through the front doors behind him.

The boy stopped to catch his breath before he spoke. "Here you go, Detective. A copy of the Ashton Hansen file."

The file was only a few pages thick.

"That's mighty white of ya," said Dan, feeling the weight of the file.

"What?"

"Never mind. A little light, don't you think?" he said, weighing the file with his hand.

"There wasn't much the officers found."

"Yeah, that's about what I thought." Dan tucked the report beneath his arm and the boy turned to head back into the building. "Hey, kid. Good work, thanks."

The boy smiled as a sense of accomplishment washed over him. He immediately tripped as he disappeared back into the building.

Dan needed to look over the file, but he refused to spend the rest of his day at the local precinct. He quickly remembered that, when he was driving in, he noticed a small bar near the edge of town. That was his next stop, one he desperately needed. He quickly drove to the German-inspired pub and walked inside. The immediate smell of beer, pool table chalk and deep-fried food filled the air; the intoxicating scent made his stomach growl and his mouth water. An empty stool near the end of the bar called his name.

A middle-aged barmaid, whose breasts were lifted up high by a blue and red corset, met him at the counter. "What'll it be?" she asked.

"Whiskey, neat, two fingers. Oh, and, uh, just some fish and chips if you got it."

"Sure do. Comin' right up." She paused for a moment and looked at him like it was a sin to have whiskey before noon, then she vanished into the kitchen. After delivering the order to the cooks, she returned and grabbed two liquor bottles from the shelf behind her. She held up a bottle of Jameson's in the detective's direction, to which he gave a polite nod. She smiled and then proceeded to pour two fingers of the Irish whiskey into a rocks glass, then set it down in front of him. "Here you go, love."

"Thank you." Dan took a sip from the glass then set it on the counter in front of him. He opened the file the boy gave him and began to peruse it. As he looked at the pictures—forgetting he was about to enjoy a hot meal—he was thankful it wasn't as gruesome as the scene that he'd left in Eugene. While still a disgusting act of aggression, it made him less queasy, without all the blood. Still, he quickly turned the pictures over and continued reading the file. He started to read the statements of the so-called "witnesses" and most held no value whatsoever. Except for one, the boy standing next to the Firebird, was quite a bit more useful.

A particular quote from the statement stood out in Dan's mind and he remembered the captain saying the same thing. *"We're going to Spokane to visit someone in the hospital."*

That alone gave him plenty to go on.

"We," as the boy had said, meant there was more than

one of them. They're "going to Spokane" meant that there were two routes most often driven from southern Oregon to Spokane, Washington. But lastly, and most importantly, the fact that they were visiting someone in the hospital gave him their destination. Somewhere to cut them off, if it came down to it. There were only so many hospitals in Spokane and fewer that would have that particular car parked outside of it.

Dan knew he needed to press on and hopefully catch them for questioning, preferably before they could reach their destination or hurt someone else. He swilled down his drink, threw a twenty onto the counter top and ran back out to his car, foregoing the delicious, greasy food he had ordered.

The old Plymouth flew down Main Street and Dan watched as the small town disappeared from his rear view mirror. He quickly merged back onto the I-5 freeway and set a course for Washington. In what was a terrifying and exhilarating realization, he felt hot on their trail. Hot on the trail of the Firebird. All Dan had to do was catch up…and have a cigarette to calm his nerves.

12

DAWN CREPT OVER the mountains, forcing the orange sunlight through the treetops of the Belle Vista Campground. The day had only begun before Taylor started stuffing their camping supplies into the Firebird.

The loud rustling quickly woke up Ben; to his surprise, the majority of their gear had already been packed.

Taylor grabbed a couple cans of corned beef hash and threw them into the edge of the fire pit. "Get up, broseph. Food's cooking, then we're off to do some fishing. I heard there's some big-ass bass a ways upriver."

"Man, you must be excited." Ben looked around and noticed the only things not shoved into the car were himself and the sleeping bag around him. He shrugged it off and stretched his arms wide like he did every morning. "I haven't been fishing in forever. There better be a ton of fish when we get there." Ben got up and sat next to the fire. "Where are we gonna cast off?"

Taylor slammed shut the trunk of his car and sat down on a log across from the Ben. "I walked over to the showers this morning. Met an old fisherman who said he just got back from a great spot upriver. He told me it's about twenty minutes from here and he filled his cooler with fish in a couple of hours. So, we drive north for about fifteen minutes, take a back road for another five and then we've got a prime fishing spot."

"I guess that's better than anything else we've come up with. Plus, it's been ages since I've scaled and gutted a fish. I'm actually kind of excited to clean and cook some." Ben's stomach rumbled. "And now I'm hungry."

Taylor picked up the pair of tongs resting on the edge of the fire pit and removed one can of hash from the coals. He placed it in front of Ben. "Careful it's hot."

"Really? I never would have guessed that something that's been sitting in the fire for ten minutes would be hot." Ben walked over to the tree line to urinate; it was time to lose all the beer he'd drunk the night before.

"Ha. Ha!" Taylor shouted at Ben, who finished peeing and sat back down. "Just eat already." He tossed a fork, can opener and a hot pad at Ben's feet.

Ben, with the hot pad in hand, picked up the can, opened the lid and started eating the hash.

They ate quickly and silently, filling their bellies and attempting to fully wake up. After finishing their meals, they tossed the cans back into the fire pit, poured a bottle of water over the smoldering wood and kicked some dirt onto the coals.

Ben rolled up his sleeping bag and stuffed it into the trunk of the car. He climbed behind the wheel and Taylor sat in the passenger seat.

As they backed out of the gravel driveway, they noticed two of the girls and one of the redneck boys from lot seventeen walking down the main road. Just as the car was about to pass them, the two girls frantically waved their hands at the car, forcing Ben to slow to a stop and roll down his window.

"Hey, 'scuse us. We're looking for a couple of our friends. They went running off into the woods last night and we haven't seen them since. You haven't seen them by chance, have you?"

"No, I'm sorry. We haven't seen much of anyone, really," said Ben.

"Are you sure? A blonde girl and a boy wearing all camo?"

Taylor leaned over Ben. "No, I haven't either. I went for a walk last night, but didn't see anyone."

"Alright, well, thanks. If you see them or hear anything, will you let the campground lady know? She has our information."

"For sure, I hope you find them. I'm sure they're just off goofing around at the river or something. I used to do the same thing." Ben wasn't too concerned about them, except for the bears that were known to reside in the woods. But bear attacks were a pretty rare occurrence.

Taylor turned away from the campers, mocked scratching his head and rubbing his temple to subtly hide his face.

Ben rolled up the car window and slowly drove away, passing the other campsites and past the obese landlady who was—once again—sitting on her porch, smoking her Marlboros.

She watched intently as they passed by, her eyes locking with theirs, looking for any signs of suspicious activity.

As they drove past, Ben could see her jotting something down on a small notepad, while still staring intently at their car. She was almost certainly keeping track of all the cars that entered and left the campground, most likely due to the missing kids. Just in case.

They turned out onto the highway and drove for a short while, keeping an eye out for any sign of the fishing spot Taylor had heard about. Luckily, they found the turnoff and made their way down the old dirt road. It was a short drive before they noticed a small clearing on their right, with the river running past it.

"See? I told you it was here," said Taylor.

If they hadn't been searching for it, they never would have seen it. A thin wall of trees kept the clearing hidden from the general public and kept the Firebird from driving any closer. Positioned a few feet from the edge of the water was a large picnic table that someone had built many years ago. The cold, damp Oregon weather had peeled away the dark green paint. Although it was left in the middle of nowhere, the table was heavy and sturdy, but due to the lack of maintenance, was beginning to rot.

They both began to pull a few supplies out of the trunk.

Ben chose to grab the grocery bags full of snack foods: chips, jerky and Cheez-Its.

Taylor lifted the cooler of beer and the two fishing rods out of the trunk. He leaned the rods up against the table, but they quickly shifted and fell to the ground. "Shit," he said, placing the cooler on top of the table. Frustrated, he picked up the rods and laid them next to the cooler.

Ben tossed the bag of groceries on to the table and everything spilled out. He walked over to the riverbank and stared across the water. Next to the clearing, jutting out from the bank, was a large formation of boulders that created a small, private peninsula. *A perfect spot to cast off*, he thought. "That's perfect, Taylor. Look." Ben grabbed one of the two pears from the cooler on the table and ran out onto the rocks. He climbed out to the point that stretched farthest out over the water and shouted, "This spot is just perfect! I'm king of the world!"

"Ben, just…just no. No *Titanic*, okay?"

Ben ignored Taylor and sat down on his rocky throne. He pulled his pocket knife out and pressed the small button on the hilt, forcing the blade to swing open and he cut into the soft, juicy pear.

Taylor grabbed two beers from the cooler and the second pear, then began making his way onto the rocks. He cautiously, and awkwardly, tiptoed across the stones to reach Ben. "This is a terrible idea, Ben. We're gonna slip, fall and die out here."

"Come on, Taylor. Find your nuts and bring me my beer already."

Taylor finally made his way to the boulder and handed Ben a beer. "Oh, man. Look at that water. I don't mean to sound gay, but it's kinda beautiful." The glimmering surface of the water was clear and translucent. All the rocks and the fish below the surface reflected back amorphous shadows.

"Yeah, it is." Ben smiled and cut another bite from the pear.

A school of small fish slowly swam upstream against the slow current. The nearest rapids were miles down the river, far enough away that the current moved slowly, nearly nonexistent.

Ben finished cutting the pear down to its core and carefully bit the last piece off of the blade before hurling the core into the river. He watched as it broke the water's surface, scattering the fish and slowly bobbed downstream. Now that he was done eating, he traded the sticky knife for the bottle opener that Taylor was holding and popped the cap off his beer.

"So, a serial killer, huh? Following someone from Oregon across the country?" Taylor took a drink, set down his beer and continued talking before Ben could answer. "You're not going to snap and slit my throat while I sleep are you?" he said, taking a bite out of the pear before examining the blade in his hand, imagining his own gruesome death.

"I don't plan on it, but I guess we don't really know that for sure, now do we?" Ben laughed and Taylor only smiled, rubbing his throat nervously. As much as he joked, Ben was never one to overreact or snap. And while he had been in a few fights, he always attempted to think of a better option first. But like anyone else, he had overreacted a few times before, but he could count the number of times he'd done it on one hand. "Did I ever tell you about the time I got in a fight at homecoming?"

"No. At homecoming, really? What happened?"

"Well, this girl I dated, Ashley, I don't think you knew her. She transferred from some high school in Beaverton. We started going out at the beginning of freshman year and a week before the dance, she fuckin' breaks up with me."

"What? What a bitch. Did she say why?"

"Nope, you know high school girls. They do and say dumb shit without any reason, whatsoever. But, I went to the dance anyway, because you know, going stag was 'cool.' But I was trying to find you and Amy, but before I could, I saw Ashley's bright purple hair out in the middle of the dance floor, grinding with some guy. So, I walked over and hit him. That's the only time I've ever thrown the first punch."

"I was wondering why you never showed up to the dance. Where'd you disappear to after that?"

"Well, I got kicked out of the gym and then stole some beer from my dad's fridge. The next day I found out that she actually went to the dance alone, too. Turns out the guy she was dancing with was that gay kid, Derek, from drama class."

Taylor fell over laughing. "You beat up the gay kid?"

"I didn't know he was gay at the time…I mean, I had my suspicions, what with the blonde tips in his hair and the way he was dancing to that song *Barbie Girl*. But anyway, she was the first girl I'd ever gotten to third base with and I was a horny high school boy. What do you expect me to do when some other guy's junk is all up in my Kool-Aid?"

"Yeah, I wish I had a story like that. I hope I never feel the need to use the word Kool-Aid when talking about a girl, but still. I've never really been in a fight before, like a real fight, not just a pushing or slapping match."

"Really? Never?"

"Nope. Back at the bar in Grants Pass, that's the first time I've done anything like that."

"I never would have guessed. I know I've wanted to punch you before. Can't believe no one else hasn't done it already." Ben laughed.

"Ah ha, see? You wanted to punch me, but you never did. Tends to be my predicament."

Ben thought for a moment and took another drink of his beer, then stood up. "Come on." He climbed down from the rocks and set his beer down on the old table.

Taylor cautiously followed him off of the rocks. "What? What are we doing?"

Ben stood a few paces away from Taylor. "Okay, we've been talking about doing this for a long time, so, it's *Fight Club* time. Hit me as hard as you can, right in the face."

"Don't be stupid, Ben. I'm not going to hit you."

"Why not?"

"Because, you're my friend and you haven't done anything to deserve it." Taylor backed away from Ben slightly.

"Come on, you've always wanted to punch someone and, now, I'm giving you that chance."

"Just…stop, Ben. I'm not going to hit you. That's it."

Ben took a step forward and punched Taylor square in the jaw. He didn't hit him as hard as possible, but hard enough that Taylor knew he had just been punched in the face.

"God damnit, Ben!" Taylor held his chin tightly. "What the hell is wrong with you?"

"There, now I've done something to deserve—" Before Ben could finish talking, Taylor swung and connected with Ben's temple. "Ah, fuck, that stings!" Ben regained his footing, shaking the ringing from his ears.

Taylor sat down on the nearby bench, taking turns rubbing his fist and his jaw.

After grabbing two fresh, cold beer bottles from the cooler, Ben pressed one against Taylor's chin until he took it. "Here, this should help. That wasn't terrible, though. Right?"

"Well, my wrist kinda hurts now. Thanks to you, I probably sprained it." Taylor winced as he put the ice-cold beer up against his jaw.

"See, now you know what it feels like to punch someone and to get punched." They removed the caps and shared a laugh, both surprised at how content they were with striking one another.

Taylor raised his bottle towards Ben, who raised his, and they clinked them together. After finishing their drinks, they moved back to their place out on the rock, Taylor carrying a fishing pole and tackle box, while Ben carried the cooler.

Now re-settled back atop their perch, Ben rubbed the side of his head where Taylor hit him. "I can't believe you hit me, man."

Taylor looked over at him in disbelief. "You hit me first!"

"Yeah, but...that's beside the point." Ben smiled and leaned back against a rock, his fingers interlaced behind his head. "So, how's Amy?"

"Really good, actually. She's been bringing up kids a lot recently, though. Leaving baby magazines and internet windows open. She thinks she's being subtle."

"Amy and subtlety never did go hand in hand." They enjoyed poking fun at their girlfriends, but that's all it was, good fun at each other's expense. Ben really did like Amy, for the most part. Sometimes she was a bit pretentious and Ben always felt that rubbed off onto Lynn. It became clear how true this was when Taylor told Ben how Amy wanted a family. Lynn had been blessed with the same ability for indirect persuasion, which was only fueled by the relentless encouragement from her friends. Ben, on the other hand, had been blessed with the gift of avoidance, something he learned from his father. Whenever Lynn would bring up sensitive subjects, such as kids or marriage, he would flawlessly skirt around the truth until something more pressing caught their attention.

"I'm actually warming up to the idea," Taylor said, staring off at the river. "I think I'm ready to settle down and start a family."

"Really? Wow." Ben was surprised at Taylor's sincerity. "That's great, man. Are you sure that's what you really want? It seems like a pretty big step."

"Yeah, we've been together forever. We've been living together since we graduated and we dated for years before that. And we've crossed pretty much everything off the list when it comes to sex."

Ben shot him a look, hoping for more details.

Taylor looked back at him and smiled. "Yup."

"You know I hate you sometimes, right?"

"It just seems like the next logical step. You know?"

"How does crossing off *everything* sexually lead you to marriage?"

"No, asshole. I mean relationship-wise. Everything we've been through, the time we've invested. Wife and kids just makes sense. Don't you think?"

"Sure." Ben couldn't help but wonder if he was ready for something like that. He and Lynn had been together since their sophomore year of high school. *Maybe it was about time to move forward.*

Every one of their friends from high school were either married or had birthed children within a few years after graduation. Each of which felt it was their duty to ask, "When are you two going to tie the knot?" This question came up every time they saw Ben and Lynn. And every time Ben attempted to answer his interrogators, they always managed to conclude that it was somehow his fault for not "taking the plunge." He never felt ready for all the responsibility that marriage or children brought along with them.

"It's weird, you know?" Ben scratched at the beer label with his thumbnail, peeling it off slightly. "It seems like just yesterday we were sitting in some shitty college bar and you were hitting on every blonde girl with two legs."

"Well, that probably was yesterday. Oh, and then there was that one girl with only one leg. But I know what you mean." Taylor looked down at the empty bottle of beer in his hand; it was time for a refill. He grabbed two more beers from the cooler and handed one to Ben. "Cheers. The last few years have just flown by, haven't they? Do you remember when I wanted to be an architect, back when I graduated from high school?"

"Oh, yeah. I forgot about that. How come you never followed that dream?"

"You know, same thing as you. Tried doing school, but that didn't work out very well. Turned out to be a waste of time and money. I got a promotion and worked all the time. Life just…got in the way. And since you're doing something that makes you happy, I figured I could live vicariously through you."

"It's not too late, you know. You could still go back to school."

"Bullshit, it *is* too late for that. I'm twenty-six years old, I've got a good job and I'm thinking of settling down. It's too late to turn back now, but I don't really care about all that anymore."

"Can't you find a way to do both?"

"I don't know, man. I don't think so, at least not right now. Maybe a little ways down the road, once I've got some money saved and a good job, then I can go back to school."

"Well, if there's anything I can do to help, just let me know. Tell you what, if I make a million dollars off my book, I'll help you go back to school."

"Deal. I can't say no to that." Taylor stretched over towards him and they clinked beer bottles again to seal the deal. He opened his tackle box and took out a jar of Power Bait. After carefully placing a ball of it onto the hook, he gripped the rod's handle and stretched it out in front of him. "Let's see if I can still do this." He placed his forefinger on the fishing line, pressing it firmly against the rod. With a swing backwards, he launched the hook through the air. It plopped into the water about fifteen feet away, right into the center of the river.

"Not bad, looks like you still got it." Ben leaned his head back and closed his eyes.

Taylor slowly spun the handle, reeling the line in. In no time at all, the hook raised out of the water. "Casting always makes you feel good. Unless it's a miserable cast, then it just sucks."

"True, true." Ben opened his eyes and snatched the rod from Taylor's hand. "Here, let me try." Ben did the same and cast the hook out into the river, near where Taylor's cast landed. Due to the water being so still, he didn't have to fight the current. The bobber slowly drifted downstream, then settled near where a fish had been spotted earlier, hopping out of the water.

The section of the river they were fishing in was one of the best locations Ben had seen in years. He watched intently as the bobber floated in place, looking for any sign of a nibble. In usual fishing fashion, nothing happened. Ben watched for a few minutes more before he stuck the base of the pole in a large crevice between the rocks. He tested it to ensure it wouldn't pop loose if anything were to bite it. Once he had it completely secure, he leaned back and closed his eyes again. The sun on his face was warm, not blistering hot, but a warm weight caressing his cheeks. The summer was nearly over, but the decent weather hadn't completely left the Pacific Northwest. He could tell it was nearing noon; the sun was high in the sky and lighting up the inside of his eyelids.

From his back pocket, Taylor pulled out a small copy of *The Sun Also Rises*, his favorite book. He always did like the classics and Hemingway was one of the greats.

Ben also enjoyed the occasional Hemingway and it helped to spur his creativity when writer's block set in.

Taylor sat with his legs crossed and started to read. He'd already read the book at least a dozen times, but for some reason he always kept a copy with him. That way he could indulge himself whenever the urge struck him.

They took a break from conversation and simply enjoyed the quiet, comforting sounds of the wilderness.

The long silence wasn't awkward or uncomfortable and neither of them felt the need to break the peacefulness.

Taylor had only read the first few pages before the tip of his fishing pole began to twitch. At first he thought nothing of it. *Just the river pulling it around.* A few moments later, the tip bent down a few inches and then the entire pole began to shake. Taylor dropped his book and grabbed the rod with both hands. "Ben, get up. We got something! Did you find a net in the trunk?" He stood up to his feet to better fight the fish.

Ben opened one eye to see Taylor struggling with the fish on the end of his line. "Did you see me bring up a net? No, I didn't think so."

"Shit, how are we gonna bring these in?"

"Alright, I'm getting up." Ben sat up and scooted over to Taylor's feet. "Just get it up onto the rocks and we'll figure it out."

Taylor's line was pulled out quite a ways before he began reeling it in. It took at least a couple minutes before it jumped out of the water and onto the boulders beneath them. He continued to reel it in until it was dangling and flailing about in front of Ben.

Ben stood up and grabbed the line about an inch above the fish's mouth and pulled it in close to his feet. He picked up his pocket knife and held the blade in his hand, the handle sticking outwards. He tried stepping on the fish's tail and after a few failed attempts he managed to stomp on it, keeping it relatively still. After kneeling down, he squinted his eyes and prepared for the part he hated the most about fishing. He slammed the handle of the pocket knife down on top of the fish's head, attempting to knock it unconscious. It twitched for a few moments more, so he hit it one more time, only harder.

The fish stopped flailing about.

Ben sat back down, the fish lying between his feet. "You get to clean it. Did you bring a fillet knife or anything in that tackle box?"

"No, sorry. You think your pocket knife will do the trick?"

"Yeah, it'll work just fine." Ben held the knife up and handed it to Taylor, who sat back down on the rock and picked up his catch. "Lucky bastard. I wish I reeled in that fish."

"Hey, don't speak too soon. There's plenty of fish in the river."

"I'm thinkin' that'll be a good start to a long day of fishing."

"Here's hoping." Taylor started slicing open his fish, tail to neck. He pulled out the guts, tossing them into the river, then began dragging the knife over the scales, against the grain, sending them soaring off in all directions.

Ben took two more beers out of the cooler to make room for Taylor's catch and any other fish they caught that day.

Taylor set the fish on top of the cleared patch of ice in the cooler.

They fished for a few more hours before giving up and deciding to enjoy the beautiful day—and drink a few too many beers—but eventually decided to pack up their belongings and return to the road. Taylor had caught one more fish and even Ben managed to reel in one. He'd hoped for more, but he was glad that he caught anything.

They needed that quiet day to take them away from the real world for a few hours and they wouldn't have traded it for the world. Although the day was nearly over and they had returned to the familiar sight of the highway they couldn't help but feel it was a day well wasted. Even

though they came out of it with a few more bruises than
they started with.

<u>13</u>

AFTER RETURNING TO the road, there was only one last place that Ben knew he had to visit before pushing through to Spokane. It had been far too long since he'd visited that small town east of Kennewick.

"Walla Walla, huh?" Taylor had never been, but remembered he had an uncle who used lived there. "My uncle Tony had a place here. My mom used to complain about him and that 'whore,' Donna, he used to live with."

"That...*really* doesn't surprise me." Ben turned onto a side street, examining the town, looking for a familiar sight to help guide him to his destination.

"Why here of all places?"

"My great grandma lives here. Has since she was young." Ben hadn't seen his great grandmother in years and the thought of seeing her again sparked a sense of nostalgia within him.

"Well, not to sound rude, but I think I'll let you tackle that one on your own. I'm gonna go find me a bar to post up in. Get a little hammered!"

"Yeah, I get it. I wouldn't want to visit another person's great grandma either."

"Oh, I cannot wait to stretch my legs." Taylor arched his back to loosen the kinks in his muscles. "We've been sitting in this car for ages." He looked around at the town around them. "How long do you think we'll be here?"

"I was thinking overnight. I called and made a reservation with one of the motels from the campground."

"Thanks for filling me in, asshole."

"I *just* told you, didn't I?"

"Fair enough. So, where does your grandma live?"

"Near some big park in the middle of town. That's about all I remember." Walla Walla was the place that spawned Ben's love of small towns, which explained his love for Grants Pass. Nothing within the county limits would make anyone think "big city," and Grants Pass was even smaller. Around the time he and Lynn were making the decision to move out of Spokane, he tried to convince her that Walla Walla was the place to live. But she was very good at convincing Ben and he only wanted her to be happy, so they settled in his hometown.

His great grandparents had lived in Walla Walla since its founding; his great grandfather even helped raise many of the buildings around town. When Ben was a boy, his grandfather often drove him around the city bragging about his exploits. "You know this town wouldn't be here if it wasn't for me" or "See that building there? Took me two whole months to build." His grandfather loved to brag. After his passing, Ben's mother often tried to convince his great grandmother to leave Walla Walla and live closer to her surviving family. But his great grandmother refused to leave the house that her husband had built so many years ago. Her stubbornness was a Keller family trait and no one would dare hold that against her.

"How do you not know exactly where she lives?" Taylor chastised.

"What, you know where *every* member of your family lives, *exactly*?"

"Well…yeah, of course I do…sort of. Okay, well, not

really. Just saying, Ben."

With a bit of luck, and the help of the map in the car door, Ben managed to find his way to the park near his great grandmother's house. *At least I remembered how to get here*, he thought. He turned off the car next to the park, across from a blue, two story home. "Other than the park, none of this looks familiar," he said to Taylor.

"So, now what are you gonna do?"

"I have an idea, actually." Ben climbed out of the car and jogged across the road, walking up to the large redwood door on the blue house. He knocked three times and waited.

No one answered for at least a minute, but, eventually, the knob began to turn. The door slowly creaked open, revealing a tiny girl who couldn't have been any older than six. Carrying a small teddy bear and wearing a full set of footie pajamas, she peeked through the open doorway.

Ben was amazed that someone would allow such a young child to answer the door alone.

"Um...hello?" the little girl whispered.

"Hi, is your mom or dad home?"

She paused for a moment and stared down at the floor, as though she were thinking about her answer. "Hang on..." She turned and ran back into the house—her small teddy bear tucked beneath her arm—leaving the door wide open.

Really? Ben thought. He was still astounded at the incompetence. *If I were a psychopath, I could just waltz in and rob the place blind, or maybe take the girl. If...I were a crazy person.* But since he wasn't, he waited. A few minutes later he could hear a man's voice yelling loudly, clearly shouting at the little girl, followed by a loud smack that echoed down the hallway.

A few moments later, a middle-aged man appeared in the doorway. "Sorry about that, can I help you?" He pulled the door nearly closed and stepped outside to speak with Ben.

"I'm sorry to bother you, but I'm not from around here and I'm looking to visit my great grandmother. Only thing is, I don't exactly know where she lives. Sharon Keller, do you know her?"

"Oh, Sharon? Yeah, she lives just up the street a ways. Are you Bryan? She talks about you all the time."

"No. I'm his son, actually." The man released the door handle and extended his hand to Ben. "I'm Ben, nice to meet you." He didn't really care about meeting the man, especially after hearing the way he treated his daughter, but he shook his hand anyway.

"Ben, got it. I'm Paul."

"So, you do know where my grandmother lives?"

"Oh, right, she lives in that burgundy house around the corner up there." He pointed towards the house. "Anyway, look, we're right in the middle of dinner, so…"

"Right, thanks for the help." Ben turned and walked down the path.

"Hey!" Paul shouted. "Tell Sharon I said hello, will you?"

"Will do, thanks again. And take care of your little girl." As Ben walked back to the car, he heard Paul yelling at someone inside the house again, swearing with every other word. "What an asshole," Ben said to himself.

"So, how'd *that* go?" Taylor asked as Ben approached the car, his arms resting on the roof of the Firebird.

"Good…I think. He knew where my great grandma lives, at least. She's just up the street." Ben climbed into the driver's seat.

"Oh, well, as much fun as hanging out with some old

lady sounds, I think I'd rather slit my wrists. So, while you go eat shitty cookies and inhale five years' worth of secondhand smoke, I'm going to go find somewhere to get that drink." Taylor leaned into the car window. "I'm just gonna walk over to where we saw those bars when we drove in. I think I saw a pretty authentic Irish pub. Irish bars are honestly the best, don't you think?"

"Whatever, man, save me a seat. I'll use you as my excuse to get the hell out of there. I love my grandma, but Jesus Christ, can she talk."

"Sounds good. See you in a bit." Taylor shoved his hands into his pockets and began to stroll down the street, away from the park and towards the pub.

Ben drove forward towards the small, dark burgundy house around the corner. In his rearview mirror, he noticed Taylor had stopped for a moment, waving at the same little girl, standing on the front porch of the blue house again. That asshole Paul grabbed her by the arm, yanking her inside and slamming shut the door. *Asshole*, he thought again. Ben put the blue house out of his mind as he pulled into his grandmother's driveway and the childhood memories began instantly flooding back into his mind.

He immediately remembered his great grandfather, taking the grandkids down to the basement of his home and measuring their heights by drawing lines on the cement wall. All the kids wanted to draw on them as well, but his great grandfather would always reply, "I built this house with my two hands. I'll draw all over the walls if I choose. When you build your own home, then you can draw on the walls all you want." He enjoyed reminding all six of his grandkids that he built the house with his own two hands. It never mattered what the conversation was about, the answer was always the same: "I built this house…"

It wasn't long before Ben thought back to playing in the garden as his great grandma tended to her plants. Ben would run around the lawn, fleeing from her yappy Jack Russell terrier, simply named "Jack." He would run until the only ground left to cover was the garden, where he would get yelled at until he finally ran back to the yard. As a young boy, Ben absolutely hated tomatoes—the texture, the taste and the fact that no one could tell him if they were fruits or vegetables while he was growing up. But from that garden, he never tasted anything he didn't like. Especially the hundreds of tiny yellow tomatoes she grew every year.

After parking in the driveway, he walked up to the metal screen door, hiding a wooden one behind it and knocked on the screen, hoping she was actually home. He could hear the sound of *The Price Is Right* with the volume turned up far too high, followed by a few loud coughs and curse words as she approached the door.

"Hello?" she hollered before opening it.

"Hey, Grandma, it's Ben. Your great grandson."

She opened the door. "Ben, is that really you? Oh, my God. Look at how big you've gotten!" she shouted as she pushed open the screen door to give him a hug.

"Hi, Grandma, how are you?"

"I'm doing okay." She removed the lit cigarette from her mouth. "I was just getting ready to go play bridge with the girls over at Evelyn's. You know, boring old people stuff. Come in, come in."

Ben followed her into the house, where the smell of an old-folk's home hid behind the thick cloud of cigarette smoke in the living room. He immediately began feeling nostalgic, absorbing the smell, the vomit green, burlap furniture, and the black and brown shag carpeting. It oddly reminded him of his dad's house, too.

"So, tell me, Benny, how have you been? What's new with you? Is there a pretty girl in your life?" She began to light up a new cigarette, forgetting about the burning one in the ashtray next to her.

"Well, yeah, but…" Ben said nervously. "I got fired from my job at the restaurant. That's why I was able to have enough time to go see my dad." He sat down on the green armchair. "Have you heard anything new about his condition?"

"Condition? What condition?" A pale, frightened look emerged on her face.

"Didn't you know he was in the hospital?"

"No! What's going on?"

Ben couldn't believe his dad never called to let her know. "He's got lung cancer; he's been in the hospital for a couple of weeks now. I'm driving up to go see him."

Her regularly happy face lost its gleefulness; she even removed the cigarette from her lips. "Oh, no. That's so awful; how come no one called me?"

"I don't know, Grandma. But, if I know my dad, he probably didn't tell anybody he didn't absolutely have to. It was like pulling teeth to get him to tell *me*. He never did like people knowing when he's weak or vulnerable."

"That stubborn…ass. I can't believe he wouldn't tell anyone."

Ben figured his dad didn't tell many people, but it was starting to seem as though he was the only one who knew. The fact made him a little bit happy, but he held back his smile and nodded in agreement.

"Tell him I said hi and that I miss him, okay? And tell him that he'd best get better, will you?"

"Of course I will, Grandma." Ben felt he needed to change the subject. "Is there anything new and exciting going on in your life?"

"Not really, I've been playing the lottery and the slots at the bars. With any luck I'll be able to move to Tahiti or Hawaii. And when I do win the lottery, I'll pay for you to come visit me sometime."

"That sounds great, but I thought you loved this house too much to leave?"

"I do. But I've been reliving old memories long enough. It just feels like it's time to let go."

"What about moving down to Grants Pass with Mom?"

Sharon glared over at Ben. "I lived near family for years before you were born. I cut that umbilical cord years ago." She laughed a bit. "Besides, your mother's not my biggest fan. If I decide to move, it's not going to be to live near her. I think a nice, warm island somewhere sounds like the dream. Don't you?" She took a long drag off her cigarette and Ben nodded in agreement with the idea. She quickly looked back at the kitchen as though she'd remembered something important and scurried off into the other room.

"Do you need help with anything, Grandma?"

Sharon didn't respond, which worried Ben for a moment, but then she returned to the living room holding a plastic grocery bag, the handles tied into a bow. "Here."

"What's this?" Ben attempted to untie the bag.

"A couple sandwiches I made earlier today and some leftovers from last night. I made meatloaf. And in the Ziploc are some of those yellow tomatoes from the garden."

Ben tore open the bag and immediately searched through it to examine what she'd given him. "Wow. Thanks, Grandma." He removed one of the small tomatoes and popped it into his mouth. It was hard for him to hide the euphoria, but he managed to avoid reverting into a giddy ten-year-old. "Mmm. I haven't had these in years."

"Well, I've always got some in the fridge, so swing by any time."

"I don't know how you've managed to keep gardening all these years. It always seemed so boring."

"When you get to my age, boring hobbies become a way of life."

"Whatever you say, Grandma. But thanks for the food; it means a lot." Ben ate another tomato and re-tied the bag. "Hey, I don't want to bother you for too long, but do you mind if I run downstairs real quick? Just to look around a bit. For old time's sake."

"No, go right ahead, sweetie." Sharon led him through the kitchen to a wooden door and opened it.

With his grandmother close behind him, Ben walked down the dark stairway, the old, wooden stairs creaking loudly beneath his feet. With his grandmother following closely behind him, he fished around on the nearby wall for a light switch. It took him a moment to remember that the bulb in the middle of the room had a chain dangling from it. "You should have someone take a look at these stairs."

"I don't like people I don't know in my house. Besides, keeping up on things like that was your grandfather's job."

Ben walked over to the light bulb dangling in the middle of the room. He didn't bother brushing away the cobwebs; he quickly tugged on the string and pulled his hand away. The light flickered on, illuminating a bare cement wall that stretched across half the room. He walked over and rubbed his hand over the scribbles. Old memories immediately resurfaced, rushing over him like tidal wave. He couldn't help but smile as he held back a few tears. The cement felt exactly the same as it did all those years ago.

"You kids were his favorite, you know?" Sharon leaned against a wall near the stairwell. "He loved you all so much that whenever your parents would yell at you for doing something stupid, he'd just say"—she attempted her best impression of her late husband—"'They're just being kids, God damnit! If I beat your ass for every stupid thing you did, they would have thrown me in prison before you hit high school.' Then he'd chase you kids all around the yard until he ran out of breath and then he'd run a little more. He was too old to run around like that." Her eyes looked as though they were lost in an old memory.

"Really? I barely remember those days anymore." He turned around to face her.

"Yup, I think he liked playing with you kids more than he enjoyed our anniversaries. But I can't say I blame him. You kids were alright." She smiled at him jokingly as she took another drag off her cigarette.

"Thanks, Grandma. You guys were alright, too." Ben took one last look at the wall before collecting himself. "Um…look, I actually gotta get going. I have to meet my friend, Taylor. He came along with me, but he's at a bar a few blocks away. I should probably go find him."

"Okay, sweetie. It was so good to see you." She walked over, wrapped her arms around Ben's neck and gave him a big, tight hug.

Ben loved his family, but didn't visit any of them very often, which made this visit all the more enjoyable. *Absence makes the heart grow fonder*, he thought to defend himself.

After she released her tight grip, they both walked back up the stairs and Sharon handed Ben the plastic bag of food that he'd left on the counter. "Take care of yourself, now."

"Thanks, and I will. Love you, Grandma."

"Love you too, sweetie." She walked him out the front door and shouted at him as he made his way to the car. "You tell your dad to give me a call and tell me he's okay, alright?"

"Of course I will." After tossing the bag into the passenger seat, Ben backed the Firebird out of the driveway. Driving away from his great grandmother's house, he could see her in the rearview waving goodbye from the front porch. He drove around the far side of the park, not noticing the ambulance parked in front of the blue house where he'd asked for directions. The young girl who'd greeted him stood on the front porch, crying, as a gurney wheeled out a covered body, the white sheet stained with spots of blood.

14

THE BAR TAYLOR walked to was only a few minutes' drive from the park. Ben pulled onto the main road and immediately noticed the Irish pub Taylor spotted as they arrived in town.

The pub was smack dab between a biker bar and an Applebee's. That small strip of road held all of the small town's entertainment, packed into one-half of a mile.

Ben parked in one of the few empty parking spaces in front of the bar.

Taylor sat at one of the designated smoking areas outside. He didn't usually smoke, but on rare occasions when the mood struck either of them, they liked to enjoy a cigarette or two.

After climbing out of the car, Ben locked it up, then walked up to Taylor, noticing only one drink on the table. "Why isn't there a beer ready for me?"

"So, it went that well, huh?"

"No, it went great. I could sure as hell use a drink though."

"Me too. You should probably get in there and buy us some. I'm almost out." Taylor took a long drag from the Newport between his fingers.

"You gonna buy?"

"I think it's your turn. I'll get us next time."

Ben raised his left eyebrow at Taylor suspiciously.

With a "Hmph," he turned and pushed his way through the swinging door. The bar smelled of old beer and smoke, regardless of the recent law to banish smoking in bars, a law forced through by non-smokers with exacerbated anxieties about secondhand smoke. Although Ben never considered himself a smoker, he enjoyed the idea of being able to go out for drinks and not be forced to freeze his ass off in the cold, just so he could enjoy a rare cigarette. Smoking and foul language in the media were both hot button issues for Ben and he applied the same logic to both arguments: if you don't like it, get the hell out. No one is forced to enter a bar and no one's being held hostage there. He leaned onto the bar and waved at the old bartender standing down near the hand-wash sink.

It took the barkeep a few minutes to wash his hands and then meander his way over to Ben.

"What'll it be, brother?"

Ben had never actually met someone with an Irish accent. He couldn't help but enjoy it. "Pitcher of hef, two glasses, please."

The barkeep began by retrieving the glassware from the cooler without any sort of reply.

"How's your day going?" Ben asked.

"Alright, still breathing. So, I can't complain, can I?"

Ben hated that answer. It always felt fake and lethargic. *How difficult is it to come up with a genuine response?* "No." Ben's reply was equally uninterested. "I guess you can't." While he waited for their drinks, he took out his Moleskine from his back pocket and jotted down a few notes about the old bartender. *Surly, monotonous...douche. Cool Irish accent.*

"What're you writin' there, brother?"

"Oh, I'm uh...just...working on a novel, taking down a few notes about the town." He quickly shut his notebook and put it away in his pocket.

The bartender set the pitcher and the two stacked glasses in front of him. "Writin' all good things, I hope?" His voice revealed his feelings towards Ben: that he was an outsider and wasn't welcome.

"Yeah, I actually love this town. My family's lived here forever and I just thought I'd stop by for a visit."

"Fourteen-fifty."

What, now you don't want to talk all of the sudden? "Damn, alright, here you go." Ben handed the man a crumpled twenty from his pocket.

"What's your book called?"

"I don't know yet. I'm not very good with titles. You got any ideas?"

"Yeah, how 'bout *The Life of a Mick Bartender*? You'll make millions."

Ben decided to accept his poor attitude and not comment on it. "I'll hold you to that."

The bartender set Ben's change on the counter and carried on with whatever miserable task he was doing before.

After grabbing his change and leaving a couple bucks on the counter—even though the barkeep didn't deserve any sort of a tip—Ben headed towards the door with the beer and the two glasses. Taylor and Ben had worked out a system where it was always customary to leave something for servers, just in case they decided to come back. It made them feel a bit classier. He walked back outside to the small beer garden where Taylor was waiting for him. "Did you talk to that bartender at all?" he asked Taylor.

"Not really, why?"

"Complete dick." Ben set the glasses on the table and filled them both to the brim; the foam rose and spilled down the sides.

"Come on man, party foul." They lifted their glasses and cautiously sipped the foam to prevent any more spillage, then took quick follow-up drinks. "Why was he such a dick?"

"I don't know, he just didn't say more than a few words to me. I tried to make conversation, but he more or less told me to fuck off."

"Yup, you're right." Taylor noticed the surprised look on Ben's face. "Just because the guy doesn't want to talk, that makes him a dick."

"Yeah, yeah. Whatever. You would have called him an asshole to his face."

"That does sound like me." Taylor took one last puff before snuffing out the stubby cigarette. "So, how was your dear old granny?"

"She was actually pretty good. I told her my dad was in the hospital and she freaked out. Apparently no one called and told her."

"From what you told me about your dad, that doesn't really surprise me."

"That's what I told her. I think she'll beat my ass if I don't have my dad call her." Ben smiled at the thought of a polite ass-whooping from his great grandmother.

"That would probably be a good idea. How long since you visited her last?"

"God, it's probably been...four, five years now."

"Holy shit, that is a hell of a long time to not visit family," said Taylor.

"I know, but life just got in the way. It's hard to keep in touch with the whole family."

They continued to drain their pint glasses.

"Yeah, I hear you. At least she's still alive, I never got the chance to tell my great grandparents goodbye. Be happy that you got to see her."

"I am." Ben looked around during a long, awkward silence. "Damn, you can be a buzzkill sometimes."

"Just don't forget to tell your dad to call her. Or else you'll end up in some deep shit."

"Believe me, I know. One time, she told me about how my dad and uncle were fighting or something like that, so she took one of my grandpa's belts and beat the hell out of 'em, then threw her shoes at them as they ran away."

"Really? Your *great* grandmother?"

"Yeah, I don't believe that little old lady has it in her, but she scares the hell out of my dad and I don't think I want to test her."

"I don't blame you. On the way back, we should stop in and update her on your dad."

"Yeah, I think she'd like that. Thanks for being so understanding about all this."

"That's what I'm here for, buddy boy." Taylor picked up the pitcher and filled their glasses.

Every time they ordered a pitcher of beer, the pitcher seemed to get smaller and smaller. Years ago, it took them hours to finish one. Now, they could polish off a pitcher within the hour. Perhaps it was because they'd built up a tolerance over the years, but they were usually careful drinkers…usually. They were well aware of their limits, but every so often they drank a little more than they could handle.

"Okay, time for an update. Anything new on your novel?" Taylor asked with excitement.

"Well, I've got a decent outline written. I just can't think of an ending. I think that's the worst part about being a writer, knowing how it ends. That's why I'm having so much trouble. My mind just doesn't want to come up with anything."

"Oh, you should have the bad guy kill off the main character. Kind of a bittersweet ending. Readers wouldn't expect that at all!"

"I thought about ending it that way, but I think it's a bit too depressing. Not sure if readers would like that very much."

"Nowadays? No, people love that sort of thing. The hero either dies in a blaze of glory or kills himself in a big twist ending." Taylor grew excited at the prospect of helping with the ending.

"Yeah, I guess that's true. I don't know, knowing how the story is going to end just seems like cheating or something. I think I'd rather just wait to write the end until, well, the end."

"That's understandable. Because, if you know how it's going to end, what's your motivation to write everything else? It loses the mystery."

"My thoughts exactly." Ben finished the half-glass of beer left in the bottom of the pitcher. "I think I've got enough to get started. Tonight I'm going to do some writing. I think I can at least get the first chapter done. Who knows, maybe a little more."

"Get it done, man. I'm ready to read it already!" Taylor chugged down the rest of his drink and slammed the glass down on the table. "I gotta piss. Be right back."

"Alright, I'm gonna get us one more pitcher before we head to the motel." Ben took his black Moleskine notebook from his back pocket and set it on the table as they both stood up and walked back into the pub.

Taylor made his way towards the restroom and Ben returned to the bar to wait for another pitcher.

The old "Mick" bartender made his way back to Ben, who held up a finger to indicate "one more," and the bartender began filling another pitcher.

Ben left fifteen dollars on the counter and carried the pitcher outside, careful not to spill any of the ice-cold, hoppy goodness. He set it down on the table and saw that Taylor had left his pack of Newports near the ashtray, with a lighter resting on top of it. Ben reached across the table and grabbed the cigarettes to shake one out for himself. Not counting the time they'd spent on the road, it had been months since Ben had smoked a cigarette, mostly because Lynn hated it and never hesitated to let him know. He lit up and inhaled deeply, filling his lungs with smoke. His eyes closed and he exhaled upwards into the sky. Enjoying the act of conforming to the cliché, smoking made him feel like a real writer. Ben often enjoyed a fantasy of himself in a small, cramped, one-room apartment, hunched over an old typewriter that he'd found at a rummage sale. Unfortunately, typewriters were much harder to come across than he expected and the only one he'd ever found was *very* expensive, seeing how they were now considered antiques. So, with his Moleskine and stained legal pad, he was his version of a writer. Words would be his art and anything he could write on, his canvas. Lynn always made irritated-wife sounds when Ben would drift off and fill out dinner napkins with story ideas.

Ben loved her, but he worried that all the advice he'd heard from married men was coming true. People used to tell him that all married people did was argue and yell at one another. For a time, that was never the case in their relationship, but that was slowly changing. They began arguing more and more, usually over little things: dirty dishes in the sink or the milk being left out of the refrigerator. But on the rare occasion, their arguments reached nuclear levels and they would fight for days, bringing up every argument they'd had previously. Before Ben left for his road trip, they hadn't fought for a month, but that day things quickly started to change. Thinking about that argument made him take a longer drag off his cigarette. The loud sizzle of the cherry burning relaxed him.

"Did you ask if you could take one of those?" Taylor walked up behind him and slapped him on the arm.

Ben immediately realized that he had gotten a dark sunburn while at the river. The distinct shape of a handprint lingered and burned intensely. "God damnit, that fucking hurt. I don't think I've had a real sunburn in years." Ben rubbed his arm vigorously.

"Well, maybe if you would leave your house once in a while, you fuckin' vampire."

"Man, you were gone for days. I was starting to think you fell in or died. Your cigarettes were your inheritance to me." Ben snuffed out the butt and lit up another Newport.

"Fair enough. I was talking to this hot-ass blonde girl in there. I think we're going to…uh…head over to the motel. You know, *before* you head over." Taylor's eyes widened as he attempted to send Ben a telepathic hint.

"Yeah, I think I got it. The motel is a ways up the road. It's a Motel Eight. Reservation's under my name." They could see the large blue sign from their table outside. "Do you need the keys to the car?"

"No." Taylor smiled as a pretty blonde girl walked out of the bar and passed by them smiling in his direction. Both men stopped talking and stared at her as she walked by and blew a kiss in their direction, leaving a hint of bright pink lipstick on her palm.

It didn't take long for Ben to realize what must have caught Taylor's initial attention.

Her breasts were pushed up high, nearly falling out of the low-cut, red dress she was wearing. Taunting Taylor with her swaying hips, she walked around the corner of the building to her car.

Taylor finally decided to speak again after she vanished from sight. "No need for the car, she's gonna drive. Isn't she fucking gorgeous?" He grabbed Ben's head and shook it around.

"Knock it off, asshole." Ben pushed Taylor off of him. "Are you sure you want to do this? What if Amy finds out?"

"She's not going to find out, unless *you* tell her." The smile left Taylor's face as he became dead serious. "Which you wouldn't do...*ever*...right?"

"No, man. You're an adult and my best friend. You can make your own decisions. As stupid as they may be."

A weak honk echoed from around the corner.

"Alright, besides if I'm gonna be taking the leap soon I should get one last hurrah before I get locked down. Consider it my bachelor party. But don't forget, Ben, bros before hoes."

Ben could tell there was no convincing him otherwise. "Bros before hoes..." he said half-heartedly.

"Okay, man, I'm out. Careful driving if you're gonna finish that pitcher. If you wreck my God-damn car, I'll kill you." Taylor had already disappeared around the corner.

Ben watched as Taylor hopped into the cherry-red PT Cruiser before it turned onto the main road and drove off in the direction of the motel. He shook his head, removing the thoughts about Taylor from his mind and opened his Moleskine. With a perfect opportunity to start powering out the first chapter of his novel finally rearing its head, Ben started writing. He began scribbling and scratching away, not forming any sort of a coherent story structure, only fleshed out interesting lines of dialogue or descriptions of beautiful West Coast locations that would be perfect for stalking and killing someone. After a few more drinks of beer, he became extremely focused on his work until the pitcher had gone flat and warm. With his opening line in mind, he started writing the first chapter of his book. In what felt like an instant, he sat outside writing for nearly two hours before his gaze broke from the page.

The day started to disappear and the sun was setting beneath the tree line, erupting in a beautiful stream of hallucinogenic colors from behind the mountaintops.

He knew it was time to hit the sack when his eyes began to burn from the stress of focusing so intently. So much, he had to rub them vigorously to calm the burn. Although it wasn't extremely late in the evening, the beer made him sleepy and he was ready for bed. *There's no way Taylor wouldn't be done with his business by now.* Focusing on his writing for so long caused his brain to feel as though it was pressing against the walls of his skull—a common side effect of the alcohol and intense concentration. There hadn't been a chance to write like this the entire trip. But after making some headway, he was ready to get some rest and an early start in the morning.

In the few minutes it took to drive to the motel, the stream of colors in the sky had dimmed and the night crept up behind him. The parking lot of the motel was nearly empty, which gave Ben a strange sense of relief. He was unsure which room was his, so he stopped in front of the office to retrieve his key.

A scrawny, brown-skinned man stood behind the counter stroking his pencil-thin mustache, staring at a small, color television locked up in a small, metal cage in the corner. As Ben entered the room, the manager refused to look away from the white-trash talk show he was watching.

"Excuse me, I have a room reserved. Benjamin Keller."

The man continued to ignore him.

"Hey!"

The man finally looked in Ben's direction.

"Ben Keller, I need to pick up my second room key; the other one was picked up earlier."

Without any words, the skinny Mexican turned and grabbed a key from one of the small hooks on the wall. He had a strange look on his face, almost surprised that someone was picking up the second key. He must have thought Taylor's "guest" was the second occupant. Or maybe he thought it was strange that two men were sharing a hotel room together, which didn't make sense with the two beds in the room.

Ben snatched the key from him, gave him a nod and headed for the door.

"Check out at eleven."

"Eleven, got it," said Ben. "See you in the morning." He turned and left the small office. The room number was printed on the obnoxious piece of plastic dangling from the key. Room twenty-seven A. It was on the side of the building opposite the office. Ben drove across the small parking lot, just in time to beat the heavy rain that began to assault the town. Room twenty-seven A was near the end of the complex, only a few rooms from the stairwell on the end. He put the key into the lock and then remembered that Taylor had beaten him to the motel. "Hey, Taylor, put your dick away. I'm comin' in." He jiggled the key a couple of times to give them a moment to make themselves presentable. Then, he slowly pushed open the door. "Ugh, smells like ass in—"

Taylor sat at the end of one of the two beds, his face hiding in his hands. They were soaked in blood.

The blonde with the pink lipstick was laying on the floor, naked, her face beaten to a pulp. Were it not for her bright pink, swollen lips and her huge tits, she would be completely unrecognizable.

"What the fuck!" Ben shouted.

Next to Taylor's feet, lay a hefty, bronze lamp, far away from its familiar spot on the nightstand between the two beds. The golden, semitransparent cord was still plugged into the wall, but shards from the broken bulb were scattered around the woman's body.

Ben couldn't move, his eyes locked on the body in front of him.

Taylor refused to look up from his stained hands. He wasn't sobbing or pleading for forgiveness; he sat completely silent, utterly shocked at whatever had taken place in the room.

"Taylor, what the fuck is this? What happened?" Ben walked closer to him, but stepped back again as he neared the girl on the floor.

On cue, the rain picked up exponentially and began slamming against the pavement like mortar fire.

Taylor finally looked up from his hands, his face marked with crimson fingerprints. He started to mouth the letter "I" over and over, but no sounds came out.

Ben crouched down next to him. "Taylor, listen to me. You have to say something."

Taylor's eyes filled up with pools of liquid, then tears quickly began to stream down his face. "I...I'm...sorry," he repeated.

"It's okay. Just tell me what happened?"

"She…" Taylor looked down at the carpet and cleared his throat, trying to dislodge the trembling in his voice. "She tried to rob me. She threatened to call her fucking pimp and that he would break my legs."

"Wha—what are you talking about?"

"I didn't know she was a hooker. I told her I didn't have any money and she got pissed, and then said that her rate had just tripled." He looked back up at Ben. "So, I told her to fuck off and everything just spiraled the fuck out of control."

"Look, it's gonna be okay, Taylor. We'll just call the police and tell them."

"No." Taylor's voice was no longer shaking and he gripped Ben's wrist tightly. "No cops. They won't understand and they'll put me on death row." He took a deep breath. "And I told you before, Amy can't find out, Ben." His eyes began to water again. "Amy can't find out about this."

"Well, what the hell do you want me to do then?" Ben pulled his wrist from Taylor's grasp.

"We need to leave. Just get up and leave." Taylor stood up and began grabbing his belongings from the nightstand. "We just need to calmly get out of here and act like nothing happened."

"They've got my name on file, Taylor and the Mexican guy in the office knows what we look like."

"You can barely understand that spic immigrant; he's nothing. We can call the police and give them an anonymous tip once we're far enough away from here."

It was a terrible plan, but Ben couldn't think of anything better. "I—I guess…"

"Okay." Taylor breathed in deep through his nose, clearing the blockages that come with crying. "Let's go." Before they had time to leave, a custodial cart pushed past the open door to their room.

Ben had forgotten to close the door.

A hefty, Mexican cleaning lady screamed at the top of her lungs and fled as fast as she could to the front office.

"Oh, shit," said Ben.

They both ran from the room, through the pouring rain and quickly started the car.

Ben backed the car out of the parking spot and floored it out of the lot.

As they passed the office, they could see the motel manager running towards them, screaming in the downpour. They couldn't understand any of the words that penetrated the sound of the rain tap dancing on the roof of the car. The words they could hear were garbled screams in angry Spanglish.

Ben approached the main road that would take them to the highway. As they pulled onto the road, at the exact moment, an old, light brown Plymouth turned into the driveway.

Time slowed to a crawl and Ben's eyes connected with the man driving the car. The connection felt as though it lasted for minutes, when in fact they only saw each other for a brief moment. His face went pale and the man in the Plymouth noticed, but had no clue as to who they were. In the back of Ben's mind, he knew the man had to be a cop. Maybe it was the adrenaline or the paranoia, but the man definitely had that look about him.

Ben stepped on the gas, hard, and they sped off north out of the city.

15

DETECTIVE SAWYER LOOKED up in his rearview mirror as the gray Firebird turned out onto the road. He slammed on the breaks as an irate Mexican man ran in front of his car, screaming at him. Dan climbed out but left the engine running. The man's screaming made no sense to him; he knew that one day he would need that Spanish he never took the time to learn. His intuition started to kick in. The screaming man, a door across the parking lot swung wide open, and the skid marks pulling out of the parking lot. *No...* Dan couldn't believe he didn't realize it faster. The gray car in his rearview had a familiar symbol on the trunk of the car. *That was the Firebird.* That was the car he'd been hunting all along.

Ignoring the motel manager, he turned around and ran out into the middle of the empty street. He stared in the direction that the car had driven in, squinting to see through the rain. The stress of losing the suspects weighed heavily on him and he frantically looked all around for any sign of the vehicle. He saw nothing. No cars, no tail lights, nothing. "Shit!" He ran back to the screaming man and attempted to have a calm conversation with him. "Calm...down. Was that..." He pointed over to the open doorway. "...their room?"

The manager shook his head up and down, still shouting.

Hoping to finally put a few pieces together, Dan ran across the parking lot, ignoring the incessant yelling. As he entered through the open doorway, he immediately saw the blonde girl sprawled out on the floor and crouched down next to her. He pressed his index and middle finger against her throat, hoping to feel some sort of pulse. *Nothing.* He kept his fingers there for another minute, inspecting his watch closely to time any pulses, just in case.

"*Ay, dios mio.*" The manager followed Dan into the room, finding more to yell about after seeing the body.

"God damnit." Dan pushed the manager out of the room and into the parking lot. "Out. No one comes in here!" The detective pointed towards the office in hopes the man would leave the area.

The manager shook his head "no" and took out his cell phone to begin making calls.

Dan ran back to his car and parked it in front of the room-turned-crime-scene. He grabbed his bag from the back seat and set it down just inside the motel room. The first thing he removed from his bag was the standard yellow police tape, using the maid's cart to quarantine the room. His second act was his least favorite part of crime scene investigation. After taking his old digital camera from the bag, he snapped a few photos of the surrounding area, including the skid marks on the pavement outside, followed by the worst part: the body.

Dan began with the blood splattered around the room. On the bed, the walls and, most prominently, the floor. As he looked closer at the body, his stomach churned and he couldn't help but feel squeamish. *It never gets any easier*, he thought, but he controlled the feelings. He crouched down next to the naked woman again. It wasn't the gruesomeness of the scene that made him ill; his nausea was caused by something deeper. He wasn't troubled by the *idea* of someone being brutally murdered. Dan was regrettably good at putting himself in the shoes of the killer and the victim. The rage that fuels an act like that began to quickly boil in his veins as he tried to think like the killers. He began to fabricate the hatred that must have flown through someone to commit such an act. His hands clenched tighter around the camera as he photographed the busted lamp lying next her. They tightened as though they were gripping the base of light fixture, prepared to use it as a makeshift weapon. He gripped so tight it became painful.

To begin photographing the body, he started with the feet, in an attempt to save the worst for last. Other than the periodic drop of blood, her feet and legs looked normal, unaffected by the tragedy. As he moved upwards and photographed the torso, he made sure to do it quickly and move on, out of respect for the poor, naked soul. As he prepared himself to capture her face, he closed his eyes and allowed for a moment of silence. After the moment passed, he took two wide shots of her face, one from either side and then increased the zoom for more detailed photos.

He captured the wound first. A large, gaping hole where her skull once stood. Jagged pieces of bone poked through the pools of liquid and brain matter.

Next were her sky-blue eyes, foggy and clouded.

After a quick photo, he moved lower, noticing her bright pink lips. He snapped a photo. It was an eerie juxtaposition between the youthful pink lipstick and the brutality of her condition. Bright white chips of broken teeth—drifting aimlessly through the pool of crimson waters that filled her mouth—drew his attention from the lipstick. The blood filled her cheeks and slowly drained out the crease of her mouth.

Dan's empathy towards the poor girl nearly made him sick; he could almost feel the beating she took in his own skull. He ran out of the motel room and sat down against the outside wall. This was the worst he'd ever felt. He came so close to the Firebird and *still* managed to lose the suspects. *Now what do I do?* he thought, racking his brain. "The motel guest book!"

The Motel Eight's manager had returned to his post in the front office, yelling into his tiny, silver flip phone.

Dan stormed across the parking lot and walked up to the office counter; his disposition had grown somber and agitated. The man virtually ignored the detective as he raved into his phone.

"Excuse me."

The manager continued his frantic conversation.

Jesus fucking Christ. Dan grabbed the cell phone and flung it into the wall behind him, splintering it into hundreds of irreparable pieces.

The manager's face was in utter shock; he was finally speechless.

"Do I have your attention now?" Dan shouted at the manager, who shook his head slowly in agreement. "Good. Because you've got a dead girl in room twenty-seven A. Who booked it?"

After standing frozen for a moment, the man fumbled for the books he kept beneath the counter. Mumbling to himself, he thumbed through the pages and drew his finger across them until he found the name. Handing the book to the detective, he pointed to the name next to the room number. "Ben-jamin Kel-ler," he said.

"Benjamin Keller," Dan repeated, reading from the page. He frantically scanned the book for any more information. "Anything else? A phone number?" The manager didn't understand, so Dan thought back to his days in high school when he'd actually taken foreign language classes. "Um…*numero de…telefono*?" He took the classes, but he never passed them.

The man answered him in quick, incomprehensible Spanish.

Although Dan could barely understand him, he didn't recognize any numbers in what the man was saying, which led him to assume the man recorded no phone number for the reservation. This was reinforced by the shaking of his head and "*Lo siento*" being repeated apologetically. "*Gracias*," Dan said back to the man. Although he'd lost the suspects, he found himself in possession of more evidence than he'd known throughout the entire investigation. He had a name and a face, in addition to the car. He'd found the party responsible for these grisly murders. Why else would someone run from the scene of a crime? But even with all the information, all the evidence, he had no clue as to what their motives could be.

This wasn't like the serial killers that Dan had learned to profile with the FBI. There was no distinct pattern to the victims, other than them residing on the same path, cutting through the Northwest. Each victim was different from the others. *Could there even be a connection? Was this just a completely arbitrary coincidence?* He knew of only two crime scenes directly connected to the gray Firebird: the one from Eugene and this one. The others were all just circumstantially linked; wrong place, wrong time. Dan had no proof, other than the car passing through each city. Dan knew he'd done all he could for the time being, other than speed off towards Spokane, hoping to beat the suspects to the hospital. *Benjamin Keller*, he thought, *who the hell are you?* He hoped that he hadn't spooked the suspects and that they would finish their trip through Washington. *They've come too far to turn back now*. He pulled out his cell phone and dialed 9-1-1. It was difficult to tell if the female operator was a bored, unmotivated state employee, or a machine recording. *Is there really a difference?* Dan told the woman who and where he was and then asked her to send a few units to the motel. When she asked if he needed an ambulance sent to the location, he simply said, "No need," then hung up the phone.

On average, a small town's response is around five minutes, depending on the severity of the emergency. In a small town like Walla Walla, which rarely saw grisly murders, the response was much quicker. In a matter of minutes two police cruisers sped into the parking lot to find Detective Sawyer standing in the doorway to room twenty-seven A. They were quickly followed by a fire truck and an ambulance.

The first officer to step out of a cruiser was a uniformed beat cop and he drew his sidearm, aiming it in Dan's direction. "Freeze!"

Dan turned around and faced the officers. He raised both hands and slowly indicated that he was going to reach into his back pocket. With his badge held high above his head, he shouted at the officers. "I'm the one that called this in, boys! I'm Detective Dan Sawyer! The vic is inside!" He turned and entered the quarantined room.

Two cops rushed in after holstering their weapons.

"I already took quite a few pictures of the body and the scene. Who's your lead?" Dan asked the first officer.

"That'd be me." A tall woman dressed in a navy-blue blazer and long skirt entered the scene and approached him. "Who might you be and why are you contaminating my crime scene?"

Dan removed his badge again and showed it to her. "I'm from the EPD. I've been tracking a vehicle that's connected to a number of other murders. When I arrived at the motel about…twenty, thirty minutes ago, I passed the gray Firebird I'd been looking for. They definitely left in quite a hurry. I didn't quite realize it was them until I noticed what was going on here. My first clue was the maid screaming her God-damn head off. By the time I ran back out to the street they were gone."

"Detective Logan, but feel free to call me Joanne. And that's the barber's little girl."

"You know her?"

"Yeah, I saw her in *Alice in Wonderland* when she was ten. She made a good Alice."

"What can you tell me about her? Nothing seems to add up; I can't establish any sort of an MO"

"Sweet girl, never got into too much trouble, but she's got a bit of a reputation for sleeping around. If I had to guess, she took a liking to one of your suspects."

"See, that's similar to one of the other victims, but there's no visible connection between the two."

"Tell you what. I've got another detective here and a couple rookies today. Why don't we let them wrap up the scene and you can debrief me on your investigation. Maybe I can help." Detective Logan turned and walked out of the room

Dan followed her. "Alright, maybe a fresh set of eyes will do some good." The two detectives climbed into Dan's car and she directed him to a small diner nearby, where they could get a much-needed cup of coffee and talk.

As they entered the oblong, steel container doubling as a diner, Joanne obviously knew the waitress and quickly flagged her down. "Evening, Cheryl. Could we get a pot of coffee over here?" She led Dan over to a corner booth and scooted in towards the wall.

Dan sat down across from her.

"Sure thing, Detective." The homely woman from behind the counter shuffled around and quickly brought them a steaming pot of coffee and poured them each a cup. "Who's your friend?" She looked at Joanne with overly inquisitive eyes.

"He's not from around here. He's actually a detective from…Eugene, right?"

"Yeah, nice to meet you," Dan said to the waitress, raising his mug in salutations.

"Well, since you're from out of town, if you try anything before you go, you have to try the rhubarb pie."

"I'll do that. Thank you." Dan wasn't much of an extrovert; he often kept to himself and only spoke when he felt it necessary. He set the thick file he'd brought in from his car on the table in front of Joanne.

"So, what do you know about your suspect?"

"Quite a bit, actually, but it still doesn't seem like enough." Dan opened the file and pulled out a couple of papers, then slid the file over to her. "Now, I finally got a name, thanks to the motel manager. Benjamin Keller." He handed her the partial image of the boy's car from Eugene. "He's driving a gray, sixty-nine Firebird. And it sounds like he may not be traveling alone. The video only showed one male suspect enter the car, but witnesses in Mt. Angel place two suspects in the Firebird."

"Oh wow. It sounds like you've got quite a bit to go on."

"That's not all. I even know where they're going."

"Where?"

"They're driving to a hospital in Spokane. I've also

got fingerprints from the crime scene in Mt. Angel." Dan pointed to another picture in the file. "And the final nail in the coffin will be the DNA results from the victims in Eugene. I should have the results back any time."

"Sounds like you've got everything you need to put these guys away. All you gotta do is catch them. Do you think that you can get them before they reach Spokane? There's no telling what they might do when they get there."

"I'm gonna try. Worst case, I know where they're going to end up, so I'm going to call for some back-up before I get into town. See if the locals can figure out which hospital they're headed to."

"That's a good idea, Detective," Joanne said before taking a sip from her coffee."

"I thought so," said Dan, smiling back.

"Any idea why they're doing all this?"

"No, I have no idea. I'm beyond stumped. So far, there haven't been any connections or similarities. But now, with the barber's daughter, there's at least a similarity. The double homicide in Eugene was more like this one than the others. Both victims were beaten to death with a blunt object." Dan excitedly fished through the file for another document. "But the young lady in Mt. Angel was a completely different story. She was viciously strangled to death. Even after she died, the killer continued to squeeze tighter and tighter, crushing her esophagus."

"That's terrible. Even in this line of work, it's hard to believe there are so many psychopaths out there."

"It really is."

"But if there are two of them, that could explain the difference in tactics."

"It would have to." Dan couldn't help but smile,

knowing he'd found a friend in a colleague so far from home. "Hey, I was keeping an ear on the scanner during the drive up here and I caught wind of some missing teens at a campground. So, I thought I would pass through and check it out and what do you think I found out when I checked in with the campground?"

"No. The Firebird?"

"Yup, exactly. I canvassed the grounds, no one but the manager recognized the vehicle. She couldn't give me much of a description—she was only able to describe Keller—but she did write down the license plate." Dan finished off his cup of coffee and sat back, exasperated from telling all he knew. "The car belongs to a Taylor Dean. I'm guessing that's our second suspect.

"So, if these teens aren't just missing, what does that bring your body count up to?"

"Six, including the two at the campground and that's just the ones I know about. It wasn't much to go off of, but I found some drag marks out in the woods there. Looked like there was a bit of a struggle. Found traces of blood too."

"Jesus Christ."

Dan ran his hands through his greasy hair. "This is…big."

"Sounds like you may have a mountain of paperwork ahead of you."

"Yeah, no shit. I'm not looking forward to tracing their path back. I'd be willing to bet this isn't their first rodeo."

Joanne hesitated for a moment, a thought on the tip of her tongue trying to make itself known. "Feel free to ignore this, but it seems like all the murders are very passionate. And excessive, beaten or strangled beyond necessity. If the kids in the woods were killed and you found signs of struggle, that means he—or they—like to be in close and do things on a very personal level. Whatever your suspects are feeling, it's escaping through them in a violent rage."

Dan hadn't thought of that before, but it was a common thread and it made sense. *God, she's good. That's kind of sexy.* "That's…outstanding. I think that makes the most sense out of anything I've found during this investigation."

"How does the motel fit into the grand scheme of things?"

"Well, I guess it was sort of similar to the double homicide. Their faces were beaten beyond recognition and she was repeatedly beaten with a lamp. And when I say repeatedly…I mean *this* was excessive. Likely more so than the double in Eugene. I'm thinkin' one guy's been doing most of the work."

"You were able to tell that just from the short time you were at the scene?"

Dan took the camera from his pocket. "Here, look at these." He handed it to Joanne and she began looking through the photos. "The wounds are jagged and deeper than if she was only struck once or twice. Also, her teeth were shattered, nearly all of them. Not just broken here and there; they were completely destroyed. It's not easy to do that. It took a lot of hatred. If there are two people doing this, it would make sense if they were taking turns."

"Will you send me a copy of these?"

"Of course, that was my plan. I'm not too shabby when it comes to CSI work, so, I thought that since I was there—with a fresh pair of eyes—I would do what I could to help. Kind of the same way you're taking a look at my case." Dan set down his coffee and looked Joanne in the eye. "Your help really has been invaluable."

"Thank you." She smiled at him and then waved the waitress back over to their table. "Could we get a couple of slices of that delicious pie, please, Cheryl?"

"Coming right up, you two." She looked over at Dan. "You'll thank me."

"I'm looking forward to it," replied Dan. As they waited for their desserts, while they ate—and after—they continued to examine the case file, bouncing ideas off one another. Their conversation slowly veered from being on topic to tangents of family and loved ones and their lives outside of police work. "You know, I could really use your help with this case."

"Isn't that what I'm doing now?"

"You know what I mean. If you didn't mind tagging along, that is. I would welcome the help."

"Yeah, I'd like that—to help. Let me just speak with the higher-ups, but I don't think that'll be a problem."

"Alright, I figure we'll take off in about an hour." Dan shoveled what was left of the pie crust into his mouth. "You know, as a kid, I hated rhubarb, but this…this is damn good pie." He smiled and looked down at the plate, stained red from the rhubarb pie. It reminded him of the scene he'd just left and it wiped the smile from his face. "Damn good pie…"

16

HALF AN HOUR outside of Walla Walla, Ben pulled hard off the road, slamming to a stop on the dusty side of the highway. Dirt and exhaust swirled around the car, dancing in front of the headlights.

"Get out of the car," Ben demanded of Taylor.

"What are you doing? Come on, let's keep driving, we're not that far from Spokane."

"Get out of the God-damn car. Now!" Ben climbed out and walked into the glare of the low beams.

Taylor hesitantly followed Ben to the front of the car. "What are you doing?"

"You need to tell me what the fuck happened back there."

Taylor sat down on the hood. "I told you..."

"The fuck you did!" Ben paused to regain his customarily calm composure, covering his mouth. "Look, just...tell me again. Please." He couldn't stop pacing in the dirt.

"Okay...well, we got to the motel and we started fooling around a bit. Then things started moving on from there." Taylor couldn't help but smile and involuntarily seek Ben's approval, which wasn't offered. "Right. When she finally told me how much she charged, *after* we were done, by the way, I didn't have enough money to pay her what she was asking." Taylor stood up and approached

Ben to reinforce his argument. "She wanted, like, six hundred dollars, man. What was I supposed to do? I don't have that kind of money."

"I don't know. But instead of *anything* else, you decide to kill her?"

"Well, no. I told her I didn't have the money and she told me she was going to go get her God-damn pimp. I grabbed her arm to stop her from walking out the door and then she pepper-sprayed me and kneed me in the fuckin' nuts. I panicked."

Ben pressed the palms of his hands against his eyes, distraught and confused.

"I couldn't let some fucking 'gangsta' piece of shit show up and break our legs or...pull a...drive-by in the middle of the night or something."

This is unbelievable, Ben thought.

"I freaked out and grabbed the first thing I saw. Everything after that is...kind of a blur."

A sharp pain shot through Ben's head; he couldn't comprehend what he was hearing. He looked over at Taylor, no tears in his eyes or remorse on his face. Ben couldn't restrain himself from storming over and socking Taylor in the jaw, knocking him back on the hood of the car.

"Ow! That fucking hurt, Ben." Taylor rubbed his jaw carefully.

"Good, I hope it did. You're lucky I only hit you once, you stupid prick!" Ben returned to his pacing, only more angrily. "I still don't understand how you could let things get *this* out of hand. Jesus fucking Christ."

Taylor knew that he deserved it, but he couldn't take Ben's accusations and grabbed him by the shirt, slamming him down on the car.

They struggled with one another, each trying to break

free of the other's grip.

In an attempt to hit Taylor again, Ben swung, missing his best friend's face, who then moved out of the way and swung back at Ben, hitting him in the temple. Ben immediately slugged him in the stomach causing them to roll down into the dirt.

Dust from the dry, farmland floor kicked up around them, spawning amorphous figures in the headlights. After a few more swings and wrestling around on the ground, they struggled to their feet, each with bloody noses and cuts on their lips and foreheads. Both men stood across from one another, panting and trying to catch their breath.

Ben wiped the blood from beneath his nose, smearing it across his cheek. "God-damn, Taylor. What the hell are we going to do?"

"I don't know." Taylor sat down on the ground, leaning against the front bumper.

"You've got to tell the police what happened."

"I know…" Taylor held his throbbing head. "But can we at least wait until after you see your dad tomorrow? This was your trip and I—I know that I fucked it all up. After we see him, I'll call the cops and explain what happened and that it was entirely my fault. Just please, please, *please* don't tell Amy."

Ben's head felt like it was going to explode. "Fine…fine, whatever." He sat down next to Taylor. "I can't believe this trip, man. All the bad shit that's happened."

"I know…Ben?"

"Yeah?"

"I'm so sorry about this—about everything."

Ben stared at the ground for a moment, then looked over at Taylor and simply nodded.

"I don't know, maybe everything'll be okay." They both knew that wasn't the case. Taylor rested his head against the car, staring up at the night sky, as if all the answers were somewhere up there.

Ben couldn't figure out how they arrived at this point in their lives. He thought back to when they were children, back in Grants Pass, looking for an answer to how this all could have happened.

Then, he remembered something. A childhood memory which, at the time, seemed entirely trivial and insignificant, but now made more sense than ever.

17

AT TEN YEARS old, the most important thing on Ben's mind was cooties, his brand-new *Super Mario* game and how to sweet-talk his parents into buying him some candy. Like every Saturday, Ben found himself sitting Indian-style in the soft, green grass of his front lawn, with a mound of mixed-and-matched Legos next to him. His non-school days were occupied by trying to recreate his favorite scenes from *Star Wars*, using various Autobots or Ninja Turtle action figures to play some of the characters.

Other than the acquaintances he'd made in school, Taylor was his only friend. They had been since they were born. Or at least it felt that way, with Taylor living just across the street from him.

On one particular Saturday, Ben was lost in his own Lego-filled, little world when Taylor came running down the sidewalk and tripped as he tried to climb through the bushes and into the lawn.

"Ben, Ben! Hey, can you play?"

"Sure, do you want Yoda or Leonardo?"

"No, I don't wanna play with Legos. That's kid stuff. Do you wanna see something cool?"

"What is it?"

"Come on, I'll show you." Taylor turned and ran back down the block the way he came.

Ben climbed to his feet, brushed off his hands and his knees and ran to catch up with him.

They walked for two blocks before reaching the dead end of the street. Between the end of the road and a large ditch—with a small creek running through it—was a guard rail, slightly taller than both of them. Taylor squeezed beneath the opening in the bottom and Ben followed. They walked along the flowing creek for a while, singing "The Bear Necessities" from their favorite Disney movie. Eventually, they arrived at a small, secluded area where the creek was shallow and crossed it, slipping only once or twice. Just past the bank of the creek was a small dog, dead and rotting behind a fallen tree. The decomposition had rendered the corpse in two, linked only by a pile of mush and bone.

Taylor straddled the tree so he could look down at it. "Cool, huh?"

"What is it?" Ben climbed up onto the tree next to him.

"I think it was Mrs. Clark's poodle."

"Gross!" As disgusting as the old, decomposing corpse of their elderly neighbor's poodle was, neither of them could look away.

Taylor picked up a stick and poked at the gaping wound nearest to the dog's head, disturbing the maggots crawling around inside it. "So cool. What do you think happened to it?"

"I dunno," said Ben.

"I dare you to touch it." Taylor pushed Ben jokingly.

"No. You touch it."

"I double-*dog*-dare you to touch it." The irony of the double-*dog*-dare was wasted on them as pre-adolescent boys.

But Ben knew he couldn't back down from a dare that had been doubled *and* dogged. He stumbled forward, climbing down from the tree and Taylor followed him. Ben cautiously knelt down next to the dog, worried the pooch was only playing dead and that it could jump up and bite him the moment he touched it. He stretched out his forefinger and aimed for a dark patch of fur on the nape of the neck. He slowly neared the spot, preparing to touch the body, when Taylor ran up behind him and pushed him over. Ben fell on top of the dog struggling to get back to his feet and keep the maggots off of him. "You jerk, Taylor! Why would you do that?"

"It was funny, that's why." Taylor moved closer to the dog, while Ben moved away to brush off the squirming larvae from his shirt. Taylor took the toe of his shoe and tapped the dog's nose a few times.

"Come on, Taylor, leave it alone. We should go home."

"Ugh…" Taylor threw his head back in a childish, animated fashion. "Fine."

The image of Taylor standing there, with his head leaned back and his hands in the air, stuck with Ben. He couldn't help but remember the image as he looked back over at Taylor, leaning against the bumper of the Firebird, holding his nose, trying to stop the bleeding. A comforting, yet eerie sense of nostalgia washed over him.

"Look, Taylor, let's just get through tomorrow and we'll figure things out from there. I'm here to help. Tomorrow we'll figure it out, together."

Taylor placed his hand on Ben's shoulder as a thank-you. "Thanks, it always makes me feel better when you say that."

Ben got up without saying another word and sat back in the driver's seat, waiting for Taylor to return to the passenger side.

The drive to Spokane, Ben's second home, was a long and quiet drive. They didn't stop at any more rest stops, or to see the sights, or even eat. They both stayed quiet until they pulled into the hospital parking lot.

"I think we should just sleep in the car for tonight," said Ben. "It's probably safer than renting a hotel room."

"Yeah, okay."

They were one of only four cars parked in the lot. Although it felt strange sleeping in the car, it felt much safer than their previous plan of staying at another hotel. *No risk of Taylor brutally murdering any more prostitutes*, Ben thought. In the morning, Ben would go see his dad, tell him about the story he'd been working on and maybe try to visit the rest of his family, while Taylor dealt with the consequences of his actions.

What would Ben say to Lynn or Amy? What could he say? *"Taylor brutally murdered a hooker because he refused to pay her!?"* Ben couldn't help but feel that he was trapped in the epitome of a rock and a hard place. Again. Stuck between Taylor and the girls, between family and the moral obligation of doing the right thing.

These thoughts kept Ben awake as Taylor sat scrunched up in the passenger seat, fast asleep and snoring away. He'd passed out almost immediately. *Did he even feel anything about what he'd done? How is it that all he could say was "Don't tell the girls"?* Then a frightening thought popped into Ben's mind. *What if Taylor was going to kill me?* As absurd as the thought was, something still didn't sit right. *Taylor could never be capable of something so inhuman...or at least I don't think he could be.* Overnight, Taylor had become something different in Ben's eyes. Even if everything worked out in the end could he even go back to the way things were? How could he keep all this from Amy, or Lynn for that matter? He just needed to sleep, and if at all possible, figure it out in the morning.

18

THE HOSPITAL PARKING lot filled with cars as Ben and Taylor slept soundly in the Firebird. As Ben awoke to the sound of a pickup truck backing into the space next to them, he vigorously rubbed his drowsy eyes and scratched the top of his head. Having parked near the front entrance, he wasn't concerned with getting a better parking spot. He picked up Taylor's phone and checked the time. "Nine-fifteen...shit," he said, rubbing his eyes again, attempting to wake up completely. As his vision cleared, the sight of Taylor peacefully drooling on the blue, leather seat got on his last nerve. *Maybe I should just...let him sleep...or something.* "Taylor!" he shouted regretfully. "Wake up!"

Wiping the drool from his cheek, Taylor jolted awake, looking all around him. "Hmm?"

"Come on. Visiting hours started fifteen minutes ago."

"Alright, I'm up."

The shadow from the hospital towered over the parking lot below, cooling their substitute hotel room. Ben hated hospitals and had since he was a boy. It was never the fear or anxiety that couples itself with health care facilities, but the feeling of helplessness once admitted. He never could grasp why an environment meant to promote healing always felt so dreary and lacked any sense of the one thing hospitals should provide: hope.

But, shaking off the chilled morning air and his contempt for the hospital, he stepped out of the car to stretch his legs and crack his back.

Taylor quickly followed Ben's lead by stretching and running his hands through his hair in an attempt to emulate cleanliness. He caught up to Ben, who had walked on ahead of him. "Morning," he said, to which Ben only nodded.

Ben walked through the sliding doors and approached the middle-aged, brunette receptionist working diligently at her desk. "Hi, room for Bryan Keller, please." He did his best to hide his hatred for the building.

"Are you family?" The receptionist refused to look up from her paperwork.

"Yeah, I'm his son," said Ben. *Does it really matter?*

"Okay, just a moment, sir." Her fingers jumped frantically across the keyboard as she searched for the proper room.

Ben glanced over at Taylor and made a face that telepathically relayed: *"She's about as happy to be here as we are."*

"Room 1304, floor six."

"Alright, thanks," said Ben, smiling awkwardly.

"Mmhmm," she grunted with her eyes still averted downwards.

Ben led the way to the elevator on the edge of the lobby and Taylor pressed the white "Up" button. After a minute of awkwardly avoiding eye contact with the sick and elderly being pushed by on gurneys and in wheelchairs, the elevator finally arrived. They walked inside, followed by two additional passengers and a short, blonde nurse. Ben and Taylor took their place in the back of the rickety sweatbox.

The elevator shook and jostled around as though they

had stepped inside the Tower of Terror and the car was about drop at ninety miles-per-hour, splattering them at the bottom of the elevator shaft.

Taylor's bony elbow jabbed Ben in the side, distracting him from the unstable elevator.

"What?" Ben whispered.

Taylor leaned in close to him and whispered, "Hey, check out the nurse in front."

Ben leaned slightly to his left to gaze between the two visitors and see the blonde-haired nurse near the front of the elevator. Per Taylor's intuition, Ben gave her a quick up-and-down, noticing her bright red underwear peeking through her thin, white scrub bottoms. Succumbing to old habits, he gave Taylor a subtle nod of approval before realizing the gravity of their situation. *How can he be so casual?* Ben thought. *Does he just not get it?*

As the elevator reached the fourth floor, the two additional visitors walked out, leaving Ben, Taylor and the blonde nurse to continue on to the sixth floor. They all exited as it arrived, Taylor's gaze locked on her backside as they reached Bryan's room.

The nurse veered off course and continued to the nursing station down the hall.

Taylor turned to Ben with big, sad eyes, performing his best sad puppy dog routine.

"Go ahead," said Ben, giving Taylor permission to pursue the hot piece of ass he'd set his heart on.

"Thanks, buddy. I'll give you some time alone with your dad," said Taylor, running off down the hallway. "You know where to find me!"

Ben turned around and peered into the window of room 1304, hesitating before going inside. His dad was fast asleep on the bed, a knit, green blanket pulled up to his chest. *I don't know if I can do this.* Seeing anyone lying in a hospital bed made him uncomfortable and queasy. After the last few days' events, he had no clue what to even say to his dad. What could he say? *Hey dad, how's the cancer?* "Actually, that's not bad." The image of Bryan lying in that hospital bed reminded him of an old memory.

At the young age of twelve, Ben had just come home from school, finding his dad passed out drunk on the couch. Bryan worked the night shift back then. He often found himself awake at six or seven in the morning, already a few beers deep. With the mornings essentially being his evenings, he would start drinking before he had to go to bed, just like anyone on a normal schedule would have some drinks in the evening. Just as he was in that memory so many years ago, Bryan was passed out in the hospital bed in a similar fashion, with one hand dangling off the side.

Although the memory wasn't an appropriate one, Ben couldn't help but smile a bit. He rubbed the scar on his temple from that day. His dad had rolled off the couch, knocking Ben into the coffee table. It cost him nine stitches. Maybe the hospital connected the two instances in his mind. His smile helped him enter the room and approach the bed.

Bryan was alone in the room; cancer patients usually got the nicer, single rooms in the hospital, although it was usually out of pity.

"Dad?" Ben stood a few feet away from the bed.

Bryan leaned up from his bed and saw his son standing close to the corner of the room. "Ben? Hey." He removed a pair bulky headphones from around his neck. "What are you doing here, son?"

"Well, I had some free time and I wanted to come see you. So, here I am." Ben shrugged like it was no big deal.

"It's a bit longer of a story than that, but that's about the size of it."

"Well, come here, Son." Bryan turned his body so that his legs were dangling over the edge. He stretched out his arms to hug his only child. "It's good to see you, boy."

Ben met Bryan's open arms with his own and they hugged tightly. "It's good to see you too, Dad. How've you been?"

"Pretty good, for the most part. I mean, as good as someone with cancer can feel. All the drugs they've got me on since the surgery make me feel like shit. They had to cut off a small chunk of my lung. It hurts like a bitch." He smiled at Ben, hoping to break the palpable tension.

Ben laughed a bit. "I don't doubt it. I'm not sure if I could let someone cut into me like that."

"Well, I don't really have much of a choice, do I? I probably hate hospitals about as much as you do. Did I ever tell you the story of when I was an MP and when we were at the hospital that you were born in? Some stupid bitch down the hall from your mother's room was trying to kill her newborn son?"

"Yeah, Dad, you've told me about that at least a thousand times. That's alright, though. I don't mind most of your stories, except when they're about you and my mom 'doin' it.'" Ben shuttered a little as he held back his gag reflex.

"Yeah, sorry 'bout that." Bryan patted Ben on the shoulder. "So, how did you get the time off to come up here?"

"Well, honestly, I don't work at Joey's anymore."

"Really? Why not?"

Ben wasn't sure which version of the story he should tell him, but something in his gut advised him to not lie to his possibly dying father. "To tell you the truth, I got fired. I got fed up with Joey's shit. He was always rude, unappreciative and I'm pretty sure a sexist prick."

"Well, Son, aren't we all a little sexist?"

"More or less, I guess," Ben said smiling. "I mean, he was a nice guy and all, but I caught him like, *pushing up* on one of the waitresses and I could tell she was uncomfortable. I tried to approach him respectfully, like a man, but he went off and threatened to can me. So, I hauled off and hit him."

"Jesus, Ben. Kind of sounds like he got what he deserved, at least."

"I guess. I haven't told Lynn the truth yet, though."

Bryan grabbed Ben's shoulder. "Listen, Son. You always stand up for what you believe in. Good or bad, you do the right thing and I will always be proud of you. And so will Lynn. Just remember that, okay?"

Ben started to feel uncomfortable with how supportive his dad was being. As though he was receiving one last lecture, just in case. "I know…hey, how are your treatments going?"

"Seems to be working. I don't have much energy afterwards, but I don't mind sleeping all day." Bryan let go of Ben's arm and leaned back onto his mound of pillows.

"There is some good to come out of all this, though. I've been taking advantage of the free time and the drive up here, and I actually started writing a novel."

"Really? That's great, Ben, you always were an excellent writer. I'd hoped you would put that to good use one day. That or become a rich rock star, like Rob Halford or one of The Ramones. But now you're going to be the next Stephen King!"

"Well, that's the plan, at least." Ben shared an uncomfortable laugh with his father and pulled up a nearby chair to sit down.

"You'll do great, Ben. You know, I have every one of his books downstairs, back home?"

"I know. I pretty much lived downstairs for three years, remember?"

"Sorry, my memory gets a little wacky sometimes."

"The drugs, right," Ben remembered. His dad used the word "sometimes," but Ben knew that Bryan often retold the same stories a lot, forgot about it and then told them again even before the cancer kicked in. "But, yeah, my friend, Taylor and I drove up here in his Firebird; he's actually looking forward to meeting you. I've told him all those awesome, stupid stories you and Grandpa used to tell me. "

"Oh, a Firebird? Lucky fucker, I love that car. He's here?"

"Yeah, he's stalking one of the nurses right now, but I'll go find him in a bit."

"And how's Lynn doing?"

"Really good, actually."

"You ever gonna marry that girl?"

"Eventually, yeah. We're just waiting for the right time. I think she is getting a little impatient, though. So, yeah, other than putting up with me, she's doing pretty well."

"Well, when you talk to her, you tell *my daughter* I said I love her and to make you get your shit together." Bryan smiled a big, genuinely happy smile.

"I will," said Ben. "Or, you could just tell her when you get out of here? Come and visit us."

"Don't patronize me, Ben. I don't have any delusions about my condition. My father had the same thing and his dad died the same way. Granted, they had less hospitals and equipment back then, but the point is, I'm not going to get my hopes up."

"Come on, Dad."

"No, Ben. What have I always told you? Hope for the best, but expect the worst."

"The odds nowadays that someone dies from stage two lung cancer are slim to none, unless you've been smoking even though they told you not to."

"I haven't *been* smoking." His guilty face gave him away. "I may have had one or two since I've been stuck in here. That small, blonde nurse caught me smoking in the stairwell. She's cute, but God-damn obnoxious with that shit. I'll tell you though, I'd rather have her bossing me around than some male-model, nurse fag."

"Can't say I blame you. She *is* cute." Ben finally remembered a message he was supposed to relay to his dad. "Oh, I saw Great Grandma. She was pretty pissed that no one told her you were in the hospital."

"Great, that's just what I need. I've got my mother all up in my shit for ending up here, now I guess its Grandma's turn."

"Yeah, she pretty much said you were a stubborn asshole and that you need to call her. You know, the usual. Oh, and she did also say to get well soon."

"Yeah, that sounds like her." Bryan had lost all the color in his face; he was clearly exhausted.

"Look dad, why don't you get a little rest. I'm not going anywhere and I'll be here when you wake up."

"Are you sure? You came all this way. I don't want to put you out."

"No, its fine, Dad. I have to go hunt down Taylor anyway. God knows what he's doing unsupervised. He's probably getting shot down by your nurse as we speak. We rode up in the elevator with her and Taylor couldn't take his eyes off her."

Bryan coughed violently until he finally caught his breath. "Okay, Son. Wake me up in a bit. I'd be happy to meet your friend. I love you, boy." His eyes closed and he turned his head away.

"Love you too, Dad."

Ben sat in the chair next to the bed and saw a small, pink pillow that had been signed by a few friends and family members. It was shaped like a pair of oversized lungs. Obviously somebody had a sense of humor about all this. Ben picked it up and read all the "Get well" messages. He took the small permanent marker that was attached to the back with Velcro and began to color in the corner of the pillow's left lung, so that it looked like a small portion had been removed. Above it he wrote *There, now you match!"* and drew an arrow pointing to the missing chunk. Ben smiled and laughed a little bit, hoping it would brighten his dad's mood when he woke up later. He set down the pillow and walked out into the hall, still able to hear his dad's snoring. *Two years of this shit must have him worn ou*t. Ben walked towards the nursing station, seeing Taylor sitting on the desk, trying to flirt with the nurse from the elevator. "Hey, 'scuse me. Bryan in room 1304, how is he doing?"

"You're his son, Ben, aren't you? He talks about you all the time." The nurse blew off Taylor and thumbed through a file cabinet, pulling out a file with Bryan's name on it.

"Yeah, that's me."

"Well, he was doing pretty well for a while, but he's been fluctuating. The cancer is in remission, but he just doesn't seem to be physically responding to the treatments. I think this visit from you will help him out. I'll bet he was sure happy to see you."

"I think so."

"I've worked here a while and sometimes the best medicine is a visit from a family member."

"Alright, thank you. I'm just going to go sit while he's sleeping."

"Okay, it was nice to meet you, Ben."

He nodded at her and walked away towards the waiting room. Trying to distract himself, he poured himself a cup of water from the jug in the corner.

Taylor followed him over and sat down on one of the uncomfortable, blue, knit-cushioned chairs.

Ben sat down across from him. "Shit, dude. I can't stand this. I've never seen him like this before. He's never been so…vulnerable. I once watched him throw himself between our two big dogs, 'cause they were ripping into one another. And not like, 'we're gay little dogs hopping around one another.' Like teeth and blood, vicious fighting. He reached in and just grabbed them both by the snout and made them stop. His hands were all cut up and bloody." Ben smiled, lost in his memory. "He just looked at me and smiled, then said, 'Hey go get me a beer, fucker,' and then just laughed, like it was nothing."

"Ha, that's awesome. I love stories about your dad. I wish I had a dad as fun as yours."

"Yeah…but I don't ever want to have to tell *this* story." Ben pointed towards his dad's room and traded in his smile for tear-filled eyes.

"I know." Taylor reached over and patted Ben's knee to comfort him. "I know. Did you tell him about your job?"

"Yeah, I would have felt shitty if I'd lied to him."

"You didn't tell him about yesterday, did you?" Taylor whispered without hesitation.

"No, of course not. Why the hell would I have brought that up? Just because I'm not going to lie to him doesn't mean I'm going to confess everything."

"Alright, calm down." Taylor leaned away from Ben. "Look, I'm going to go get that nurse's phone number, then we're going to go wake your dad up and have a beer. Why don't you go grab the cooler out of the car?" He was trying to keep Ben's mind preoccupied to avoid dwelling on his dad.

"Yeah, alright," Ben smiled. "He'll like that. He probably hasn't had a beer since he was admitted." After Taylor walked away, Ben stood up and walked over to the elevator. He rode it down to the lobby, jogged out to the car and popped the trunk. As he picked up the cooler, he could smell the stench of warm, dead fish filling up the trunk. The ice had completely melted overnight, allowing the fish to bake inside the car. He took out a few beers and stuffed one into each pocket and the third securely in the waist of his pants. The walk back to his dad's room was a treacherous one and he nearly lost the third bottle a couple of times. Eventually he arrived upstairs and walked back into Bryan's room, finding his dad still sleeping. He sat back in the corner chair and popped the cap off one of the beers and downed half of it in one drink. "Love you, Dad. You need to get better soon, okay?" He leaned back and waited for another five minutes before he heard a faint knock on the door.

Taylor cracked it open and walked in. "Hey, he awake yet?"

"No, he's passed out still," Ben whispered handing him a bottle.

"You're right; it is weird seeing someone in a hospital bed like this. These places always give me the heebie-jeebies." Taylor walked around to the opposite side of the bed.

"I know the feeling. I get that the nurse was just trying to be nice, but I wish she just could have told me the truth.

No bullshit." Ben stared down at the bottle; he'd already scratched off most of the label. "Sorry, you probably don't want to hear me keep complaining. So...did you get her phone number or what?"

"Umm...yeah. And we talked for a minute about your dad." The look on his face said he was hiding something.

"What were you talking about him for?"

"I don't know how to tell you this, man, but you were right. She was lying a bit. Your dad's dying, dude."

"What? What the hell are you talking about? You're not even related to him. Why wouldn't she tell me that?"

"Shhh," Taylor hissed. "I don't know, but I did tell her I was his family too. But she said something kind of messed up. At first it didn't sit right with me, but now, seeing him, it's starting to make sense."

"What? What'd she say?" Ben stood up across from Taylor.

"She said...she said that someone should put him out of his misery and that he was suffering."

"Are you fucking kidding me? That's sick." Ben stormed over to look through the window in the door. He fiercely scanned the hall for that bitch of a nurse.

Taylor walked up behind him and put his hand on Ben's shoulder.

"I know. That's what I thought, too. But don't worry, I took care of it. That stupid bitch won't say anything like that to anyone ever again."

Ben's face dropped, speechless.

Taylor turned Ben around and stared him in the eyes. "But I'm starting to think she was right, brother."

Ben's face was frozen. He couldn't believe what he'd just heard. "What do you mean you took care of it?"

"I mean just that. She had no right to talk so inconsiderately about others' lives." Taylor walked back over to Bryan and stood over him.

"I...I...what the fuck, Taylor?"

"Something like that should only be talked about by the people who know him. The people that love him. Not some carefree fucking *cunt*, who thinks that she gets to decide who lives or dies."

"You don't even know him. How can you even think she might be right?"

"Because, you're my family, Ben. I love you, and because he's you're dad, I love him, too. If there's anything I can do to take care of my family...I'll do it in a fucking heartbeat!"

Ben took a cautious step towards him. "Where the hell is all of this coming from? This doesn't sound like you." He began to realize how out of the ordinary Taylor had been acting during their whole trip. His thoughts jumped back to their argument in the desert, the dead girl in their room and even the missing kids at the campground. It finally dawned on him, that the murders weren't just some crazy, random happenstance as they drove north. It was them. Taylor was the only constant in every situation. Even with Ashton. He was there, every time. "It's you...It really has been *you*, this entire time, hasn't it?"

"What has been?"

Ben stepped backwards. "Have you been...killing people this whole time?" he whispered.

"I had to, Ben. They all deserved it. And more than that, you *needed* something to write about and I gave it to you. You wanted a murder and now you've got one. Hell, you've got half a dozen to choose from! All you have to do is leave our real names out of it."

"But don't you think that someone might notice if I write—in detail, mind you—about half a dozen unsolved murders?"

"You're a writer, Ben." Taylor smiled that wide smile. "You said it yourself, 'Write about what you know.' You took an event, a real event and created a purely 'fictitious' story from it. I told you that I was going to help you write your book, didn't I?"

"Yeah, you did, but...Jesus, Taylor. Not like this! What the hell were you thinking? What if I write about something that was never released to the press, huh? You didn't think this through at all, Taylor. Fuck!" Ben crouched down and covered his head with his arms, hiding from Taylor's bullshit.

"Ben, look, it's okay." Taylor crouched down to Ben's level and smiled. "Look, you only know about some of the murders. The 'Highway Slasher'—terrible name by the way—has more notches on his belt than you know. You just need to be vague about the ones that you do know about." Taylor laughed and threw his arms up as though he'd solved all of Ben's problems.

"There's more? Who?" Ben shuffled back across the floor until his back pressed up against the door. "How long has this been going on?"

"Since we left Grants Pass."

"You didn't even know what I was going to write about then. I didn't even know. What the hell is wrong with you?"

"Nothing...!" Taylor screamed, "...is fucking wrong with me, Ben! Not a God-damn thing. Every one of them was asking for it. Leading us on, being rude, or threatening our lives." He straightened his back up, like he was about to say something important. "And you needed this just as much as I did. Like that old prick at the gas station, you would have been happy to just let him walk all over us and steal our money. So, I took his money and I walked all over him."

"Jesus." Ben was disgusted. He stood back up and froze for a moment, feeling around on the door, hoping to find the handle and his escape route. As his hand touched the cold, steel handle, he had an intense moment of hope for his best friend and stormed over to Taylor, grabbing him by the shoulders. "Look, you need to just go. If you're not going to turn yourself in, you need to just go."

"I'm sorry, Ben, I can't. I'm not done yet."

"What do you mean you're not done yet?"

"Your dad is sick. *Our* dad is sick, and in pain. I can't leave until he's not suffering anymore."

"You fucking psycho." Ben shoved Taylor hard into the wall, still gripping his shoulders. "You're not going to kill anybody else!" He slammed his fist into Taylor's jaw.

"God damnit, Ben." Taylor struggled with him, fiercely trying to break free. "It has to be done; you know it as well as I do. Wouldn't this be a better story to tell than him dying weak and helpless from some fucking disease?"

Ben paused briefly, as though it were a moment of clarity, only to be interrupted by a sucker punch to the gut and then in the face. Blood gushed from his nose, but he quickly regained his grip on his friend's shoulders.

They continued to struggle until Ben's hands made their way to Taylor's throat and he began squeezing tightly.

"Ben, what are you doing? Knock it off," Taylor spit out.

"No more, Taylor. No one else." He felt an intense burst of adrenaline as he squeezed Taylor's throat. Ashton's face quickly replaced Taylor's, forcing Ben to relive the horror of losing her. The thought of Taylor wringing the life from her only made Ben more furious.

"You...can't...kill me, Ben."

"Ben? What are you doing?" Bryan woke up from the commotion and shouted across the room. Still struggling, Ben refused to acknowledge his father's cries. "Ben!" His plea finally broke through and Ben turned his head to look at him.

Taylor took advantage of the distraction and kicked Ben square in the knee, which buckled under the pain. He quickly moved away from Ben and stood between the father and son.

"Son? Son, are you okay? What's going on?"

"Yeah, Ben. *You* okay?" said Taylor, snarling.

Ben stood up and turned to find Taylor standing in front of the bed, staring back at him, his eyes glazed over and crazed.

"You did just try to kill me, Ben...But please, are you okay?"

"What the fuck!? What happened to you?" Ben yelled, stepping backwards frightfully, until he collided with the wall again.

Bryan continued to call out to Ben, but his voice was muffled by Taylor's, repeating the same phrase over and over again. "Are you okay, Ben?"

19

"YOUR DAD'S IN a lot of pain. Cancer is a nasty disease." Taylor walked over and stood within a few inches of Ben's face. "You need to put him out of his misery."

"No. I can't. This...this is all too much. Just go away!" Tears streamed down Ben's face as Taylor leaned in closer. "Why? Why would you do this, Taylor?"

"Jesus fucking Christ, Ben. I'm not the one who's forcing you to do this. When are you going to get that through your thick skull?"

Ben's tears stopped. "Huh?"

"You're the one who wanted me to do this, Ben. What would you do without me?" Taylor walked back over to Bryan's bedside and stared down at him. "I could see it in your eyes. You needed me to do the things that you couldn't, the things you would never do for yourself. I've known you since before I can remember, Ben. I knew you didn't have the balls to do what needed to be done and that's why I came along for the ride. That's why *I* am your best friend."

"How many people did you kill? How many others were there, God damnit!?"

"Oh, there's been a few others, Ben. That old prick at the gas station and the college kids you know about. That bookstore girl..."

Son of a bitch, Ben thought.

"She would have tried to pull our friendship apart, Ben. And Lynn's a different story. At least she's not trying to take you away from me. I actually really like her."

"You stay away from her. You stay away from all our friends."

"You know…you're really gonna hate to hear this, and I'm going to hate saying it out loud, but I—I had to kill Brandon."

"What? Why the hell would you do that? He was our best friend!" Ben was too panicked to hold back the tears that continued to stream down his cheeks.

"Really, you don't remember? We were all pretty smashed, but you and Brandon got in a huge argument about Lynn. He called her a bitch and told you to break up with her and all you could do was storm off like a little girl. So, I took care of it, again. I had your back like I always have. The note was a nice touch, don't you think?"

"What makes you think I would have wanted you to do that?"

"Don't worry, Ben." Taylor tried to calm him. "I'm starting to think I know what you want, even before you do. I may have gone a bit overboard, but what are you gonna do? No point in crying over spilled…well, Brandon," he laughed.

Ben hid his head deep in his hands. "No, no. This can't be happening; this has to be a bad dream."

"Ben! Ben, talk to me, Son. You're talking nonsense." Bryan was sitting up in his bed, frightened and concerned. "What the hell is going on?"

"Since I can tell you need me to and you clearly can't do it, I'll do this one last thing for you, Ben. But then you need to start taking care of yourself, okay?"

"What one last thing?"

"Your, dad, Ben. He's dying. Don't you ever pay attention? You can't just let him wither away like some helpless plant."

"I can't, Taylor...I can't."

"Son, talk to me God damnit!"

"Yes, you can, Ben. Trust me, when have I ever steered you wrong?" Taylor thought for a moment. "Other than the dead hooker. That was an...error in judgment."

"I...guess you haven't." Ben walked towards Taylor and stopped next to him and his father.

"Exactly."

Ben stood an arm's length away from his dad, whose pleading words were only a muffled hum.

"Do you want me to do it for you, Ben?"

"No."

"Are you sure? You think you can do this?"

"No...I...NO!" Ben erupted, lunging at Taylor and throwing him to the ground. They struggled, rolling around on the floor until Ben picked him up and slammed him into the wall.

Taylor pushed Ben backwards into a small table.

Ben fought back, landing two quick punches into Taylor's nose, sending blood spewing out onto the checkered linoleum.

"Help! Help!" Bryan shouted at the door, pressing the assist button on the side of the bed.

Taylor grabbed Ben by the neck and pulled him down onto his dad's lap.

Ben's arms flailed around until they finally grabbed Taylor's head, spinning him around, landing Taylor on top of Bryan's legs. Before Taylor could react, Ben wrapped his hands around Taylor's neck for the last time and started to squeeze. His grip tightened, giving Taylor a taste of his own medicine for what he'd done to Ashton.

"Ben, what are you doing? This is…pointless," Taylor gargled out.

Ben refused to answer him, continuing to squeeze tighter and tighter until Taylor's face turned the color of a freshly ripened plum. Ben could feel Taylor's windpipe collapsing beneath his fingers.

"Ben, stop it…" Bryan croaked. "Ben, God…damnit." He struggled to get out of the bed, but couldn't break free.

In response to the frantic mashing of the assistance button, a male orderly knocked on the door and opened it slowly. "Alright, Mr. Keller, what's going on in he— what the hell? Help! Somebody, help! Call the police!" The orderly was pushed out of the way by a middle-aged man wearing a dark brown coat.

"Benjamin Keller, police! Stop what you're doing. Now!" shouted the detective, aiming his pistol at Ben, who continued to ignore his surroundings.

Stopping Taylor was all that mattered to Ben.

Detective Sawyer holstered his weapon and ran up to Ben, wrapping his arms around him, but Ben broke loose, shoving Dan back towards the door. Concerned for the man in the hospital bed, Dan frantically looked around the room and snatched the fire extinguisher off the wall. Ben glanced over as the detective charged at him with the extinguisher in hand. Dan raised the makeshift weapon high above his head and slammed it into Ben's temple, sending his body falling limp onto the bed.

As Ben lost consciousness and the world around him drifted off into darkness, the last thing he could see were his own two hands releasing their grip from his own father's neck.

The exhausted detective, adrenaline still pumping through his veins, dropped the extinguisher and ran over to Bryan, who lay on the bed unconscious. Barely responsive to Dan's touch, Bryan's throat wore a dark purple abrasion where Ben's hands had tightened like a noose around it. Dan placed two fingers on the patient's neck, held his breath and closed his eyes, hoping for a pulse. Finally, he exhaled.

20

AS BEN SLOWLY awoke from his unconsciousness, he attempted the seemingly impossible task of prying apart his heavy eyelids. The fog clouding his vision began to clear and Ben was finally able to make out a steel table in front of him and a blurry figure on the other side. His head pulsated; with each blink he could feel his brain pressing against the walls of his skull.

I hope I don't sneeze. My brain might explode and leak red goo from every hole, Ben thought. With his vision no longer clouded, he realized the man sitting across from him was the man in the brown coat. The man from the hospital.

The detective's hair was pushed back and grimy having not been washed for days. He just sat there, without saying a word, continuously tapping something on the table.

Tap.

Tap.

Tap.

Ben's head throbbed with every beat. "Did you hit me with a fire extinguisher?" he said, rubbing the bump on his head.

Detective Sawyer stared at him, still without a word.

As Ben stared into his interrogator's eyes, he immediately remembered that same stare gawking at him through the car window as they fled from Walla Walla.

"You fully awake yet?" Dan asked.

"Um…yeah, what's going on?"

"Can you tell me where you are?" Dan looked down at the open file in front of him.

"Yeah, we're in Spokane," Ben replied. "Aren't we?"

"Yes, but do you know where you are right now? At this exact moment."

"No, I just woke up." Ben was thoroughly confused. While he looked around the room to regain his bearings, he finally realized his left arm had been handcuffed to the steel chair beneath him, which was bolted to the ground. "Are we…at the police station?"

"Yes," Dan callously answered.

Tap.

Tap.

Taylor! Ben suddenly remembered what had just happened. "Oh God, where's Taylor? Did you catch him?"

"Taylor who?"

"He was in the room at the hospital with me. We were fighting when…wait, you really did hit me. Why did you hit me with the fire extinguisher?"

"Well, I'm glad to see that your memory isn't completely fucked up."

Tap.

Tap.

Tap.

"God, what the *hell* is that?" Ben shouted.

"Calm down." The detective quit beating his small, metal Zippo against the tabletop and set it down. "I had to. You didn't really leave me much of a choice. You scared a lot of people, you know."

"I'm sorry, I had to stop him. He was going to kill my dad. Like he did to all the others. You have him locked up, right?"

"It's Ben, right?" Dan continued before Ben could answer. "Where are you from, Ben?"

"From Grants Pass, in Oregon. Taylor and I grew up there."

"Grants Pass, okay. That makes sense." Dan wrote something down in the file. "And you were driving up here to, what? Visit your dad in the hospital?" The detective's questioning felt very cryptic.

"Yeah, he has lung cancer. He just got out of surgery the other day, so we planned to get up here afterwards." Ben struggled to make his bound hand more comfortable. "I'm sorry. Are these handcuffs really necessary?"

"Well, I'm sorry, but I think they are necessary. Are they too uncomfortable?"

"Yeah, a bit."

"I'd take them off if I could, Ben, but this is standard operating procedure for interrogations." Dan stood up and walked around behind Ben, who couldn't see exactly what the detective was doing. He stared into the large glass mirror on the wall for a moment, building the tension in the room with an uncomfortable silence. After a moment, he reached down and unlocked the handcuffs. "Better?"

Ben rubbed his sore wrist and then his temple where he'd been struck. "Yeah, thanks."

The detective returned to his seat and picked up the lighter again, fidgeting with it in his hand. "Where'd you go after you left Grants Pass?"

"We stopped for gas at a little Gas-n-Go; the old guy there was an asshole, by the way. But then we went on to Eugene. Our friend, Brandon, owns a bar there and we hadn't seen him in a while, so we decided to stop in…I'm sorry, but what's this all about? These questions are kind of strange."

"I'm just trying to understand everything, from the beginning to where we ended up at the hospital, that's all."

"Oh, okay, that makes sense, I guess. I'm still trying to figure it all out, too." Ben leaned forward on the table to continue recounting the events of the past few days. "Then we went camping for a night at some campground, I can't remember the name. Um…oh, before that we stopped in Mt. Angel. It's actually a nice small town. Have you ever been through there?"

"Once, not too long ago during an investigation. It's hard to enjoy the little things when you're working." Dan reached into his coat and pulled out his crumpled pack of Pall Malls and removed one with his lips. He held the pack outwards towards Ben, offering him one.

"No, thanks, though. Are you sure you can smoke in here?"

"I'm a cop. I can do whatever I want in here, Benjamin." Dan changed the subject again. "Tell me about your time in Mt. Angel."

"Well, we bought some beer and relaxed in the park while I tried to do some writing."

"Writing?"

"Yeah, I'm trying to be a writer. This whole trip was supposed to be about me working on my first novel. So, we took the scenic route so I could get some inspiration."

"Did you do anything else while you were in town?" The detective sounded like he was searching for something specific.

"No, that was pretty much it."

"Did you cross paths with a young girl there?" Dan scanned over the file. "Her name was Ashton."

"Yeah…I met her at the bookstore, where she worked." Ben hoped he could forget about Ashton. "We

talked quite a bit and she showed me where the park was."
He thought about her shy smile again. "I actually *really*
liked her. She died, right?"

"Huh, yeah, she did." Dan wrote down more notes. "I
thought you might have known who she was." He held
out the pack of cigarettes again. "You sure you don't want
one? May not get another chance for a little while."

"No, I'm okay." Ben grew increasingly quiet.

"So, tell me, do you know what happened to the
bookstore girl?" Dan flicked the flint on his Zippo, lit up
his cigarette, then placed the lighter back onto the table.

The question troubled Ben. He couldn't decide if
protecting his best friend or throwing him under the bus
was the right thing to do. *Taylor had his chance. He knew
what he was doing all along.* Ben felt that he had no
choice but to tell the detective the truth. "When I heard
she'd been murdered, I didn't really know what happened.
But yesterday, in the hospital, Taylor told me that
he...that he did it...that he killed her."

Dan set down his pen. "What can you tell me about
Taylor Dean?"

"Well...what do you want to know? I thought he was
a normal, nice guy. I mean, we grew up together. And
then he goes and does all this shit..." Ben rubbed his
forehead. "I'm sorry, I feel like I don't know him that well
at all anymore." He ran his hands through his hair and
exhaled deeply.

"You're doing fine. Tell you what, I arrived in Walla
Walla just as you two were leaving. Can you tell me what
you were doing there and about the motel incident?"

"I wanted to visit my great grandmother for a little
while and while I did that, he waited for me at one of the
nearby bars. He met some woman there and they decided
to go back to the hotel without me. He told me that she

was a hooker, but she didn't tell him that she was before they...well, you know."

"I can tell you right now, Ben, she was no hooker."

"What? Of course she was."

"No, she wasn't. She was the local barber's little girl. She came home from college for the weekend to visit her family."

"I...he said she was..."

"Please," Dan interrupted. "Continue. Tell me what else happened."

"Um...okay." Just thinking about it made Ben sick to his stomach. "After a couple hours, I decided to go to the hotel. I knocked on the door, just in case they were still busy and went in. He was sitting on the bed, nearly in tears. He was scared and panicked. And when we were trying to figure out what to do, the maid walked by the room and screamed. We got freaked out and ran. That's when I saw you."

Dan hadn't taken a drag off of his half-burnt cigarette in minutes. "Tell me about the hospital, Ben."

"Um...I don't remember everything, but we decided to sleep in the car. I went in to visit my dad the next morning and Taylor followed some blonde nurse around. He can't help but flirt, if that's what he was actually doing."

Dan stopped taking notes and listened intently. "Then what happened?"

"He came in to meet my dad and then said that nurse wanted my dad to die. I don't know why, but he told me that he 'took care of' the nurse. Then he told me that we had to put my dad out of his misery. He was going to kill him, Detective." Ben's eyes filled with tears. "How could he say something like that to me? Then, to top it all off, he actually tried to do it! So, I blew up and hit him. I was so scared that he would kill both of us if I didn't do something. Then you came in and, well, you know the rest from there."

Not knowing what to say, Dan continued to sit there, staring across the table. To him, Ben's story sounded like an elaborate fairy tale. It sounded too convenient. He continued to stare intently at Ben, who was awkwardly squirming from being watched so intently. After what felt like a lifetime of uncomfortable eye contact, three quick knocks echoed through the room.

Detective Logan peered through the small, square window in the door and waved her hand to have Dan meet her in the hallway.

"Ben." Dan closed shut the folder in front of him. "In Walla Walla and the hospital..." He paused, looking for any sign that Ben was guilty. "...there was no one with you."

Ben's face turned to an empty and shocked shade of pale white.

"*You* were the one in the car when we crossed paths at the hotel. And the reason I hit you with the fire extinguisher instead of *Taylor* is because you had your hands—nobody else's—wrapped around Bryan Keller's neck." Dan stood up, calmly pushed in his chair and walked over to Ben. "Your hands were choking the life out of your own father. Maybe you should reconsider this 'my best friend did it' story." He reached down and snapped the handcuff back around Ben's wrist, then walked out of the room, slamming shut the door.

"Get anything out of him?" Detective Logan asked.

"Nothing useful. I just told him he was going down for the attempted murder of his father. I'm going to let him stew for a few minutes. See if he decides to come clean."

"Looks like I've got some good news then. I got in touch with the Eugene PD, while you were in there. They had your partner, a Detective…" Joanne scanned over a stack of papers in her hand. "…Lyle, send over the DNA result from your double homicide. And they even matched the prints you pulled from the bookstore in Mt. Angel. I think you're going to want to read this." She handed him the stack of papers.

Dan read over them intently. The results answered so many questions and hammered the final nail into Ben's proverbial coffin.

The first of the DNA results returned the name "Brandon Hemsworth." That was no surprise. "Brandon Hemsworth was the owner of the Irish-bar-turned-crime-scene." It wasn't until he read the second victim's name that a sharp chill shot up Dan's spine. "Taylor Dean," he read aloud. "So, there really is a Taylor."

"That's who he said was at the hospital, right?" Logan said confused by Ben's story.

"And at the hotel and the bookstore. It was all Taylor, according to the suspect."

"He's obviously lying, Dan. Go in there and call him on his bullshit."

"Oh, I plan on it. There's just something about him. I'm starting to think that he truly believes all his bullshit. That or he's a damn good actor. He was genuinely concerned about whether or not we had *Taylor* in custody."

"I think he's well aware of what he did. There's no way that he brutally murdered his best friend and still thinks that he can get away with blaming it on him. I'll bet that he thinks we don't know that Taylor Dean was killed in Eugene."

"That's the only other thing I can think of. He's just playing this game as long as he can, hoping to get away with it."

"Does he know you're from Eugene?"

"No, I haven't specifically told him that, yet."

"There you go. Maybe, it's about time you let him know where you're from and what you know." She did make a valid point, but something still wasn't sitting right with Dan.

"Alright, I'm gonna give him a minute longer to squirm, then I'll go back in there. He'll crack eventually."

Dan and Joanne entered the tiny space next door to the interrogation room. They sat down behind a small desk and watched through the two-way mirror, while examining the rest of the evidence.

"He'll crack."

21

STILL SITTING IN the interrogation room, gripping the arms of the chair so tightly his fingers were ready to fall off, Ben sat stupefied in his steel, handcuffed prison. It was impossible for him to comprehend what the detective had said: *"No one else was there."*

"'I am Jack's complete lack of surprise.'" Taylor's voice erupted from behind him, causing Ben to jump as high as he could while still attached to the chair. "What the hell do you think he meant by that?"

Ben was shocked to see Taylor leaning against the wall behind him, but a small part of him wasn't surprised.

Taylor walked around the table and took a seat in the detective's chair.

"What...the *hell*...are you doing in here?" said Ben.

"I came to make sure you were doing okay without me." Taylor leaned back in the chair and kicked his feet up onto the table.

"Doing okay? Are you fucking kidding me? Where the hell have you been?"

"Not getting caught. Unlike some people I know." Taylor smiled that stupid toothy grin, like Ben was the butt of a running joke.

"Would you *please* go tell them what happened!" Ben sat back down to have a conversation with his old friend. "Tell them what you did."

"I heard you sell me out. Send me up shit creek without a paddle. Now tell me, why should I have your back when you didn't have mine?" Taylor set his feet back down on the floor and leaned in close to Ben, intently awaiting his answer.

Ben was speechless. "After all the years we've known each other..." He could only think of one reason why Taylor should turn himself in. "Because you're the one who did it, Taylor. That's why."

"That's where you're wrong, 'brother.'"

What? "You *did* do it, Taylor. You fucking told me so."

"I'm not that depraved, Ben. It was all you, pally." Satisfied with his position, Taylor kicked his feet back up onto the table.

Ben's jaw dropped, speechlessly hitting the floor. "Th—that doesn't make any sense. How could it have been me?"

"I dunno. It just was." Taylor picked up the Zippo that was left on the table and began flicking the lid open and shut, over and over.

"Bullshit."

"Think real, real hard, Ben." In an attempt to keep himself preoccupied with the boring situation, Taylor flicked the flint a few times, trying to ignite the lighter. After countless failed attempts he irritably threw the Zippo back onto the table. "I have an idea. Think back to the hooker at the motel."

"She wasn't a hooker, Taylor!"

"Irrelevant. Just try to remember when she was still alive."

Ben thought hard about it, but wasn't sure what he was supposed to remember. "What good is that going to do, Taylor? The only time I saw her alive was when you were leaving the bar."

"Wrong again, pally. I said think real, *real* hard."

With his eyes closed, Ben thought as hard as possible, trying to remember something he never saw. And like a brick through a plate glass window, it hit him. He remembered her face, then her tits…and then her voice. *I never heard her voice*. The memories continued to flood into his aching mind. Although it was impossible, he remembered approaching her in the bar. He sat next to her and struck up a conversation, like it was no big deal. Like he was Taylor. After they left the bar together, the night's events played out like an old movie in his head.

Ben saw himself talking to an empty chair outside the bar, informing no one that he was heading to the motel. Things began to make a frightening sort of sense, like why the hotel manager was so surprised when Ben returned to pick up the second key. Hitting him like a punch to the face and then to the groin, the memory of them having sex washed over him. He could feel how firm her tits were and how soft her lips and skin felt. He relived every moment, including thrusting himself deep inside of her. The moment when Ben walked into the motel room, finding Taylor sitting on the edge of the bed, was replaced with himself standing over the dead body, talking to no one. He had cleaned up, left the room, nonchalantly retrieved the second key and returned to "discover" a dead woman in his room.

"That's right, Ben…now you've got it." Taylor smiled a wide, accomplished smile.

Everything Taylor had seen and done over the past few days swarmed into Ben's mind. One by one, they mutated and changed, replacing Taylor with a dark and twisted version of himself. Even the good memories changed. What began as an enjoyable day on the river, filled with fishing and drinking, transformed into him sitting alone on the bank, talking to absolutely no one. He'd hand a bottle of beer to the air and not notice as it crashed to the ground. Ben's mind felt like an overworked VCR, replaying events he was never there for. They began like a VHS tape, grainy and fuzzy, but slowly revealed the whole, high-definition picture.

First it was Taylor dragging the bodies through the woods and with a flash Ben replaced him committing the acts. He remembered stalking the two college-aged kids through the woods and then stomping on their bodies as he swung the small hatchet down on them repeatedly. After disposing of the bodies, he watched another strange sight. He stood at the edge of their campsite, any sign of humanity long gone from his eyes as he stared at an empty sleeping bag by the fire.

"How is this even possible? We left the bar together; the girls knew we were going out *together*." Tears streamed down Ben's face as his anger grew.

"Well, yeah, of course we left Grants Pass together. We even had a great night hanging out with Brandon…well, until you took a cinder block to both of us."

"I…couldn't have…I…" Ben's eyes lifted up as he remembered. "I *did* kill you, didn't I? I remember it now."

"That's right. We were all beyond smashed, and Brandon called Lynn a…controlling, self-righteous…"

"…know-it-all bitch." Ben finished.

"So, even though we could have left Eugene without any problems and you wouldn't have to see Brandon ever again—if you were so inclined—you had to snap and smash his face in. Then you did me. While I was taking a piss, dude! How fucked up is that?" Taylor smiled with enjoyment as he retold the tale of his death.

As Ben gazed over at Taylor, a grisly fact became clear. He glanced down, fighting the urge to remember what had happened, but as he look back up at Taylor, his best friend had been replaced by the horrifying hallucination of Taylor's body beaten and bloody, his skull nearly nonexistent. Ben Looked away and clenched his eyes tight. As they opened again, a "lively" Taylor sat across the table, smiling back at him.

"What? You look like you've seen a ghost."

The memories continuing to flood into Ben's mind, he arrived at the shocking realization that he truly was present for the one event he swore he knew nothing about: Ashton's death. That nightmare Ben had in the car as they left Mt. Angel, it wasn't a dream. He killed her. He stalked her back to the bookstore and clenched his hands tight around her throat. He was the dark figure in his nightmare. Every second of it was real. There was no vicious beast of a man slaughtering all those people, no one else to blame. Only him. Ashton, the horny teens in the woods, the old asshole at the Gas-n-Go. *The Gas-n-Go?*

"Checkmate." Taylor snapped his fingers. "You sacked up and you taught that old prick a lesson in customer appreciation, while I patiently waited by the car."

"But why me? Why have you been following me around and doing all of this?"

"Because you needed me, Ben. You didn't have the balls to do what was necessary to stand up for yourself. You needed to find a way to come up with some good content and some publicity for that book you keep claiming you're going to write."

"Taylor, that's the most insane thing I've ever heard."

"I told you, Ben. I'm not really Taylor." He stood up and started pacing. "You really need to learn to stand up for yourself once in a while. Like with Mister Detective behind the glass. You let him walk all over you back there." Taylor noticed Dan walk in front of the door to the interrogation room. "Oh, great, here he comes now."

"Taylor, no. I need you to help me here. What the hell do I say?"

Detective Sawyer stormed back into the room and sat down in his chair. "Alright, Benjamin. It's time you stopped feeding me this line of bullshit."

"Wh—what do you mean? I don't know what you're talking about." Ben was frantic.

"Come on, Ben, tell him. Tell him everything," Taylor whispered in Ben's ear. "Tell him that if he doesn't let you go, you'll fuckin' kill him, too.

"You keep telling me that this 'Taylor' was with you all along." The detective paused a moment, waiting for another lie from his suspect. "That's a load of shit."

"Wha—what do you mean?"

"Back in Eugene, behind your friend's bar…"

"Y—Yeah?" Ben knew what was coming.

"We found Taylor Dean's body in the alley behind the building."

"You really found his body…"

"Him and a Brandon Hemsworth. I take it that was your friend who owned the bar?"

"Brandon's really dead too?" A few tears streamed down Ben's face as he thought about everything he'd done and what was about to happen to him.

"Listen, kid. I need you to tell me the truth. If you do that, I may be able to inform the judge of your cooperation. Maybe he'll grant leniency."

"Oh, what a crock of shit!" Taylor yelled in Ben's ear.

"You've seen enough cop shows to know that he's just spewing typical cop garbage." He slammed his hands down on the table, his eyes staring daggers at the detective. "Show him you know he's lying. Jump across the table and wring his fucking neck!"

"I don't...I..." Ben couldn't bring himself to form a full sentence.

Dan's gaze was firmly locked on Ben, seemingly raising the temperature in the room. "Okay, Ben. I'm just going to be straight with you. We know it was you who killed all those people. Now, you're going to tell me about each and every one of them."

"Oh, big deal, of course I killed them. Hell, I'll bet you there's even a few you don't know about. Now, let Ben...*me*...go!" Taylor's words spewed from Ben's mouth.

"Let you go? You're joking, right?" Dan laughed. "You just confessed to murder. You're fucked now, kid. You must be crazy if you think I'm letting you go."

Ben snapped and leapt to his feet, nearly breaking his still-cuffed wrist. He slammed his free hand down on the table. "I am *not* fucking crazy!" Taylor's words again. Ben felt like he was going insane.

"Sit down!" Dan stood up and met Ben's stare.

"I killed her too, you know."

"Killed who, Ben?"

"That cunt nurse, who said she was going to 'take care' of Bryan."

"Your dad's nurse?"

Ben was no longer in control of his words or his actions. Every word vomited from his mouth was no longer his own and he couldn't do anything to stop them from spilling out.

Taylor was doing what he said he would. He stepped

in to "help."

"Stupid bitch said he was in so much pain and it would be better if he just died. So, after getting a little hot and heavy in the stairwell, we went down to the bottom floor and I snapped her God-damn neck." As the words left his mouth, the violent memory played out before him.

The nurse ran her hand up the inside of his thigh, lightly kissing his collar bone. As her hand approached his crotch, he grasped the nape of her neck with one hand and with the other, twisted her head around. She died instantly. He buried her beneath a pile of gurney mattresses stored at the bottom of the stairs and left her there.

Detective Logan listened from behind the mirror. She instinctively pulled out her cell phone and called the uniforms stationed at the hospital. "This is Detective Logan. Check the stairwell for a blonde nurse. She may be missing, presumably deceased. Call me if you find anything." Her nerves began to eat away at her as she waited for a return call. She had to know if her temporary partner was sitting across from a great liar, or a mad man.

"How many, Ben?"

"I don't know." Ben looked at Dan like he was an imbecile. "I lost count somewhere around…half a dozen. But there had to have been a few more." He didn't blink, only averted his gaze in an attempt to recall the correct count.

Logan's phone started to vibrate. "Yeah?" She listened to the officer on the other end of the line. "Alright, thanks." She shut the phone and stormed into the small interrogation room. Without even a glance in Ben's direction, she made a direct route for Dan and whispered in his ear. "We got him. The girl from the hospital, she's dead. That's a body, confession and all the evidence we need." After informing him, she stood against the mirror and stared over at Ben.

"What the fuck are you glaring at, whore?" Ben snarled at her.

"Shut your God-damn mouth." Dan moved closer to his perp. "This is it. Your last chance. Tell me everything, starting with your friend you killed, Taylor. You got that, Ben?

"Stop saying that!"

Dan was confused. "Stop saying what?"

"Ben?" asked detective Logan. "Stop saying Ben?"

"Yes!" Ben shouted with relief.

"Why would we not call you 'Ben'?"

"He didn't do any of this." Ben saw the last few days like he never had before. Sometimes he was himself. Other times, he was a twisted interpretation of his oldest friend, watching a hallucination of Ben that didn't truly exist. Their arguments and fist fights, that seemed so real at the time, transformed into disturbing images of self-abuse and flailing about with an invisible doppelganger. He was fighting with nothing but the wind. "I killed those people, not Ben. I'm the one that rescued Bryan from his pain and misery, and I silenced that ignorant candy striper. So stop trying to blame him for all this."

"Be—Look, Bryan Keller survived. He's a little worse for the wear, but he's still kicking. Whatever you were trying to do, you failed, pal."

Ben's relief at his father's safety didn't show on his face, but it was there. Buried deep beneath the surface. Hidden behind the images of the lives he gruesomely snuffed out. But the image of his own hands wrapped around his dad's neck made his brain feel as though it were moments from erupting, spraying brain matter and red chunks across the walls and his interrogators.

"At least tell me something. You keep telling me not to blame Ben. But if I can't blame him, then who the hell do we pin this on?"

One last thought crossed Ben's mind. *Thank you, Taylor*. And before he could answer, whatever was left of Ben withdrew from his body, no longer a tenant in Taylor's house of mirrors. He surrendered his voice and body and, finally, his mind.

"What're you, high? You've already got me handcuffed in here. You can blame me." With nothing left to do or worry about, Ben finally left, disappearing like a forgotten memory.

"What the hell's wrong with you?" shouted Detective Logan. "We've *been* blaming you this whole time."

"Hang on," said Dan, confused and concerned. "Who do you think you are? What's your name?"

"You're just as thick as she is. You've been torturing the hell out of me with your incessant questioning, and you don't even know my name!?" Ben laughed and rolled his head backwards. "Ben left a while back. He's gone; he went home. My name is Taylor, you colossal ass hat. Taylor Dean."

Epilogue

DETECTIVE SAWYER MADE his way through the Eugene police station, acknowledging his coworker's adoring glances for his part in catching a sick and twisted serial killer. Not typically one for praise, he gave the passing officers a half-hearted, two-fingered salute or a simple nod and a smile. He walked towards the back of the station and entered the tombs, the jail cells where they kept their collars.

The cells were all empty except for two. The second cell on the right housed a local drunk, passed out with a massive bruise on his forehead from colliding with a streetlamp outside his favorite bar. Near the back of the room, the last cell on the left, held Dan's most recent catch: a twisted young man, wanted for the homicide of over half a dozen serial murders throughout the Pacific Northwest.

Dan walked up to the cage and banged his keys on the bars. "Get up. It's time for you to go."

"Where am I going?" asked Ben.

"You're being transferred to the state pen. You're going away for a long time." Dan unlocked the cell door and slid it open. "I hope it was all worth it."

"Oh, fuck off. You've got nothing. Why don't you come back with that hot piece of ass you work with? Your partner, I think."

"Nothing?" Dan held up an evidence bag containing a wrinkled legal pad covered in scribbles and writings and a worn, pocket-sized Moleskine notebook. "We found this in your car, filled with detailed accounts of at least eight murders. Murders you've been linked to. This is about as good as a nail in the coffin gets."

"Oh, sure. Big, bad detective thinks he has it all figured out. Everything on that pad is a work of fiction. So, suck it."

"Why don't you just get the hell up, Benjamin? Don't make me come in there and pick you up."

"Oh, my God!" Ben yelled, venting his apparent frustration with the detective. "This is why you got nothing. Ben's not here, dumbass. He went home to his girl and he's not comin' back, bro."

"I hate to break it to ya, kid. Things are never the way they used to be. You can never really go home. Especially not after something like this."

"Whatever," said Ben as he lay back down on the bench.

"Alright, that's it." Dan stormed over and grabbed Ben by the front of his shirt, stretching out the collar as he "helped" him to his feet. "I've had enough of your schizo, multiple-personality bullshit. It's not gonna work on me and it's not going to hold up in court either." He slapped a pair of cold, steel bracelets onto Ben's wrists and dragged him out of the jail cell. Dan walked him out of the tombs and through the main floor of the station.

A number of officers and detectives gave him a genuine slow clap as he passed and a few even shouted, "Great job, Dan!"

Slightly embarrassed, although expectedly indifferent to their praise, Dan simply nodded and smiled, and continued on through the station.

Detective Lyle walked up to him in the lobby of the precinct. "Hey, transport's all set to go. You ready to do this?"

"No," interrupted Ben.

Dan jerked him forward for his insubordinate attitude. "Yeah, let's do this." He followed Lyle out of the precinct, pushing Ben along in front of him.

A short, white bus with the words "Oregon State Penitentiary" on the side waited in front of the building with the rear door open, awaiting their prisoner. One guard, holding a shotgun, waited outside the bus. Another unarmed guard stood inside to help restrain Ben.

Dan lifted Ben's restrained hands and passed the makeshift leash to the guard standing inside the bus.

Ben stepped up the retractable steps and entered the transport.

The guard immediately began to recite the prison's rules and regulations as he chained Ben to the floor. "Inmate, you will stay completely seated for the duration of the trip. Once the vehicle comes to a complete stop, you will stay seated until a corrections officer removes you from the bus. Upon exiting the bus, you will stand ten feet away and face the bus at all times."

"Oh, shut up!" shouted Ben. "Can you just put some music on or something?"

"Inmate!" the guard yelled. "You will remain sile—"

"No! I will not!" Ben began humming Taylor's favorite rap song loudly, ignoring the frustrated guard.

The guard on the outside of the bus closed the back door, muffling Ben's incessant humming. "You're the guy that caught him, right?" he asked Dan.

"Yeah."

"I know you were just doing your job, but good work." The guard reached out and shook Dan's hand firmly.

"Yeah, thank you."

"Please," said Lyle. "He did all this single-handedly and pursued the perp all the way to Washington. It was definitely above and beyond." She smiled at Dan, hoping to make him blush.

"Knock it off." Dan turned back to the guard. "Thanks. You guys take care. And don't listen to him, he's a habitual bullshitter."

"Got it, Detective." The guard walked around the front of the bus and climbed into the driver's seat after securing his weapon on the rack next to the door. The bus sputtered to life and slowly pulled out of the police station parking lot.

Dan stood on the front steps, watching the bus, ensuring nothing would go wrong before it disappeared behind the municipal buildings. He could finally exhale. The worst of this past week was finally behind him.

"Why don't you call it a day? I told Sheila I'd try to get you home as soon as possible," said Lyle.

"Yeah, I think I might. Lord knows I'm fucking exhausted."

"You should do something nice with her. Unwind."

"Yeah, maybe I will. I just gotta go grab my coat." Dan opened the door for Lyle and followed her inside. They walked up the stairs and over to his desk. He passed the incriminating notepad over to Lyle. "Do you mind?"

"Nah, I'll cover for ya." She looked at the notepad. "It's weird isn't it? This kid's life didn't seem that bad, but a lot of little things add up and someone becomes capable of something like this."

"Weird is an understatement. And people are capable of a lot worse."

"This crazy, fucked up world, huh?"

"Yeah, you're tellin' me."

"But forget about all that. It's over. Head home and don't worry, I think the boss-man'll understand that you just needed a little 'you' time." Lyle sat down, tossed the evidence bag onto her desk and leaned back in her chair, nonchalantly texting Sheila that Dan was headed home.

"Thanks, Lyle. I'll see you in the morning." Dan glanced down and noticed a long orange envelope sitting on his desk. "What's this?"

"I'm not sure, it wasn't there earlier."

Dan looked at the envelope, the words *"ATTN: Detective Dan Sawyer"* written by hand on the front, next to a poorly drawn smiley face. He opened it and removed a white sheet of paper, completely blank. "There's nothing on it." Until he looked a bit closer. "It looks like there's some sort of a watermark on it. Probably from whoever sent it."

"Maybe they sent the wrong thing."

"I don't know, they'll send it again if it's important. I'll hang on to it, just in case." He folded the paper in half and stuffed it into his coat pocket.

"Alright, I'll see ya. Don't have too much fun with Sheila, now." She smirked deviously at him.

Dan smiled and turned away, walking out to the parking garage ant then climbing into his Plymouth. He drove home as quickly as he could, ignoring a few posted speed limit signs. As he pulled into the driveway, the house looked peaceful and comforting as though he'd never left. *It's good to be home*. The car slowed to a stop and Dan stepped out, ignoring the trash the floor had accumulated over the past week and quickly made his way up to the front door. He walked inside and was immediately greeted with the scent of juicy, delicious roast beef and potatoes. Without hesitation, he made his way to the dining room, only to find the table adorned

233

with tall, burning candles surrounded by flowers, glasses of wine, and two plates stuffed to the edges with their aromatic dinner. "Sheila?" He tossed his keys onto the dinner table. "Sweetheart? This smells delicious." He used his fingers to tear off a small piece of roast beef, then tossed it into his mouth. "Mmmmm. Amazing," he whispered, not caring that the meat was a little cold. Still no reply from his wife, he walked back towards the bedroom. He slowly pushed open the door, expecting to find his wife lying on the bed, wearing her favorite pink teddy. But to his surprise, he found no one in the bedroom. "Huh, that's weird. She must be at the store or something." Hoping to take a moment for himself, Dan pulled off his coat and walked over to the dresser on the far side of the room. Before he could set it down, something moved out of the corner of his eye.

Sheila was tied to a tipped-over chair on the ground, her mouth gagged and her favorite pink teddy torn and bloodied. Her eyes were wide with terror and filled to the brim with tears.

"Son of a bitch. Sheila, what happened?" Dan took a step towards her and heard the bedroom door squeal closed. He turned his head and was met with a police baton to the temple, sending him plummeting to the floor.

Sheila cried out in agony, her screams muffled by the makeshift gag.

The intruder's footsteps were loud on the bare, wood floor as he walked behind Dan. "I hear you like to chase serial killers," said a low, sinister voice. His footsteps grew louder as he stepped over Dan's head and walked over to Sheila. The intruder wore a pitch-black ski mask and all-black clothes. In one hand he held Dan's old police baton from when he was a beat cop and in the other he held a long, straight blade with a simplistic handle. The sleeve on the arm holding the knife was pushed upwards, revealing ornate, twin scythes tattooed around his forearm. The hilts stretched from his elbow to his wrist, where the long, curved blades coiled around it. He tossed the baton onto the bed and picked up Sheila, standing the chair upright. Without saying another word, he walked around her, lightly dragging the blade across her collar bone and the back of her neck, not cutting her, only teasing her.

Dan's vision faded in and out of darkness, only catching glimpses of the man with the scythe tattoo. "Who are you?"

The intruder said nothing.

"God damnit, answer me!" Dan shouted. "Why are you doing this?"

"I'm not. You are," hissed the intruder. "You've been all over the news the last few days. Everyone's saying how good you are, how you're a hero. When in reality, you did nothing."

"What the hell are you talking about?" asked Dan as he held his throbbing head.

"You didn't catch some big-shit serial killer. You caught some stupid kid who lost his mind and his temper. A small fish in a big, God-damn ocean." The intruder pressed the blade down on Sheila's collar bone, drawing a small amount of blood.

"Okay, stop." Dan held his hands out in surrender. "Please, stop. You're right. But I don't want the praise, I swear. They can go to hell for all I care. Just leave and I won't tell anyone about this."

The intruder lifted the blade from Sheila's neck. "You won't tell anyone?" he said surprised.

"No, I promise. Not a soul," Dan pleaded.

After setting the knife on the bed, the intruder walked

over to Dan and fell to his knees, staring Dan straight in the eyes. "You swear? You promise you won't tell anyone?"

"Yes! I swear! Just let us g—"

"Well, what fucking good does that do me!?" shouted the intruder. "You and this...fucking *boy* are all over the news. I want that. I want to be all over the God-damn news, because I deserve to be!"

"Wha..."

The intruder ripped off his ski mask, his dark black hair falling down into his face, shrouding the mad look in his piercing blue eyes. "Let's do that, let's get on the news, Detective." The crazy man climbed to his feet and walked behind Sheila, picking up a small jerry can, hidden beneath the bed and began pouring gasoline over her.

Sheila's cries grew louder as her muffled plea attempts fell on deaf ears.

"No, stop it!" shouted Dan. "Kill me! Kill me, you sick son of a bitch!"

The crazed man didn't say another word. He walked over to Dan and kicked him in the face, forcing him back to the floor.

"I...won't...tell anyone..."

"What was that?" asked the crazed man.

"If you do this, I won't tell a damn soul." Blood dripped from the corner of Dan's mouth.

The man stepped closer to Dan and bent down. His breathing calmed and the excited look on his face disappeared, replaced with an intense, grim stare. "You won't have to." He turned and removed a book of matches from his pocket. After striking one, he lit the book on fire and tossed it onto Sheila's lap, her teddy igniting instantly, engulfing her in flames.

"No! No, you mother fucker. I'll kill you." Dan tried

to climb to his feet, but was still dazed from the blows to the head.

The intruder picked up the knife from the bed and walked around the room, standing behind Dan.

Flames from Dan's wife lit up the entire room, igniting small pools of gasoline on the floor.

Dan watched his wife burn alive in front of him, her screaming muffled from the gag, until it burned away and they turned to howls. He noticed the blank piece of paper on the floor above his head; it had fallen out of his coat when he fell. The flames from the fire grew nearer to Dan and the paper, the heat slowly revealing something on it. The haunting image of the crossed scythes appeared, the same image on the intruder's arm. Three handwritten words emerged below the image as the heat became more intense: *"See you soon."* The ink grew darker as the flames neared, until the paper caught fire, incinerating in an instant.

The intruder knelt down behind Dan and placed a hand on the back of the detective's head. "I know we're going to have a lot of fun, you and me," he whispered into Dan's ear. The blade in the man's hand found its way to Dan's abdomen and pierced the flesh on the right side of his stomach. He leaned in close to Dan again and whispered before ripping out the knife, "Catch me if you can, Detective."

"Stagnancy and listlessness have a way of affecting all of us. When life doesn't turn out the way you imagined, the way you dreamed it would all turn out, you hold on as long as you can, but sometimes, you just can't take it anymore and you do something stupid."

~Sean Kelly

Made in the USA
San Bernardino, CA
11 January 2017